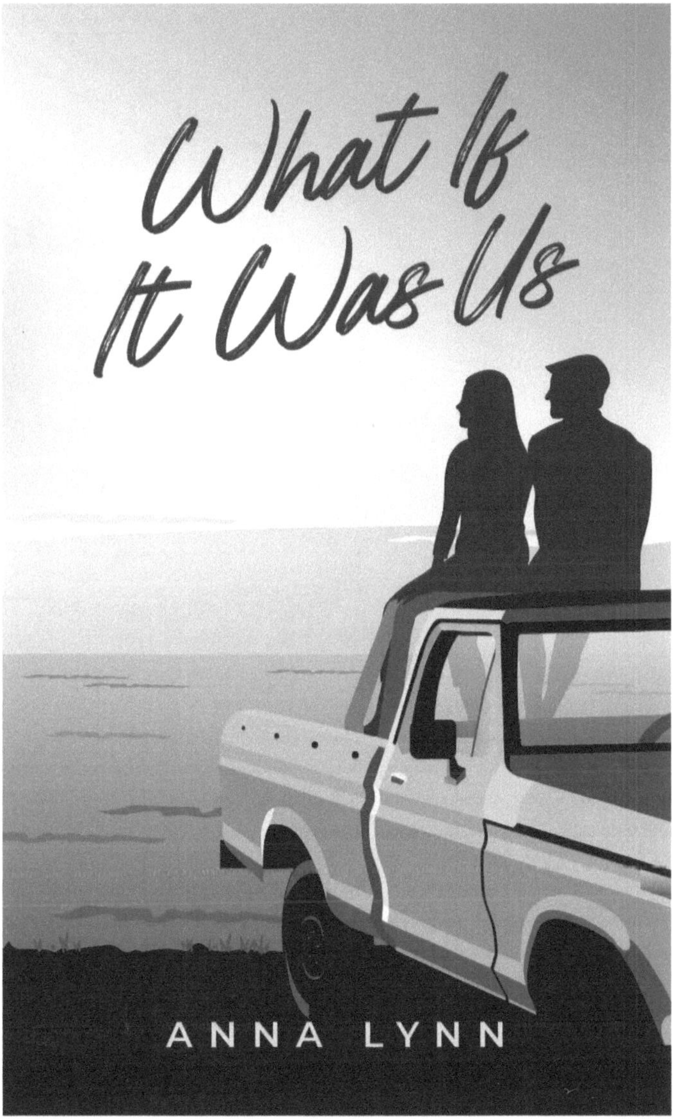
What If
It Was Us
ANNA LYNN

Copyright © 2026 by Anna Lynn

Cover Art by Kalyn Allen

All rights reserved.

No part of this publication may be reproduced, stored or transmitted in any form or by any means, electronic, mechanical, photocopying, recording, scanning, or otherwise without written permission from the publisher. It is illegal to copy this book, post it to a website, or distribute it by any other means without permission.

This novel is entirely a work of fiction. The names, characters and incidents portrayed in it are the work of the author's imagination. Any resemblance to actual persons, living or dead, events or localities is entirely coincidental.

Anna Lynn asserts the moral right to be identified as the author of this work.

Anna Lynn has no responsibility for the persistence or accuracy of URLs for external or third-party Internet Websites referred to in this publication and does not guarantee that any content on such Websites is, or will remain, accurate or appropriate.

Contents

Dedication	VI
Preface	VIII
1. Chapter 1	1
2. Chapter 2	8
3. Chapter 3	24
4. Chapter 4	27
5. Chapter 5	33
6. Chapter 6	39
7. Chapter 7	48
8. Chapter 8	55
9. Chapter 9	62
10. Chapter 10	68
11. Chapter 11	75
12. Chapter 12	84
13. Chapter 13	92
14. Chapter 14	100
15. Chapter 15	106
16. Chapter 16	113

17. Chapter 17   121
18. Chapter 18   128
19. Chapter 19   137
20. Chapter 20   146
21. Chapter 21   154
22. Chapter 22   162
23. Chapter 23   167
24. Chapter 24   176
25. Chapter 25   186
26. Chapter 26   196
27. Chapter 27   203
28. Chapter 28   210
29. Chapter 29   218
30. Chapter 30   223
31. Chapter 31   232
32. Chapter 32   243
33. Chapter 33   249
34. Chapter 34   253
35. Chapter 35   262
36. Chapter 36   274
37. Chapter 37   282
38. Chapter 38   287
39. Chapter 39   293

Epilogue   300

Afterword	305
Acknowledgements	306
About the author	309

WHAT IF IT WAS US

For anyone who's had every reason to give up and kept going anyway

And to all the parents that made your home a safe space for every child that walked through their door, especially my parents, thank you for existing

Preface

I'm beyond grateful you've chosen to read this book. This story deals with topics such as parental abandonment, addiction, and mention of physical harm. If any of these topics mentioned are triggering for you, please proceed with caution.

Much love, Anna Lynn.

Chapter 1

NOW

June

My stomach lurched as I approached the four-way stop that would take me back to my childhood town. I had been driving for fifteen hours, and I *still* wasn't ready to face the house I had grown up in. Why? Because there were only two reasons anyone ever came back to the place they were raised—a wedding or a death. My reason was the latter.

There were no cars at the other stop signs, so I let my attention linger on the sign that pointed left for Tostela, and right for Highland. *Just turn right. The house is right.* I tapped my fingers against the steering wheel in a nervous rhythm while my brain fought back and forth with the devil on my shoulder. Something in my heart tugged at me to turn left; to head to Tostela, and to the one place that had actually felt like a real home to me.

"Fuck it," I breathed out as I turned left.

I drove slowly down Main Street and into downtown. Most of the businesses were closed since it was a Sunday morning, but it didn't look like much had changed in the ten years since I'd last been here.

The ice cream parlor windows were still painted with pictures of ice cream cones, and a melting sundae with dancing bananas. The shoe store still had the same footprints etched into the door, leading to the sign above. I felt like I had been transported straight back in time—until I spotted Delvecchios' Restaurant.

The awning was blue instead of red, and the once-cursive signage was now a block font. I wondered if the Delvecchio family still owned the restaurant and updated it, or if they'd sold it to new owners. I couldn't imagine the family wanting to change anything, and I felt a pinch in my chest. I'd spent all my high school years inside that restaurant. I spent more time with that family than my own—and I hadn't talked to any of them since the night of my high school graduation.

I parked my car across the street and stared at the building. I still had the key to the back door on my key ring. The locks had probably been changed since then, but I couldn't get rid of it. Every time I felt the etched D on the key, it reminded me why I'd never come back here . . . and why I shouldn't even be thinking about going in now.

The back of my throat started to sting. I couldn't believe how emotional I was getting just *looking* at this place. Mrs. Delvecchio always did inventory on Sundays, and I couldn't help but wonder if she was inside, walking around with a clipboard, marking off her checklist and counting wine bottles behind the bar.

I got out the car and walked to the front door, which was now gold instead of green. There was a sign taped to it that said "Closed today for engagement party."

Underneath, the restaurant's hours were written in white vinyl. They were open on Sundays now; they had *never*, not once in all the years I worked here, been open on a Sunday. There was no way the family still owned it.

I leaned forward and cupped my eyes against the glass. It didn't seem like anyone was inside, and the overwhelming nostalgia was begging me to see if the door was unlocked. I pushed the handle down and let out a small laugh when it opened. I felt like I was fourteen again, stepping inside for the first time.

They had the A/C running on high, and I walked past the hostess stand, drawn by the familiar sight of the dining room. The lights weren't on, but even in the dark I could tell it was exactly the same, down to the floral carpeting. I could smell bread baking in the back; that, along with the quiet hum of the song "Pink Pony Club" by Chappell Roan, meant someone was definitely in the kitchen.

Before I could turn and run out the restaurant, a figure came flying through the swinging kitchen doors.

We both stopped in our tracks, sizing each other up from opposite ends of the restaurant. I knew I was fully illuminated from where I was standing, but I couldn't see the face of the person in the back.

"Addison?" It was a woman's voice, and before I could register whose it was, she was hurrying toward me with a smile on her face, her dark-brown hair swishing back and forth behind her in a blur.

"Julie?" I said with a laugh before I was wrapped up in a crushing hug. She was embracing me like it hadn't been a decade since the last time I saw her, or gave her a hug.

"Are you a ghost?" she said before leaning back to survey my face. "Oh my god." I examined her facial expression; there was no hint of animosity there. She just looked ... *happy* to see me. My heart warmed. Julie didn't hate me.

She was still just as beautiful as she had been at eighteen, when I first met her. Her long, dark-brown hair from her teens was now curled in perfect short waves at her shoulders, and she was wearing a pink floral dress that cut off at her knees.

"I didn't know if you guys still owned the restaurant," I said as I let myself fully look around, noticing a stack of little dinner napkins on the table closest to us with "J & S" printed on them.

"Jackson owns it now." Her features softened as she waited to see my reaction. I was shocked to hear Jackson owned it—he'd acted like he hated this place when we worked here. He treated it like a death sentence, while I found it a sanctuary.

"That's great," I said as I managed a smile. "Are you getting married?" I asked as I picked up one of the napkins. I looked down to her left hand, finding a princess cut diamond on a gold band. And it was *huge*. "Who's the lucky S to your J?" I teased.

"Oh. Um, I'm not the one getting married," she said as she licked her lips nervously. "I'm already married."

"Oh, is Sam back?"

"Addie, it's—"

The kitchen doors flew open behind her, cutting her off mid-sentence. The lights in the dining room turned on, and I looked past Julie's shoulder to find a face I hadn't been sure I'd ever see again. Every emotion I had buried deep in my chest over the past ten years was suddenly fighting for my attention. I felt betrayal, hurt, and confusion, but what surprised me most was how *relieved* I was to see him. The boy who broke my heart was standing ten feet away from me—and he looked just as relieved to see me as I was him.

"Addie?" The sound of his deep voice reverberated through me, from the top of my head to the tips of my toes. He was grown now, and so very adult. The past ten years had been good to him. His black hair was cut shorter—no longer wavy, and falling over his forehead. He looked taller, broader, and he was dressed in a short-sleeve blue polo and black pants. His right arm was filled with black tattoos now, and he still had a silver hoop in his left nostril that was a mirror image to the one in mine. The memory of us getting our noses pierced together as teenagers smacked against my brain.

"Jackson." My voice came out airy; I didn't even sound like myself. It was almost as if I'd exhaled, and his name was the sound my breaths were made of.

He walked toward me slowly, like he was trying to figure out if I was actually here or if I was just a mirage. He stopped four feet away from me, and his eyes bounced down to my feet, then back up to my face.

"What, um . . . What are you doing here?" Jackson asked. His fingers twitched nervously at his sides. When had Jackson *ever* been nervous around me?

I cleared my throat awkwardly. "Peter, ya know."

"We were so sorry to hear about him," Julie said quickly, eyes moving from Jackson to me. Jackson didn't add anything, his eyes studying me for a reaction.

"The funeral was three months ago," he said slowly. Had he expected to see me? Did his whole family go? Should I ask if my mom went?

Julie's eyes flicked between the two of us. "I gotta go check on those rolls," Julie said before disappearing back through the kitchen door.

The second it swung shut, Jackson pulled me into a hug. It took me so by surprise that it almost knocked me over, and I stumbled back as he tightened his hold on me to keep me close. I clasped my hands around the middle of his back, and exhaled at the feel of his breath against my neck.

I couldn't be the first to let go; I couldn't believe I'd forgotten how good it felt to be in his embrace. His heart was beating in time with mine, and I imagined us at eighteen years old—the last time he'd held me like this. I lost track of how long we stood like that before he finally stepped back and cleared his throat.

"Why are you here?" Jackson asked again, more firmly this time.

I shrugged and let out a deep breath. "He left me the house. I didn't even know he owned it."

Jackson crossed his arms, leaning back against the wall as he processed the words. His stance gave me a clear view of the Delvecchio tattoo plastered across his right forearm, a familiar sight among all the new ones.

"That's interesting."

"Yep," I confirmed. I shoved my hands in my hoodie pocket. "Did you go to the funeral?"

I watched him tense, clenching and unclenching his fists. "Marie, Jules, and I went. We thought maybe we'd see you."

I swayed uncomfortably from side to side. After all this time, they'd wanted to see *me*.

"Was . . . Um, was my mom there?" I asked timidly.

He pulled in his lips, rubbing them together before letting out a long breath. "Yeah. She was."

I nodded, not knowing how to feel about this information.

"She didn't call you, did she?" he asked.

I shook my head no. I had no idea Peter had passed away until I got the call from our mom about the house being left to me.

Jackson mumbled something under his breath, but I didn't catch the words.

"What?" I asked.

He shook his head, rubbing a hand down his face. "Nothing. So, how's the house looking?"

I gave a weak smile. "No idea. I haven't been there yet. This was my first stop."

His eyes softened, and a genuine smile spread across his face. A mixture of excitement and nerves swirled in my stomach at the sight of that smile. I noticed a scar running through his right eyebrow, a line missing straight through it. It took everything in me not to reach forward and run a finger over it.

Jackson opened his mouth to say something, but the front door swung open and I turned to see a woman walking through with a box of flowers in her arms. Her face was obscured by the bouquets, but I heard her say, "Little help here!"

Jackson hurried over to help her, and when he took the box from her, she kissed him right on the lips before turning and facing me. Her smile fell abruptly off her face, and I couldn't stop my jaw from dropping. I may have thought I'd never see the Delvecchios again, but I definitely never thought I'd see *her* again.

The S and J—it was clicking together, finally. Jackson was engaged to Sophie Waters.

Chapter 2

BEFORE

August, Fourteen Years Ago

The summer before my freshman year of high school was when shit officially hit the fan in my family. It had been hovering for years—and when I say years, I mean approximately fourteen. Because the day things started falling apart in my family was the day I was born.

My brother, Peter, was eight years older than me, and I was the product of our mom cheating on his dad with a one-night stand. Peter's dad left our mom when the truth came to fruition, and became a raging alcoholic as a by-product. He died two years after the split—something Peter says I'm to blame for.

Mom found a new boyfriend earlier this year whom she up and left us for, moving three hours away to Traverse City. Of course, Peter blamed me for that, too. The screaming in the house between Peter and Mom that had been the soundtrack to my life quieted the first few months after she left, but now Peter had turned all his focus on me. I had conditioned myself to cover my ears through their screaming matches, but I couldn't do that when the yelling was in *my* face.

Just last weekend he'd screamed at me that he was *not* going to break his back supporting me. That I shouldn't expect him to cook for me, or dish out money when I needed it. I was still fourteen, and with the labor laws for minors, nobody was tripping over themselves to hire me, but if Peter wasn't going to help me anymore, I had to find *something*.

I didn't have a résumé, so I went to the library and did my best to write a cover letter. At the top was my name, Addison Bianchi, in a bold blue font. I had read online that choosing a visually appealing color would make your name stand out in a pile of résumés, and I figured it couldn't hurt to try. After passing them out to every store and restaurant in town, I decided to ride my bike to the next town over; it was two miles, which wasn't too bad on my bike, but it was especially hot, even for August. The humidity was killer, and by the time I made it, I was sweaty and unpresentable.

My white-blonde hair was sticking to my neck, and I tied it up in a ponytail, even though I thought it looked prettier when I wore it down. I had on my longest pair of denim shorts, which I hoped would look professional since they reached farther than my fingertips if I kept my hands at my sides. My top wasn't much better—I was wearing a T-shirt that I got from freshman orientation. It was light blue with Maple High School written in gold lettering across the front.

It wasn't until after I arrived that I remembered it was a Sunday; most of the businesses in Tostela would be closed. I just wasted my time riding my bike here for no reason. I looked up from where I sat moping on my bike, and saw an Italian restaurant named Delvecchios' Restaurant on the corner of the block. The name was written in white cursive lettering over a red awning and a green door. There were no hours written on the door, so I tried the handle, finding it unlocked and pushing through into the sudden wave of air conditioning.

The front entrance led straight to the hostess stand, and behind it, a dining room with low lighting and a floral-patterned carpet. There was a bar against the far wall lined with various wine bottles, and on either side behind it were swinging doors that I assumed must lead to the kitchen. I thought maybe I had been here as a kid; maybe this was where we went after Peter's high school graduation a few years ago.

Someone stood up from behind the bar, and we both screamed at the sudden sight of another person.

"Oh honey, you scared me!" the woman said with a hand to her chest. She had black hair pulled back into a ponytail, and right away I could tell she was Italian. She was short, olive-skinned, and beautiful in that effortless type of way. She walked around the bar and came over to where I was hovering by the hostess stand. "We're closed on Sundays; I'm just in here for inventory."

She smiled at me with the type of smile that looked motherly. I glanced down at her left hand, finding a huge rock of a diamond on her finger. For a split second, I wondered what it would be like to have someone like this as a mom. Someone who looked put together, who called me honey when she didn't even know me, and who smiled at me like I wasn't a stranger.

"I was wondering if you were hiring. I have a cover letter." I self-consciously wiped sweat from my upper lip, holding out my last cover letter to her.

She glanced at it briefly before looking at me. "We're not really looking to hire." She had the decency to frown at me empathetically. I felt defeated; I was starting to think it wasn't possible for me to find a job before school started. Peter was going to be pissed. If he wasn't going to give me any more money, what was I going to do?

I tried to say, "That's okay," but instead, it tumbled out in a mess of words, followed by a choked sob.

"Oh," the lady said, clearly caught off-guard by the teenager bursting into tears in the middle of her restaurant. She started rubbing my arm. "What's the matter?"

I hurried to wipe the tears off my face, letting out a self-deprecating laugh. "I'm so sorry," I said as I took a step back. "I just really need a job."

She looked back down at the cover letter before settling her eyes back on me. "Follow me, sweetheart."

She guided me over to the dining room, taking the seat across from me in one of the booths that lined the wall.

"Bianchi?" she said with a smile. "You Italian?"

I nodded. Half Italian, anyways. I had no idea what my father was, and my mom gave me her maiden name.

"Well, that's at least one thing we have in common." She winked at me before nodding toward my shirt. "You go to Maple?"

I swiped my hand under my nose, clearing my throat. "I start in two weeks."

"My son is starting his freshman year, too. Did you go to Oaks for middle school?"

"No, I didn't grow up here. I live in Highland. Maple is closer to my house though, so it'll be easier for me to bike there."

She nodded again, eyes flicking down to my paper to read it before looking back up at me.

"You're fourteen already, yes?"

I nodded again.

"You could work a couple nights a week for a few hours," she mumbled to herself, "but my kids typically work those shifts since we're slower during the week. Fridays and Saturdays are our busiest nights, and we're closed Sundays. We could probably use another set of hands on the weekends . . . Tell you what, whatever weekends you can spare a three to ten o'clock shift, they're yours."

I physically sagged in relief. "You're serious?" It almost sounded too good to be true. I hated weekends because Peter was off work, lazing around the house, drinking, and yelling at me whenever he got the chance. This was a perfect scenario.

"Come by next Friday at two thirty for training. I'll have your polo and apron for you. The dress code is black pants, and any type of black sneakers. We're not picky; we just want you to be comfortable. You'll be a busser, so you'll be cleaning tables and helping the wait staff. It's a great first job."

"Thank you, thank you so much!" I jumped up from the booth, trying to contain how excited I was that this actually worked out.

She laughed as she folded the paper in half. "I'm Marie Delvecchio, by the way. It was a pleasure to meet you, Addison. I'll see you next week, okay?"

"Thank you, Marie! Seriously, thank you so much."

She placed a hand on my arm again, and walked me out of the restaurant. I rode my bike home, and not even the heat could melt my smile off my face.

***

I rushed out the door on Friday wearing black jeans and my high-top black Converse, ready to go for my first shift at Delvecchios'. My stomach was rolling with nerves, and I was so anxious about being late that I arrived at two fifteen. I stood outside in the sun for the next fifteen minutes until my watch read two thirty on the dot. I could feel my arms beginning to burn by the time I opened the front door, and that sudden cool rush of air conditioning caused me to let out a relieved exhale. I stood in the front entrance, watching as two women and one man set white tablecloths across the tables until a door on the right opened and Marie stepped out.

"Hi honey, come on into my office." I followed Marie in, and we quickly went through paperwork. She handed me a black polo that had "Delvecchios' Restaurant" written on the left side of the chest in cursive, and a black apron with white stripes.

"Go ahead and get changed in the bathroom. I'll meet you in the kitchen when you're done. Enter either side."

The bathroom had cherry-scented soap, and I put some on a crumble of paper towels, quickly rubbing behind my neck to hopefully mask the smell of my sweat from my bike ride. I switched my T-shirt for the polo, then redid my ponytail so that it was situated at the nape of my neck, and pulled out some pieces to cover my ears. I wasn't wearing any makeup, and decided that was a good decision since I probably would have sweat off the mascara anyways.

I shoved my T-shirt into my backpack, then left the bathroom to push my way through the doors of the kitchen.

When I entered, there was a girl with long, wavy brown hair sitting on one of the kitchen counters with her legs criss-crossed, eating a cannoli. The powdered sugar was leaving flecks of white all over her black apron. Next to her, a boy with shaggy hair that was so dark it was almost black was leaning against the dishwasher, his legs crossed at his ankles while he stared at his phone.

"Um, hi," I said as I walked up to them. Both of them flicked their eyes toward me, and the boy put his phone into his back pocket. The three buttons of his polo were undone, and I could see a freckle on his collarbone. I looked back and forth between them, their brown eyes examining me as I did the same to them.

The girl shoved the rest of the cannoli into her mouth and wiped the powdered sugar off her apron as best she could before jumping off the counter.

"New employee, right?" she asked with her mouth full.

I nodded. "I'm Addie. I'm gonna be a busser."

The boy looked me up and down before crossing his arms and looking over at the girl. "Does Marie think I'm slow or something?"

I could feel my cheeks turn pink.

"She mentioned her kids work hard during the week and the restaurant needed more help on the weekends," I said as I placed my hands in the apron's pockets. It was a half-truth. She probably wanted her kids to have the weekends off since it seemed like they worked a lot throughout the week.

The girl opened her mouth to say something, but the boy cut her off. "Oh yeah, I heard the daughter is a real bitch," the boy said, deadpan.

The girl scoffed and turned toward the boy with an eye roll. "I heard the son is a real prick; he's a cocky little piece of shit."

My eyes widened. "Oh?" I said as I looked back and forth between them. Marie seemed like a saint. I couldn't imagine her kids being horrible people.

"I actually heard the son is really cool, and super handsome," the boy said as he leaned back against the dishwasher again, fixing a lock of dark hair in the process.

"That's funny. I heard he failed kindergarten." The girl turned toward me again. "I actually heard the daughter is beautiful. Like, some would even say stunning." She twisted her hair up before grabbing a claw clip out of her apron and clipping it into her hair.

"Fuck off," the boy said, ears turning red.

The kitchen door flung open, and Mrs. Delvecchio walked through, cutting off the conversation.

"Oh Addison, I see you've met my lovely children, Julie and Jackson."

I cocked my head to the side in surprise as Julie and Jackson smirked at each other. Julie placed an arm around her brother. "I meant every word I said."

"Shut up," Jackson said as he pushed his sister away, but he was still smiling. I couldn't stop looking back and forth between them. They were just joking around with each other? I hadn't seen a sibling relationship like this before. If Peter said the same things they did, it would've been ten times louder, and with one hundred percent truth. And *definitely* without a smile.

"I swear they love each other," Marie said as she gave them a look that seemed to say *I'm watching you two*. "Julie is one of our waitresses, but she'll be bussing with you and Jackson tonight to help you get trained. It's a little after three right now, and we open in an hour. They'll show you as much as they can beforehand, and everything else you'll just learn along the way. You're in good hands." She smiled at me before walking back out through the kitchen doors.

"Stick with me, girl. Trust me, Jackson does *not* have good hands. He was picking his nose until like, five minutes ago," Julie said as she grabbed my arm to lead me toward a basket of silverware.

"Jules, can you actually just shut the fuck up?" Jackson said as he stomped out of the kitchen.

Julie giggled at his tantrum before grabbing a fork, knife, and spoon. "He's so sensitive sometimes. Do you have a brother?"

I said yes, not willing to give away any more information.

"So you get it then. I have two."

I actually didn't get it, because my brother and I did *not* interact the way they did.

Julie showed me how to roll silverware, letting me try a few times until I got it perfect, then she gave me a full tour of the restaurant. There was a bulletin board in the back, which was covered with Polaroid pictures of the employees during work, and what looked like holiday parties. I wondered if I'd ever make it onto that wall.

The job seemed pretty simple; we would just be clearing tables for the wait staff, and occasionally bringing bread or drinks to patrons if we were slammed and the wait staff needed the help. Julie passed me a handful of straws to stuff in my apron pockets, telling me I wouldn't believe the amount of times someone would stop me to ask for one.

"You don't even have to worry about closing duties since you'll be out at ten," Julie said.

Jackson left us alone while Julie showed me around, and by the time it hit four there was hardly a chance to sit until my break. We each got a thirty-minute break, and Julie opted to take hers with me.

I was drenched in sweat from how hard we were working. I gulped down half my glass of water as soon as we sat on the curb in the alley behind the restaurant.

"Next time you come to work you can come through this back door; it leads right through the kitchen," Julie said from beside me. She stifled a yawn with the back of her hand. "So, what's your story?"

I didn't know how to answer. What did "story" mean?

"What do you mean?"

She stretched her legs out, crossing them at the ankles. "Like, tell me about yourself. Mom said you're starting at Maple High but you live in Highland. She asked Jackson if he knew who you were since you're in the same grade, but he said no."

I shrugged. "Maple is closer to my house, so I can ride my bike. That's what my older brother said, anyways. He graduated in 2007 from Highland."

"So did my older brother, Samuel, but he went to Maple. Huge football star, super annoying. He's studying to be a lawyer in New York now, so we hardly see him. I bet your brother knows him since the schools are rivals."

I just shrugged again in response. She looked toward me, and I was worried she'd ask another question, so I hurried to ask her, "What about you?"

She let out a loud *hmmm* before saying, "I just graduated in the spring, and I go to the community college. Getting my associates degree there before moving to wherever the wind takes me. Samuel thinks he's the shit since he got into law school, so I kinda want to do that, too, just to show him it's not that hard. I just feel bad leaving Jackson here. Our parents will probably try to convince him to take over the restaurant if I leave, too, 'cause none of us want it."

"You guys don't like the restaurant?"

Julie let out a long breath before checking her phone for the time. Our break was almost over. "Our entire life just revolves around this place. None of us want to stay chained to it like our parents have."

"Where did your mom go? And why'd Jackson call her Marie?"

"She mostly works from home. Occasionally she'll waitress, or work in the kitchen if someone calls off. Phil does, too. That's my dad. We call them by their first names; it just started off as a joke 'cause they have such adult names, and we just never stopped." She said this with a smile, and I ached for what it must be like to have a family like that.

I drank the rest of my water before we both stood up to head back inside. The rest of the shift flew by, with everything mostly wrapped around nine thirty, most of the patrons settling up their checks and being considerate of the ten o'clock close.

"Damn, that was one of the busiest Fridays we've had in a while. Good thing you were here, Addie," Jackson said as he grabbed a paper towel to wipe the sweat that had accumulated on his neck. His polo was buttoned up now, hiding that freckle I had spotted earlier. The compliment caused something to flutter in my stomach.

"Seriously, you were a huge help today. I would've never believed this was your first job," Julie told me before pulling off her polo, leaving herself in a hot-pink tank top. "I'm dying." She grabbed a menu to fan herself.

Most of the kitchen staff were finishing up with putting the dishes in the dishwasher, and Jackson and Julie said their goodbyes to them. The waitresses and waiter I saw earlier gave us a portion of their tips for the night, and I tried to hide my surprise at the extra cash, which I quickly stuffed into my back pocket.

"You can get out of here. Do you need to call a ride?" Julie asked.

"Oh, I rode my bike here."

Jackson raised an eyebrow at me while Julie's mouth dropped open. "It's ten o'clock. We are not letting you ride your bike home by yourself."

I nervously scratched my arm. "Seriously, it's fine."

Jackson started chewing on his thumbnail as he looked over at Julie.

"Listen, why don't you stay and close with us? I have a truck; we can throw your bike in the back and take you home," Julie offered.

My heart rate started to pick up. I didn't want them to go out of their way, and I definitely didn't want them to see the house Peter and I lived in. And I *especially* didn't want to risk them seeing Peter.

Peter developed a drinking problem after our mom left, which was ironic because he'd always claimed he would never be like his father; that he would never turn to the bottle because of a woman. His claim was quickly proven false, because mom leaving us really fucked him up. I knew he'd be drunk by the time we finished closing—if he wasn't already—and I didn't want Jackson and Julie anywhere near him.

"Honestly, it's fine," I said.

Jackson shook his head. "Why don't you at least give me your cellphone number, in case anything happens on the way home." He was making eye contact with me for the first time tonight, and it caused butterflies to start flapping their wings inside me.

"I don't have a cellphone, but I can call you from my house phone," I offered lamely.

"You don't have a cellphone!?" Julie screeched. "My mom would kill us if we let you leave this late on your bike. Seriously, call your parents and let them know we'll take you home if they can't pick you up."

I could feel my lower back starting to sweat. There was nobody I needed to call, and hearing the words "your parents" caused a sharp pain in my heart.

Jackson and Julie were still staring at me, waiting for me to agree to the ride home.

"Okay, if you're really sure it's fine?" I tried my hardest to not sound as timid as a mouse, but I did not accomplish that.

"We're so sure," Jackson offered with a smile. "Do you want to use my phone?" He pulled it out of his pocket and held it out for me.

I shook my head no. "It's all good."

"Now that that's settled, get ready to learn closing!" Julie said, clapping her hands together. "It's kind of like a game for me and Jackson. We each pick three songs, and try to get everything done before they're all over. We have to take off the last of the tablecloths, vacuum the floors, and mop the entrance, the kitchen, and the bathrooms. Sometimes we'll roll silverware if we don't feel like doing it the next day." She turned to Jackson, who was already plugging his phone into the speaker. "You pick three songs already?"

"We should each do two, let Addie pick, too." He looked up at me. "We always leave the songs a surprise."

"I don't have to pick any. I don't really listen to music." I gave him a squeamish smile. I knew a lot of popular songs, but had no idea what their names were, or even who sung them.

"We are definitely going to change that," Julie said as she took the phone from Jackson. "I'm a huge Swiftie."

I laughed while Jackson audibly groaned. "I seriously have every song of hers memorized because of how much Julie plays her."

Julie laughed wickedly, picking her three songs before pressing play.

A rap song started playing, and Julie and Jackson immediately started singing along. Jackson was singing the main parts, and Julie was doing the background vocals. I couldn't stop laughing at the lyrics, and the fact that both of them were singing such a provocative song as we started the closing duties.

Julie and I started removing all the tablecloths while Jackson got the vacuum. "Don't be shy, go ahead and sing!" Julie said as we carried the first pile of laundry to the back of the kitchen.

"I don't know this song," I admitted.

"You've never heard 'No Hands' by Waka Flocka Flame?" she gasped.

I furrowed my eyebrows. "Waka who?"

"Oh lord, that's bad," Julie said with a laugh.

The next song started playing, and this one I actually recognized. It was "Sing For The Moment" by Eminem. I mouthed the words, not confident enough to actually rap like Julie and Jackson were both doing while we all worked in tandem. I knew the next song after that, but didn't know the name.

"'Stronger' by Kanye West," Jackson called out over the speakers. "Have you ever seen the movie *Never Back Down*? This song is in it; it's my favorite movie!" I shook my head no and Jackson playfully rolled his eyes.

While we were getting the mops ready, Julie's song picks started playing, and she started shaking her hips as Taylor Swift's voice blasted through the speakers.

"Please tell me you've heard 'Enchanted'!" she yelled over the music. I laughed as I shook my head no. Even Jackson was singing, and I was laughing so hard at both of them that I had to clutch my stomach.

They were twirling around the room using the mops as microphones, and when the last bridge of the song began, both of them dropped to their knees to belt out the words. When it was done, I clapped dramatically for them as they stood and bowed for me.

Jackson cleaned the men's bathroom while us girls cleaned the women's, then we met in the kitchen to unplug Jackson's phone from the speaker.

"And look at that, we're already done with closing. We don't even need to listen to the last song Julie picked," Jackson said with a wicked grin.

Julie let out a long, exaggerated laugh. "Guess we'll just have to listen to it on the way home! And you can sit in the middle!"

Jackson stuck his tongue out at Julie before grabbing my backpack off its hook and handing it to me.

"When he picks music first, he purposely chooses long songs so that we never make it to all of mine." She bent down to whisper in my ear, "Jokes on him because the only CDs in my car are Taylor Swift."

Julie locked up the back door, and I followed them to her truck. It was one of those old trucks that didn't have backseats, so Jackson really did have to sit between us. Our thighs were touching, and I tried my hardest not to hyperfocus on that bit of contact. Julie drove around to the front of the street where my bike was still leaning against the rack.

"I'll get it," Jackson said before I could open the passenger door. He crawled over me to get out of the truck, and I felt frozen to the seat as his bangs swiped across my forehead on his way out. I tried to act nonchalant, like that closeness didn't send me completely off-kilter. I looked over at Julie without moving my head, but she was just mouthing along to the song she had started playing.

I watched in the side mirror as Jackson picked up my bike and placed it in the bed of the truck. His biceps were illuminated under the streetlights, and I swallowed in an attempt to get the sudden dryness out of my throat. When I saw him walking back toward the car, I hurried to jump out for him before he could crawl over me again.

We didn't speak on the way home; the two of them continued to sing along theatrically to the music, and I just pointed out where to turn when needed. When they pulled into my driveway, I was relieved to see that Peter's car was gone. He was probably out at a bar. "Thanks for the ride."

"We'll see you tomorrow! Have two songs ready!" Julie said.

I hopped out of the truck but before I could shut the door, Jackson stopped it with his arm, jumping out after me and getting my bike out of the truck bed before I could even protest.

"Thanks," I said as he followed me to the side of the house. "You can just leave it behind the gate."

I crossed my arms as Jackson fixed his wavy hair.

"Have a good night, Addie. It was really nice meeting you."

I nodded back, trying to calm down that fizziness that reappeared in my stomach. "See you tomorrow, Jackson."

He smiled at me before walking back to Julie's truck. I waved at both of them from the front porch as they backed out, and I could hear the faint sound of Julie's music as they drove down the block.

I smiled—for the first time since Mom left, I felt like things might actually be okay.

Chapter 3

NOW

June

Goddammit. Sophie was still fucking gorgeous. Her red hair was pinned up, her curtain bangs framing her face. She was wearing a long, flowy white dress that made her blue eyes pop. The blush on her cheeks made her look like a perfect porcelain doll. I looked like a sewer rat compared to her. My white-blonde hair was stringy and loose down my back, and I had been sweating all through my drive from North Carolina. My ratty hoodie and biker shorts weren't much help, either. I don't even think my Converse were laced.

"Hey, Sophie. You look great," I said, hoping the cheeriness in my voice sounded real.

She smiled at me, and we both knew it was fake.

"Addison. What a surprise to see you." She didn't even sound like a bitch when she said it—just confused and intrigued. Her eyes moved from Jackson to me, waiting for one of us to explain.

"I'm on my way out, actually. Congrats on your engagement!" My voice chirped so high I would've laughed if I wasn't absolutely mortified.

I squeezed between the two of them, not able to breathe until I was out the front door. I stepped on one of my untied laces, almost eating shit on the concrete. That sure would've been the cherry on top.

"Hey—hey, wait up!" My hand was on the handle of my car door, and I so badly wanted to pretend I didn't hear Jackson running after me. *Act natural.*

I turned around, leaning back against my car.

"You're getting married," I managed to choke out with a smile. "That's amazing. Sophie Waters. You guys were always such a great couple." Lie, lie, lie.

Jackson just pursed his lips. He knew I was bullshitting. "You're still a terrible liar." He was smiling.

"You don't know me anymore, Jackson," I shot back.

He ignored the dig. His eyes roamed my face, like he was trying to find any differences from the last time he saw me.

"How long are you in town for?"

I rolled my eyes and shrugged. "I have no idea. Maybe the entire summer. I don't know how shitty the house is going to be. It's Peter, so the place is probably a dump."

"Do you need help?"

I tried not to scoff. Help from who? Jackson? Yeah, right.

"I'm good, Jackson. I'm sure you're busy with wedding planning."

He looked apologetic, and it absolutely wrecked me. Neither of us said anything else; we just stared at each other, and I focused on that scar across his eyebrow. I didn't know this man. I had no idea what type of person he was now. And I shouldn't *want* to know. He had been here this whole time, exactly where I left him. Without a word I got into my car, and Jackson stepped back so I could pull away from the curb. I watched in my rearview mirror as he stayed in the street, watching me as I drove away.

Chapter 4

BEFORE

September, Fourteen Years Ago

I was a nervous wreck the first day of high school. I'd walked the path from the front door to my locker three times during freshman orientation, and probably practiced my locker combination close to fifty times so I would have it memorized, but I was still anxious. There wasn't a single person I knew besides Jackson Delvecchio, and we had only worked together four times. Plus, we didn't have any classes together, so I doubted I would even run into him.

After English, math, and chemistry, I had lunch. My stomach was a fluster of nerves over not knowing anyone, and I tried to get a view of the cafeteria as I went through the lunch line.

I looked at the person behind me to see if they noticed the lunch lady giving me my lunch for free after I read her my student ID number. They were on their phone scrolling through Twitter, totally oblivious. I had to stop being so paranoid.

My knees were practically knocking together as I looked around the lunch room, trying to find an empty seat. Out the corner of my eye,

I noticed someone waving their hand above their head, and I looked to see who it was attached to. Jackson Delvecchio was motioning for me to sit next to him, and I cocked an eyebrow in surprise. I even turned around to make sure no one was behind me. When I turned back toward him, he cupped his hands around his mouth and yelled, "Yes, Addison Bianchi, I'm waving at you!"

I was sure my entire face flushed red. A few students turned to look in my direction, and I put my head down as I rushed over to Jackson's table. He had headphones in, and when I approached, he pulled both buds out of his ears and shoved them into his back pocket. Something about it made my stomach flutter, that he stopped listening to music in order to give me his full attention.

"What's up, Jackson?" I asked shyly. We had only been working together for two weeks; I wouldn't even say we were friends, and I was surprised he was acknowledging me.

His eyes bounced from me to the open seat next to him. His eyes crinkled, and he let out a low chuckle. "Addie, you can sit."

The heat returned to my cheeks as I set down my tray and crawled my legs over the bench. Jackson picked up the bag of apple slices from my tray, opening it and taking a slice as if we'd had lunch together a million times before.

"How's your day going?" I asked as I grabbed an apple slice for myself.

"It's good. This school is like, just a bunch of different squares. I accidentally walked in the same circle three times until I realized the numbers on the doors were the same every time. I was late to second hour," he said.

I giggled, and we fell into an easy conversation about our classes. A few other kids joined our table and Jackson introduced me to each one, even though I knew I wouldn't remember their names. All of them were wearing football jerseys, and I looked at Jackson, wondering if he was a jock, too.

"Do you play on the football team, too?" I asked Jackson.

Everyone at the table laughed, even Jackson.

"Nah, football was more my brother Sam's thing."

I nodded my head.

"Are you guys coming to the game after school?" one of the guys asked.

Jackson looked at me, acting the same way he had when he took one of my apple slices. "Do you want to go to the game?" he asked, as if we'd hung out plenty of times before.

"I guess so."

Jackson turned back to the guys and they continued to talk about the game. I smiled to myself as I finished my lunch. He wanted to hang out with me.

***

After school, I met Jackson outside the fence to the football field, and we walked up the stands together.

"Did you get lost finding any of your other classes?" I asked as we leaned our backs against the bench behind us. The sight of Jackson's bare legs crossed on the bench in front of us made me realize I'd only seen him in work clothes before this. My eyes traveled up his body from his khaki shorts to his gray shirt, which had a red pocket with an Aztec design.

"Nope, I finally figured it out." He smiled at me and unzipped his backpack next to him. "Hey, do you have Cash for math, too?"

I nodded. "Yeah, I have her second hour."

He pulled out a blue folder and pointed at a worksheet. "Did you have trouble with this?" It was the homework assignment from class today.

"Not really." I shrugged one shoulder and he shoved the folder back in his backpack.

"I'm walking to the restaurant after the game; do you want to come with me? Jules is working tonight, and I'm craving pizza. Do you think you could help me with that homework, too?"

Jackson was so easy to be around, and it made my stomach flutter. "Yeah sure."

"Sweet." He pulled his cellphone out of his pocket. "I know you don't have a phone. Did you want to call your parents?"

This was the second time he had said "your parents" as if I had people at home who cared about my whereabouts.

I averted my eyes and pushed his phone away from me. "I don't live with my parents; it's just me and my brother," I said, as if it wasn't a big deal.

I acted like I was interested in the football warm ups, and when Jackson didn't respond, I looked at him out of my peripheral vision.

"Did they, um . . . die?" Jackson asked quietly.

A laugh burst out of me, and Jackson looked horrified at my reaction.

"Oh my god, sorry, no, they didn't die. It's not that dramatic. My mom lives up in Traverse City with her boyfriend, and I've never met my dad," I said quickly. I covered my mouth and turned toward the field.

"Oh, that's interesting," he said, finally. It wasn't demeaning, the way he said it—more like he was confused and trying to understand. "So, you just live with an older brother?"

"Peter, yeah, he's twenty-two."

"Is he kind of like your dad?" Jackson asked.

Another laugh escaped me, because yeah, right. Peter was in no way, shape, or form like a father figure.

"No, he either yells at me like I'm a complete inconvenience in his life, or pretends like I don't exist," I said. I couldn't believe I was admitting all of this to Jackson, but he was listening and asking questions like he actually gave a shit. It was *nice,* and so, so refreshing.

"Is he your only sibling?"

"That I know of," I said lightheartedly. "We have the same mom but different dads."

Jackson made a sound of confirmation, then stopped badgering me with questions.

"Sorry for being all invasive in your business," he added.

"You weren't, it's not a big deal." I gave him a smile to let him know it was all good, and he gave me a one-sided grin that made my stomach somersault.

The game started, and Jackson explained the rules so I could attempt to follow along. It started to get chilly by the third quarter, and I pulled my hoodie on, tucking up my legs and holding them to my chest.

"We don't have to stay for the whole thing if you're cold. Let's head to the restaurant," Jackson suggested.

We walked around to the front of the school so I could grab my bike, and I rode it slowly next to Jackson as he walked.

When we got to Delvecchios' we sat at a corner booth, spreading out our notebooks while Julie served us pizza.

Our homework sheets quickly became fingerprinted with pizza grease, and at the end of the night, Julie brought us a few cannoli to snack on. I couldn't take more than a bite, and Jackson ended up finishing them off for me.

We stayed after the restaurant closed, finishing up our homework while Julie blasted music through the speakers as she cleaned.

I didn't even have to ask if they would be taking me home and putting my bike in the back of the truck. I already knew they wouldn't let me ride it home by myself in the dark.

On the way home we listened to one of Julie's Taylor Swift CDs, and as they belted out the lyrics to "You Belong With Me", I mouthed the words, feeling a little bit more comfortable with showing my full self to them. Jackson knew all my family issues now, and he still wanted to hang out with me. I smiled the whole drive home as we sang, realizing that Jackson Delvecchio wasn't just my coworker anymore—he was my friend now. Maybe he would even become my best friend.

Chapter 5

NOW

June

The next morning, I woke up to three loud knocks on my driver's side window. When I got to Peter's house last night, I couldn't find the courage to go in. Instead, I went to Wendy's to get a meal, use their bathroom, and take advantage of their free Wi-Fi all day. When I pulled into the driveway, I still couldn't make myself go in, so I slept in my car, which I was no stranger to doing.

I rubbed my hands down my face before sitting the seat up straight. My neck ached, and every joint in my body was stiff. I blinked at the person standing outside my car. Jackson fucking Delvecchio. I turned on the car and rolled down the window.

"Why the hell are you sleeping in your car?"

I ran my fingers through my hair. I didn't want to risk looking in the mirror to see how awful I looked.

"I wasn't ready to go inside yet."

He looked me up and down. "Come on, I'll go with you." I went to argue, but he cut me off. "I brought snacks." He held up a white plastic bag, then scrunched his nose. "And seriously, you need a shower."

I scoffed. "Always the charmer." I rolled up my window and tried to ignore him, but he didn't step away. Instead, he pulled on my door handle, and I cursed myself for leaving it unlocked.

I stayed in the seat and stared up at him, his arm resting on the top of the door frame, waiting for me to get up. I silently cursed Peter before lifting myself out of the car. Why did he have to leave me the house?

I grabbed my suitcases out the trunk, and Jackson carried one up to the house for me. I unlocked the door and inhaled a deep breath. "He didn't even change the locks," I mumbled.

"Maybe he thought you'd come back," Jackson said softly. Had Jackson thought I'd come back, too? No, most likely not.

"Honestly, fuck Peter. I don't want to deal with this," I groaned as I stomped a foot on the porch.

Jackson slipped past me to open the door, walking in while I stood on the porch, peering in over his shoulder.

"Your brother was a real piece of work," Jackson scoffed as he kicked an empty bottle out of the walkway. I took a step inside, finding exactly what I expected.

The place truly was a dump. The leather couch in the family room was peeling, the paint on the walls was chipped and stained, and the kitchen counter was lined with empty bottles.

"I can't believe I've never been in here," Jackson said from the family room. He set the snacks he'd brought down on the coffee table, crossing his arms and looking around.

In all the years I had known Jackson, I'd never let him or anyone else in his family set foot inside this house.

"Well, you weren't missing much," I said with a sigh. I couldn't even bring myself to walk down the short hallway to my old room. "Peter's room was in the basement. I'm sure it's even worse down there."

He pulled out a box of Cheez-Itz from the bag on the table and threw it to me. "Eat something, and then let's decide what to tackle first."

My stomach growled as I opened the box and popped a Cheez-It into my mouth. "And you're helping me because . . . ?"

He scratched at his jaw before meeting my eyes. "Because I want to."

I couldn't stand how sincere he looked. "Don't you have like, a restaurant to run?"

He laughed at me as he shook his head. "Believe it or not, I'm hardly there. Remember Rami?"

I nodded. I loved Rami; he was one of the waiters who had started working at Delvecchios' when he was a teenager. He was at least a good ten years older than us, and had been almost thirty by the time I started working there.

"He manages the place alongside Sophie. I do everything from home, mostly."

I ate another Cheez-It while I accepted this information. "What's up with Phil and Marie?" I asked. *And how the hell did they convince Jackson to buy the restaurant?*

Jackson chewed on his lip while he watched me, then gave a pained smile. "Marie is down in Texas with her sister. She moved down there after Phil died."

I choked. I put a fist over my mouth, trying to clear my throat. "Phil?" I loved their dad—he was one of the nicest men I had ever met. Marie and Phil were the best parents, too. They were so loving and generous, and one of the only couples I had ever seen that were truly in love. They had treated me like one of their own children.

"Heart attack, two years ago," Jackson confirmed.

I shook my head in disbelief.

"Damn." I wondered if that was why Jackson bought the restaurant. To keep it in the family, since Phil was gone and Marie left. "I'm so sorry."

Jackson gave a one shouldered shrug. "Yeah . . . Me, too." He ran a hand through his short hair. "So, where should we start?"

He clearly didn't want to talk about it anymore, but I couldn't fully process this information yet. Phil *died,* and Jackson still didn't try to contact me. It started to confirm what I'd always feared, I wasn't as important to the Delvecchios as they had been to me.

I wiped the Cheeze-It dust off my palms before clearing my throat, pursing my lips as I looked around the room. "Start from the bottom up? Maybe we can go through his clothes and donate them."

Jackson followed me down the stairs into the basement. It was an open floor plan with a washer and dryer in a small alcove off to the side, and Peter's bed, TV, and dresser in one corner. There was still a pile of dirty clothes on the ground.

Jackson started picking up the pile. "Let's just toss anything dirty." He ran back upstairs to get trash bags.

My eyes started to glaze over as I looked around the room. I didn't want to have to do this. When Jackson came back downstairs, I wiped at my eyes quickly.

"Sorry," I said as I used my hoodie sleeve to wipe under my nose. "It's just . . . a lot to do, and I don't want to do it."

He looked around the room before meeting my eyes again. "I have an idea: Let's do the same thing we did in high school. We'll pick a time frame for a task, and choose songs to listen to. When the songs are over, we take a break. Take a walk, or just sit and relax. It'll make it more manageable," Jackson suggested.

It actually wasn't a terrible idea. And it made the whole thing seem less overwhelming.

"Okay, but I definitely need a drink first." I grabbed a half-drunk bottle of whiskey off Peter's dresser and took the cap off before shuddering at the smell. I couldn't put my lips to the bottle to drink it, knowing Peter had probably done the same. I raised it up, fountaining the liquor into my mouth without touching the bottle against my lips. I drank it in one quick gulp. "Ugh, disgusting." I wiped my mouth and handed it over to Jackson, but he shook his head. "Too early to drink?" I joked.

He itched his right eyebrow right over the scar before meeting my eyes. "I, um . . . I don't drink anymore."

I laughed, assuming he was joking. Then I met his gaze, and my jaw snapped shut the second I realized he was looking at me sincerely. "Oh, you're serious?"

He nodded awkwardly. "I've been sober for five years."

"Oh, shit," I said as I turned around and shoved the bottle behind the bed frame. "I'm so sorry. I had no idea."

Jackson laughed at how flustered I was. "Addie, I can be around it. Sophie still drinks."

I turned around and pushed my flyaway hairs out of my face. "Let's just . . . pick the playlist for the task," I said to change the subject. "I hate to say it, but I've been listening to Taylor Swift's new albums with all her rerecorded versions. I bet Julie had a field day over those when they were released."

Jackson laughed as he took my phone out of my hand. "You have no idea. I took her to The Eras Tour for her birthday last year, in

California. I let her pick my outfit and put glitter on my face and everything."

"Oh, please tell me you have pictures of that," I begged. "So, Julie stayed in California, huh?"

Jackson nodded. "Yeah, she got married three years ago. She's a big fancy lawyer now, and she and her wife live in LA."

"Well, the first song on today's playlist has to be 'Enchanted', then. Taylor's Version, obviously. It was the first song Julie played on my first shift."

Jackson smiled down at my phone at my request. "You remember that, huh?"

"My first shift at my first job? Of course I do." The real reason it was such a deep memory was because it was the day I met Jackson and Julie. But I wasn't brave enough to tell him that.

He handed my phone back to me. "I added my number to your contacts."

I wanted to say something like, "I'll delete it as soon as you leave," but we both would've known it was a lie.

Chapter 6

BEFORE

December, Fourteen Years Ago

By the time December came around, I was in a steady routine with the Delvecchio family. The first month I worked there I'd ride my bike to the restaurant, and Jackson and Julie would drive me home in the truck. On Fridays, Jackson and I would walk from school to the restaurant, where we'd change in the bathroom before getting ready to work. When it rained or the weather got too cold, I allowed them to pick me up for my shift.

Julie started waitressing again once I was fully trained, so Jackson and I worked in a perfect tandem on Fridays and Saturdays as the only bussers. Closing the restaurant with them was *fun;* they made work feel like a hangout instead of a job. They showed me so much music, and I wasn't shy around them anymore. Now I was dancing on the tables and singing into mop handles with them.

On occasional Saturdays, Phil and Marie would pop in during the dinner rush, and I couldn't believe what a force Marie could be in the kitchen. Her quiet demeanor disappeared and she turned into a fierce woman, barking orders. She never lost her cool, and she stayed professional while telling everyone what to do.

Jackson, I'd learned, was one of those guys that was friends with everyone. He didn't have a specific friend group—instead, he rotated between the jocks, the stoners, the band kids, the drama kids, and even the brainy students. He asked genuine questions, and he knew how to make people laugh without even trying. Every day I walked into the cafeteria at lunch not knowing where he'd be sitting. He didn't seem to have a routine or a schedule for where he sat each day; he just joined whoever he happened to talk to in the hallway before lunch. But *every* day he waved me over to sit with him, wherever he was. His energy was addicting, and it wasn't long before I realized I had a crush on him. It wasn't like he was going out of his way for me or anything. He was nice to everyone, but I couldn't help feeling special that I was *one* of the people who got to revolve in his orbit.

On the Sunday before Christmas, the Delvecchios threw a staff Christmas party at the bowling alley in Tostela. It felt like an actual family Christmas party. I had never enjoyed the holiday with Peter and my mom as much as I was enjoying my night with my coworkers.

Mom had invited us up to Traverse City for Christmas, but there was no way I could sit in a car with Peter for three hours, and the thought of being trapped in her boyfriend's house for an entire weekend made my stomach hurt. Peter still hadn't even decided if he was going yet.

At the end of the employee Christmas party, Jackson pulled me aside. "Hey, you know Ezra from the football team?"

I had to wrack my brain for who Jackson was talking about. Each friend group of his was organized in my head by the little traits I could remember. Finally, it clicked. "Ezra, the one who broke his arm at the homecoming game?"

Jackson nodded. "He's having a party tonight. Do you want to come with me?"

It was Christmas break, and if I didn't have to go home to Peter, that was a plus. We mostly avoided each other throughout the week since he worked from two to ten pm, so when I woke up for school he was still sleeping, and I always made sure I was in my room before he got home. On Saturdays he was typically at a bar, so that left Sundays as my least favorite day of the week.

"Sure," I said.

This would be my first high school party, and Ezra was a junior, so I assumed it would be mostly older kids. Jackson wasn't just friends with kids from every social group, but from every grade, too. I think it was because he had two siblings who were both older than him: Julie by four years, and Sam by seven. And Julie wasn't joking that first day I met them; Jackson really *did* get held back in kindergarten, so he was already fifteen when he started freshman year.

Julie was nice enough to drop us off at the party, and I followed Jackson into the basement. It was mostly kids from the junior varsity and varsity football teams, along with some of the cheerleaders. Everyone seemed to say hi to Jackson at the same time, and someone brought him a red Solo Cup. I declined when he offered me a sip—the only time I had ever drank was after we had a busy shift at the restaurant before Thanksgiving, when Julie sneaked us each a glass of wine while we were closing.

Everyone was sitting in a circle in the middle of the room, with two stacks of cards in the middle. "We're playing seven minutes in heaven," Ezra told us with a waggle of his eyebrows.

Jackson laughed. "Come on, we're freshmen and even we're not that juvenile." I looked up at Jackson, wondering what he usually did at the other parties he had been to. Or how many girls he had kissed, for that matter.

"Oh, don't be a lame ass, join the circle. You too, Addie." I was surprised Ezra remembered my name, and I hesitantly looked over at Jackson. He just shrugged at me and pulled me down next to him.

"We're just waiting for Paul and Emily to come back," the girl next to me said. I tapped my fingers nervously against my kneecaps. Jackson took a few large gulps from his cup until the couple who had been in the closet came back with smiles on their faces.

"So the way we're playing is a guy grabs a card from this deck," Ezra explained as he pointed to the stack of cards on the left. "And then all the girls grab from the right deck. Whichever girl has the same card as the guy has to go in the closet."

I looked up at Jackson warily, but he just smiled back at me like it was no big deal.

"Jackson, you may do the honors," Ezra said as he lifted his cup.

Jackson shuffled the cards on the left before settling with his pick. I nervously watched all the girls reach forward for a card in the other pile. Jackson elbowed me, motioning for me to grab the last card. I tried to keep my fingers from shaking as I picked it up.

Jackson looked around the circle mischievously before dramatically slapping his card down. I looked back and forth between his card and mine, my eyes widening when I saw we both had the queen of diamonds.

All the other girls put down their cards face up, and I watched as Jackson looked around at all of them. I didn't want to put my card down. I could feel my face heating, and my hands hadn't stopped shaking. Jackson's smile turned to a frown when he realized none of the cards on the floor were a match. He finally looked over at me, pinching his eyebrows together when he noticed I still had my card in my hands. He smirked before plucking the card right out of my fingers. When he realized we both had the same card, his eyes widened, too. His gaze cut to mine, his lips parting in shock.

"Oh shit, Addie has the match!" one of the boys from the football team said, and everyone started hollering and cheering. I gave Jackson a nervous smile, and he chugged the rest of the beer in his cup before throwing it down theatrically and grabbing my hand to drag me to the closet.

"Have fun, kiddos!" another girl called after us.

When Jackson and I stepped into the closet, we just stared at each other in the dark for a moment until our eyes adjusted. There were at least three feet between us, and it felt like we were daring each other to close the distance. I expected him to say we didn't have to do this—that it was a silly game, and nobody actually expected us to kiss.

"So, how do we do this?" he asked as he took a step toward me.

What!?

My heart was ricocheting in my chest like a damn pinball machine. "You've kissed someone before, right?" I asked, raising my eyebrow.

Jackson let out a small laugh. "Nope, have you?"

I shook my head. Jackson hadn't had his first kiss either? Considering he could probably ask out any girl he wanted and she would say yes, this came as a shock. "Um, I don't know, what do they do in the movies?"

He took another hesitant step toward me, and I watched as he lifted his right hand to cup my neck. "Something like this, right?" His voice came out in a whisper. His hand was warm, and the sensation traveled throughout my entire body. He held my face with such confidence. Every nerve ending in my body lit up, and I knew I'd never recover. There was no way I could get rid of my crush now. We were about to have our first kiss together—something we would share forever.

"Yep, that seems good," I whispered back. I stared up at him, and I swear, the look in his eyes was telling me he wanted this; game or not, he wanted to kiss me. He rubbed his thumb against the length of my jaw, and I felt like I was slipping into a pot of boiling water. Bubbles popped and burst in my stomach, spreading out into every limb.

He swallowed deeply. "Okay, then. Are you ready?" I nodded slowly, and then his face was so close to mine I could feel his breath against my lips. I could smell the beer he just drank, and I wanted to taste it for myself. We stayed like that for a moment—his nose against mine, his lips a hairsbreadth away.

"I'm nervous," I whispered against his lips.

"I'm not," Jackson said before breaking the distance.

His lips were on mine in an instant. I couldn't help the sound that came from the back of my throat. I reached forward to fist his T-shirt in my hands, and he angled my face upward to deepen the kiss and slide his tongue into my mouth. Oh my god, I had to thank the person who suggested playing this game. Seven minutes in heaven just became my new favorite game.

His other hand pulled at my waist, pressing my hips flush against his, and every graze of his fingers against my skin made me crave more. I wanted his shirt gone. I wanted to see the freckle that I knew sat on his left collarbone. I wanted my shirt gone, too, I just wanted Jackson's skin against mine. I wanted more than kissing.

I got lost in the kiss. The only thing my brain could process was *Jackson, Jackson, Jackson*. My mind drifted back to the first day I met him, when he crawled over me in the truck and his hair brushed against my forehead. That was it, I realized suddenly. That was the moment that he'd lodged himself in my brain, and he'd been living there ever since.

Three loud bangs against the door caused us to flinch away from each other, our eyes wild as reality settled back in. At some point I must've run my hands through Jackson's hair; it was sticking out in every different direction. I wiped a finger against my lips, and a shiver ran through me when I remembered the sensation of Jackson moving his mouth against mine. I could still taste the beer from his tongue.

"What the hell are you guys doing? It's been almost fifteen minutes! Eight-minute penalty!"

"Oh my god," slipped out of Jackson's mouth as we both scrambled to fix our hair before busting out of the closet.

I giggled when I saw the group of wide-eyed people standing outside the door.

"What were you guys doing in there?" someone asked.

I opened my mouth to answer, but Jackson cut me off. "Nothing, we were just talking about how stupid this game is."

My eyes snapped up to his, but he wouldn't look at me. I wanted to tell everyone that he was a fucking liar. Was he embarrassed that we kissed? Or embarrassed that he liked it? He was the one that wanted to follow through with the game!

I didn't say anything. Instead, I mumbled something about having to use the bathroom, then I ran upstairs and out the front door.

That was the first time Jackson ever hurt me—and it wouldn't be the last. It was just the beginning.

***

I paced up and down the block, replaying the kiss over and over again in my head. The way Jackson said he wasn't nervous, then grabbed my hip and pulled me toward him. Why did he have to act like a jerk after?

Snow had begun to fall around me, and I wrapped my arms tighter around myself.

"Jesus, Addie, I've been looking everywhere for you."

I turned around to find Jackson walking up behind me, pulling the hood of his jacket over his head to block the snow.

"I said I had to use the bathroom," I said lamely as I continued my walk. I had this entire block memorized from how long I had been walking. Five houses to the end of the block one way, ten the opposite way to loop around the cul-de-sac.

"Yeah, and you never came back. I sat outside the door for thirty minutes before I realized nobody was in there."

Something pinched in my chest. Why did he have to act like he cared?

"It sucks when someone disappoints you, doesn't it?" I was attempting to sound tough, but it just came out pathetic.

Jackson shoved his hands in his pockets, unable to meet my eyes as he kicked his toes against the layer of snow on the sidewalk. "Addie, I'm—"

A car honked behind me, and I turned around to find Julie's truck.

"I called her to come get us. The party was stupid," Jackson said. What was he going to say before that?

I didn't turn back around to look at him as I opened the passenger door, letting him get in the truck first. I reluctantly jumped in after him, keeping myself as close to the door as I could so that our thighs didn't have to touch.

Julie was asking about the party on our way home, but I kept my mouth shut. She kept saying she was happy we weren't drunk; that we were too young to start drinking, and she was proud that we were being responsible. I zoned out for most of it, trying not to think of Jackson holding me in the closet.

Peter's car was in the driveway when we pulled up. The light from his room in the basement was turned on, which was a relief because that meant I didn't have to walk past him to get to my room. The Delvecchios knew I lived with just my brother now—Jackson had shared the information with them after I explained my situation to him. I pretended not to notice that they started giving me free food from work after they found out.

"Thanks, guys," I said before hopping out of the truck.

"Have a good Christmas," Jackson called out from the window. I didn't turn around to respond, and instead just raised my arm in a goodbye.

Chapter 7

BEFORE

December, Fourteen Years Ago

Christmas morning fell on a Sunday this year, and I was sitting on the couch reading a book when I heard a loud knock on the door. I sighed and closed my book. Peter left yesterday morning to drive out to our mom's house, and he wouldn't be back until tomorrow morning. I'd expected to have a quiet weekend alone. Would I never have a single moment of peace in this house?

I walked to the front door, peering behind the curtain and gasping when I saw Marie and Jackson standing on the porch. I pulled down the hem of my sleep shorts, making sure they weren't scrunched up on my thighs, and ran my fingers through my greasy hair before pulling open the front door.

I hadn't talked to Jackson since he and Julie dropped me off after the party, yet he was standing on the porch, smiling at me like nothing had happened. I was actually happy to see Jackson, regardless; the restaurant was closed for the holidays, and this was the first weekend

I hadn't worked. I hadn't expected to see any of the Delvecchios until the following weekend.

"Merry Christmas," Jackson said as he held out a present. It was wrapped in green paper with holly leaves printed all over it. My name was written in Sharpie across the top—I could tell by the cursive that Julie had written it.

"Oh, thank you," I said as I took it from him. "I didn't get you anything."

"It's from my entire family, we didn't expect anything in return," Jackson said with an adorable smile. He shoved his hands in the front pockets of his winter jacket, his deep-brown eyes twinkling with the reflection of the snow outside. I looked at both of them, letting myself smile.

"Go ahead and open it, sweetheart," Marie said with a laugh. I ignored the bite of cold wind and the goose bumps rising on my bare legs as I unwrapped the paper, letting it fall to the floor behind me.

I raised an eyebrow when I held the unwrapped package in my hands. It was a cellphone. Nothing extravagant by any means, but a cellphone—my first cellphone. I looked up at them, my mouth hanging open, and they both smiled at me.

"You guys got me a cellphone? This is incredible, thank you," I said in amazement.

Jackson chuckled at me, reaching forward to rip off the plastic for me. "It's just a prepaid phone, nothing crazy. But now we can call and text." He was acting like it was no big deal, but he didn't understand how much this meant to me. Jackson wanted to be able to call and text me? My heart felt like it went into an arrhythmia.

Marie shivered from the next gust of wind, and I watched as she peeked behind me, trying to look around. They were both standing on the porch in the December air, but I didn't want to invite them inside. "Where's your brother, honey?"

I awkwardly clasped my hands behind my back, focusing on Jackson as he opened my new phone. "He went up north to visit our mom."

Both Marie's eyes and Jackson's came to meet mine, and I tried to plaster on a smile. Jackson looked at his mom, then back to me. "You've been by yourself all weekend?" he asked.

I nodded, feeling like Kevin McCallister, minus the family that actually loved him.

"How about you come over? We just finished presents at our house, and Phil is whipping up breakfast as we speak," Marie said as she placed an arm on Jackson's shoulder.

Christmas with the Delvecchios? Now *that* sounded like the perfect Christmas present. "Oh, I wouldn't want to intrude," I said, trying not to sound too eager over their offer. "And I don't even have anything nice to wear."

Jackson reached down and pinched at the fabric of the plaid pajama pants he was wearing. "We stay in our pajamas all day on Christmas."

Before I could counter, Marie cut me off. "Go get changed, we'll meet you in the car." She grabbed Jackson's arm and they both turned to walk down the driveway. Jackson still had my new phone in his hands. They didn't even give me the option to say no again.

I rushed to my room to change into a hoodie and a pair of black yoga pants. I pulled my hair back into a low bun and put a layer of mascara on my lashes. I didn't even tie my Converse before running out the front door and sliding into the backseat of Marie's car.

On the way to their house, Jackson programmed my phone for me, making sure to put his phone number in. "I'm number one in your favorites now, too," he said with a wink. I tried not to blush. I couldn't even stay mad at him about the party.

He added the restaurant, Mr. and Mrs. Delvecchio, and Julie to my contacts next.

When we got to the house the smell of bacon and eggs hit my senses, and my stomach growled. Julie was at their kitchen table drinking orange juice in her Christmas pajamas, her hair braided into two long French braids down her back. She yelped when she saw me, running over and wrapping me in a hug. "Merry Christmas! What are you doing here?"

"I was forced here against my will," I said with a giggle. "Thanks for the phone."

"Of course, of course. I would've added you to our family phone plan if I could have."

Phil was at the stove flipping pancakes, and a tall, broad man with hair as dark as Jackson's was sitting on the couch watching TV in their family room.

"Let me give you a tour," Jackson said as he grabbed my arm.

I had never been in their house before, and I tried not to gawk at the open floor plan. The kitchen was the first thing you walked into from the garage—Peter and I didn't even have a garage at our house.

They had black countertops with white cabinets, and one of those fancy hood fans above the stove. The kitchen was connected to their family room, which had a vaulted ceiling and sleek, black leather couches. There was a floor-to-ceiling window on the far wall, and their entire backyard was wooded, with a playset that I could picture Julie and Jackson playing on for hours as kids.

"That's Sam," Jackson said, motioning toward his brother. He looked like the grown-up version of Jackson, with sharp features and a broad chest. I remembered Julie saying he played football, and that was apparent by looking at him. He was handsome, but I still thought Jackson was more attractive.

"Samuel," he said with a nod. He stood up to shake my hand before sitting back down. Jackson rolled his eyes, muttering under his breath about being corrected. I remembered Julie telling me that Samuel was studying law, and I couldn't help but think that he seemed like a professional lawyer already.

"I'm Addie," I said back.

I followed Jackson up a staircase to the second floor, which had a balcony looking down on the lower level. We had a bird's-eye view of Sam on the couch, and Julie, Phil, and Marie in the kitchen. Julie lifted her head from her seat at the table and waved to me. I laughed and waved back. Jackson pointed out each person's room until we made it to the end of the hallway.

"This one's mine." It was the last room on the floor, tucked behind a short corner.

I grabbed the handle and pushed it open. What kind of person was Jackson outside of the restaurant and school? I was filled with anticipation to get to know this side of him.

He had a full-sized bed pushed against the far wall with a messy heap of blankets on top, a dark-blue dresser on the opposite side with different knickknacks on top, and a drum set beside it.

"You play the drums?"

"Sure do," Jackson said bashfully as he messed with the hair that was laying across his forehead.

"Well, prove it!" I said with a laugh.

"I'll show you later. Come on, let's go eat breakfast." I followed him out of his room, closing the door behind us.

I sat at the table between Julie and Jackson, and Marie stacked my plate with pancakes, eggs, and bacon. I felt like I could burst by the time we were done eating. The six of us played a game of Monopoly after, then Jackson showed me how to use my phone. He even took a picture of us with the camera and set it as his contact picture. Julie and I posed for him while he took pictures of us, and he even got one of Mr. and Mrs. Delvecchio to set as their contact photo. True to his promise, he let me watch him play the drums until he had sweat running down his temple and had to shower. I was *obsessed*.

At the end of the night, his parents and Sam went to sleep, leaving me, Julie, and Jackson in the family room to watch a movie together. Julie was sleeping soundly in the recliner while Jackson and I sat on the couch. I was leaning against the arm rest with my legs stretched out, while Jackson was on the other side, sitting cross-legged. We weren't touching, but I could almost feel the heat of his thigh next to my toes. We were sharing a blanket, and I had to keep reminding myself to focus on the movie and not the fact that Jackson and I had kissed a week ago. Or the fact that I wanted to do it again.

I felt Jackson's fingers tentatively touch my ankle, and I swallowed deeply as I struggled to keep my attention on the screen. He slowly crept his hand up the leg of my yoga pants, trailing up my calf, pausing on my kneecap. He started rubbing circles around the top of my knee where it met my thigh. It was taking everything in me not to beg him to put his hand higher, to keep touching more, more, *more*.

I sneaked a glance over at him, but he was looking at the TV. I noticed the way his chest was moving up and down, breathing deeply while he touched me. I slid an inch toward him, giving him more access to my body. I watched as he swallowed thickly, his hand moving an inch higher, then another inch, only stopping when he reached my mid-thigh. It was physically impossible for him to reach up any higher because of the tight fabric, but the pulsing between my legs was begging for him to try. I placed my hand over his, the thin piece of material the only thing preventing our hands from touching. He continued rubbing slow circles against my skin, and I lifted my hips slightly. I slid a foot into his lap, and his jaw tightened when I pressed against the hardness between his legs.

"I can't believe I fell asleep," Julie said from the recliner, causing both Jackson and I to tense. I turned my head toward where she was stretching out, and Jackson slowly inched his hand out from inside my pants, staring at the TV like nothing was happening beneath the blanket. I pulled my shaking legs away from him, acting like I was readjusting into a more comfortable position.

Julie stood up and rubbed her eyes. "I should probably take you home now, before I get way too tired later."

I threw off the blanket, not looking at Jackson as I followed her out the door. Jackson didn't move to join us.

On the way home, Julie played her music at an ear-piercing level to keep herself alert. I was thankful we didn't have to talk.

I crawled into bed when I got home, snuggling under the covers and placing my hand over the spot on my thigh where Jackson had touched me. I rubbed my thumb back and forth, pretending it was his.

Chapter 8

BEFORE

December, Fourteen Years Ago

I didn't see the Delvecchios until the following Friday when Julie and Jackson picked me up for my shift. Jackson sat between us in the truck, and he smiled at me when I squeezed in beside him. I tried not to blush when our eyes met.

He was tapping his fingers on his thighs to the beat of the music, but his pinky kept grazing across the top of my thigh.

When we got to the restaurant, Julie tapped the corkboard with the Polaroids. "You officially made the board," she said with a wink. I dragged my eyes over the Polaroids, finding a picture of me between Jackson and Julie at the Christmas party, their arms wrapped around me. There was another photo right beneath it of me sitting at the bowling alley, tying the laces of one of my Converse, and laughing with my eyes closed. Jackson was standing next to me in the photo, his arms crossed, smiling down at me. I wanted to take the photo off the wall, stuff it in my pocket, and hide it under my pillow at home. I wanted to keep that photo forever, to remind myself every night of the way he was looking at me; that it was real and someone had captured it.

We were slammed tonight, and our shift was flying by. It was the Friday before New Year's Eve, and apparently everyone and their mom was craving Italian. Jackson and I were rushing around all night, clearing tables and running out food for the wait staff. Every time we cleaned the same table, his hand somehow found mine. It wasn't much contact, but it felt intentional every time our fingers grazed, or whenever he placed a hand on my arm or back as we passed each other in the kitchen.

I started doing it back to him, purposely brushing my arm against his if I had to walk by, reaching into the same bucket for a wet rag, and acting like I didn't realize we were about to grab the same set of silverware. I was addicted to the way his skin felt against mine. All I wanted to do was touch him.

At the end of the night after all the other employees left, Julie poured us each a small glass of wine. "That was a day," she said as she drained the entire thing in one big gulp. Jackson passed his phone around so we could each pick songs to close to.

"You two pick the music, I'm going to run home really quick to shower and change. I have a party to get to tonight. I'll come pick you guys up and take you home."

Julie had never left the two of us to close by ourselves, but I didn't mind. We had our routine down to a T; it wouldn't take too much longer without her, especially if we weren't fooling around and singing.

When Julie left, I started taking off the tablecloths while Jackson started vacuuming. "Lollipop" by Lil Wayne was playing at an obnoxious volume over the speakers, and Jackson sang to himself as I shoved the last of the tablecloths in the laundry hamper.

"Crazy In Love" by Beyoncé started next, and on my way back out to the dining room, I accidentally kicked the foot of a shelf that held empty food containers, causing three to tumble to the floor. I reached up to replace the last of the containers I'd knocked down, but I couldn't get it to balance. I stood up on my tiptoes, jumping up to try to get it to stay.

"I'll get it."

I could hear Jackson's shoes scuffling across the kitchen tile until he was right behind me. He reached up to place his hand over mine, his chest pressed against my back as he pushed the container into place.

The feeling of his breath on my neck and the hardness of his chest pressing into my shoulder caused me to arch my back and press into him. He sucked in a large gasp of air, and his hands gripped the shelf on either side of me. I spun around but neither of us made any attempt to move away from the other. We were close enough for me to feel the hardness that was growing under his belt.

Memories of us kissing in the closet flashed through my mind like a runaway train, and I gripped the shelf behind me, the sides of my hands resting up against his thumbs where he still held the shelf, blocking me in place. His hands moved down to hold my hips against him just like he did in the closet, and every rational thought left my mind. I hiked up one of my legs to rest on the counter behind Jackson, and his erection pressed against the perfect spot between my legs. We both gasped at the pressure.

He pressed himself more firmly against me, and I let out a small whimper. We were grinding against each other, the hormones and the want that had been building up since the party overtaking any other thought in my brain. Part of me wanted to kiss him again, but I was addicted to the sound of his small gasps; I wasn't ready to silence them just yet. I could get drunk off those sounds he made.

I could feel the pressure building, and I was almost sent over the edge by the way he gruffly choked out, "Addison." I loved the way he said my full name, like he couldn't believe this was happening. Our eyes locked again, and he finally leaned forward to kiss me. I closed my eyes to meet him when the sound of the back door opening caused us to fling apart like opposite magnets.

Jackson started messing with his pants and turned his back to Julie as she stepped into the kitchen.

Her eyes shot back and forth between the two of us, and I tried to slow my breathing as the last bridge of "Crazy In Love" blasted through the speakers. My heart was surely jumping out of my chest.

"I, uh . . . forgot my phone," she said as she continued to look at both of us.

"I gotta go to the bathroom," Jackson mumbled before leaving the kitchen.

I didn't say a word, and I watched as Julie walked to the counter that my foot had just been propped on. I could see the footprint from my Converse on the edge. *Oh God.* She looked out the kitchen doors before turning to face me again.

"Listen Addie, I don't know what I just walked in on. But nothing can happen between you and Jackson, okay?"

I could feel my cheeks burning up, and I stared at my shoes as I nodded my head.

"Promise me, okay? My mom would flip. She caught me kissing one of the bartenders one time, and it wasn't pretty." She placed a hand on my shoulder, forcing me to meet her eyes. "Our family really likes you, and I know you need this job. Don't fuck it up by screwing around with Jackson."

"O-okay. I promise, Julie." I was mortified, and I knew my neck was covered in a flush.

She nodded at me again just as Jackson came back into the kitchen. Her eyes narrowed at him, and I felt my skin prickle with discomfort. "Don't touch her again," Julie demanded. Then she walked out the back door.

Jackson and I split off in opposite directions. We finished the rest of the close without even a glance at each other. When we climbed into Julie's truck at the end of the night, Jackson didn't so much as touch me with his pinky again.

***

After our shift the next day, Jackson invited me to a New Year's Eve party. This time it was hosted by a drama kid named Priscilla. She had just played Alice in the school's production of *Alice in Wonderland*.

I had on a pair of jeans and a long-sleeve gray shirt with my high-top Converse, looking out of place beside all the other kids, who were dressed in formal attire. The boys were wearing button-up dress shirts with slacks, and the girls were in a variety of sparkles and cocktail dresses.

"I didn't realize it was fancy," Jackson said, leaning down to talk in my ear. His breath against the shell of my ear caused me to shiver. He was wearing jeans, too, with a pair of red Vans and a black hoodie.

"At least we stick out together."

I met his eyes, and I almost melted at the smile he was giving me. I could dip into those brown eyes and be content with whatever small piece of himself he was willing to offer me.

Don't fuck it up by screwing around with Jackson.

What was more important? Jackson or my job? Definitely my job. He just had to stop *smiling* at me like that.

"I'm going to get something to drink," I said as I turned away from him. I recognized one of the girls by the beverages, and she struck up a conversation with me. I ended up sitting with her at the table, playing a game of Catch Phrase with three other kids.

Jackson stayed on the other side of the room, sitting on the couch with a separate group of kids. There wasn't alcohol at this party, and I liked the setting. The theater students did not lack confidence. Every few seconds someone would break out in song, and everyone else would join in. Nobody was worried about making a fool of themselves, and I liked to watch Jackson sing along with them, too. Every now and then Jackson's eyes would meet mine while we sang, and a burst of heat would blast through my stomach like a blowtorch.

When there was a minute left until midnight, everyone gathered around the TV. Everyone was screaming the countdown, and when the screen flashed "Happy New Year", I looked through the throng of people for Jackson.

A few kids were throwing confetti, while couples started kissing. I pulled a piece of confetti out of my eyelash, and found Jackson watching me from across the room. For a moment I thought maybe he'd ignore Julie's request to not touch me again, because the way he was looking at me now was the same way he'd looked at me in the closet. He studied my face as he clenched and unclenched his fists, like he was having an internal battle with himself. I took a step forward, and even though we were ten feet away from each other, he took a step back. Then he slowly shook his head at me. I froze where I stood, his eyes pleading for me to stay put, like he wouldn't be able to tell me no again.

His features softened, and for a second, he looked like he was changing his mind. He leaned forward hesitantly, and a surge of adrenaline bolted through my stomach. It was going to happen—he was going to come kiss me. He straightened at the last second, and instead, he turned to the right and tapped the girl next to him. She turned around with a smile, and said something to him I couldn't hear.

Then I watched as Jackson kissed someone else.

Chapter 9

NOW

June

Jackson and I had just finished filling up a third bag when the playlist ended, so we decided it was time to take a break. "Enchanted" by Taylor Swift, "You Should See Me Now" by Neck Deep, and "Nothing Changes" by Simple Plan had been my picks. I might have been subtly giving him messages, but that's just speculation.

He'd chosen "No Hands" by Waka Flocka Flame, which I knew was an homage to the first shift I worked with him and Julie, when they were both shocked that I had never heard the song before. After that was "Circles" by Mac Miller, followed by "The First Time" by Damiano David. It felt like a message back to me, but I wouldn't let myself overthink it. The entire playlist was barely half an hour.

When the room filled with silence I stared at the scar over Jackson's right eye as he tied all the bags. How did he get it? What had I missed in his life these past ten years?

"Do you have something to say?" Jackson joked when he caught me staring for the hundredth time. "You have your thinking face on."

"Do I?" I asked as I reared my head back.

Jackson smirked. "You always raise your left eyebrow when you're focusing hard on something." He reached forward and smoothed his thumb over my eyebrow.

When our eyes met, he dropped his smile and snapped his arm back. Ten years, and he still remembered that detail about me. I pointed toward his scarred eyebrow, not daring to touch him. "When did you get that scar?"

He ran a finger over it before putting his hands on his hips and looking away. "I got it when I was eighteen."

I let out a small laugh. "Jackson, I knew you when you were eighteen."

He looked up at me and pinched his mouth to the side. "Not during those last two months."

I was already in North Carolina by the time Jackson turned nineteen. He must have gotten it sometime between June and August.

"What happened?"

He started picking up the bags as he answered. "Car accident. It was no big deal. Just a piece of glass."

I stood up from my spot on the floor to follow him up the steps, telling myself not to pressure him for more details. I needed to keep him at arm's length, which I was failing at miserably.

"I'll take these to Goodwill. Why don't you take a shower while I'm gone." He was out the front door before I could say anything.

I grabbed my toiletries bag and walked toward the bathroom. Peter's shampoo and body wash were still in the shower, and his toothbrush and razor were on the sink. I quickly threw all of it in the trash. The house had well water, and I had to let it run for a while until the pipes seemed clear enough to shower. I didn't even want to think about tackling the bathroom; the sink and tub were both stained with copper and rust from the well water. That was going to take forever to scrub off with rust remover. That was an adventure for another day.

I wasn't used to the smell of well water anymore, but at least it was warm, and it felt good to clean myself of the dried sweat that covered my body. I scrubbed myself until I felt like a new woman, and brushed my hair until all the tangles were out. I ran my hand across the mirror to gaze at my reflection. I still had purple bags under my eyes, and a few freckles sprinkled across my cheeks from the sun. I debated curling my pin-straight hair, but decided to let it air dry since today was going to be humid and the curls would inevitably get frizzy.

When I walked out of the bathroom Jackson was already back, sitting at the kitchen table and scrolling through his phone. "Feel better?" he asked as I approached.

I nodded, crossing my arms and joining him at the table.

"I got smoothies."

I had to force myself not to smile, because I already knew it would be a peanut butter banana smoothie from the ice cream shop in downtown Tostela.

"Thanks," I mumbled as I unwrapped a straw and placed it in the lid. The smoothie was thick and chunky, just the way I remembered. I let out a sound of pleasure from the taste. Nowhere in Wilmington had ever lived up to this. Jackson laughed at me, then took a sip from his own cup.

"So how can you be here the whole summer? Are you taking time off work?" Jackson asked.

I crossed my legs in the chair, putting my hair behind my ears. "I always have the summers off. I'm a nanny, and the mom is a teacher so she doesn't work summers."

"Yeah? How'd you get that job?"

I smiled, picturing the curly haired girl that I'd watched grow up. She was almost thirteen now. I missed Mia so much. "The family is amazing. It was pure luck that I got the job. I was only in North Carolina for a week, and happened to be sitting at a coffee shop next to her mom, Wren. Mia was only two at the time, and she kept looking over at me and smiling. She ended up walking over to my table and asking me if I'd come play with her. Wren had taken off teaching when Mia was born and was planning to go back to work in the fall. She was thinking about hiring a nanny. I emailed her my résumé immediately, and she hired me the next day. I've been with them ever since."

Mia was getting older, and Wren and I had a conversation before I left about if they would need me for much longer. I had lived with them for ten years—it was probably time I thought about moving out. I looked around the kitchen. I owned *this* house. It had fallen into my lap. I could live here if I wanted, but the thought of being in Peter's house caused a shiver to run down my spine. My last memory here made me feel sick.

I looked over at Jackson, and he was staring at me with a smile. I looked away and dug my nail under a piece of the table that was chipping. "So, since Marie moved what happened to your house?" I asked.

"She sold it. Sam, Jules, Sophie, and I had to move everything out for her. It was really sad, but she couldn't bear to be in it for long without Phil."

The piece I had been scraping at popped off from the table, and I played with it between my fingers. "I loved that house. Did you keep your drum set?"

Jackson laughed. "Of course I did. Sophie keeps begging me to get rid of it."

"Can't imagine why. Not like it's the loudest instrument ever invented," I said sarcastically, even though watching Jackson play the drums was one of my favorite pastimes back then.

Jackson laughed again. "It's a great stress reliever. Whenever I feel like drinking, I play."

I felt awful for making a joke now, and a part of me was mad at Sophie for wanting him to get rid of it. If it helped with his sobriety, why would she want it gone?

I tried to think of anything to say to change the subject, but I was at a loss for words.

"You wouldn't believe some of the stuff we found at the house." Jackson covered his mouth to suppress a laugh. I raised my eyebrow.

"Julie found a pair of your underwear in my dresser."

I choked on my smoothie, standing up quickly and patting my chest. Jackson didn't try to cover his laugh this time, content with himself for making me flustered.

"Jesus Jackson, you didn't need to tell me that." My cheeks were red, and I went over to the sink to splash water on my face.

"I still have them."

I whipped around and flicked water at him.

He wiped it off his face and bent over with laughter. "I'm fucking with you, Addie. We threw them away. Sophie just about murdered me."

"Good! You're a freak, Jackson." My legs felt wobbly. I knew *exactly* what pair he had, and why. I tried—and failed—to clear the memory of him taking them off me from my brain.

He laughed at me again before standing straight. He crossed his arms and settled his eyes on me with a smile. "I just wanted to make you laugh."

"Well, you didn't. That wasn't funny."

I leaned back against the sink, staring him down with my angriest glare.

The smile on his face didn't falter. "I have to go." He shook his head and grabbed his smoothie. "I'll text you."

"No, you really shouldn't," I said.

"Bye, Addie." He gave me one last wave before walking out the front door. I turned the dead bolt before he even made it down the porch.

Chapter 10

BEFORE

February, Thirteen Years Ago

The Saturday after my fifteenth birthday, Julie picked me up for my shift without Jackson. Nothing had happened between us again since the day Julie caught us in the kitchen. We didn't even acknowledge that anything had happened at all; it was a mutual understanding that I needed this job, and messing around wasn't worth it. It didn't mean I didn't *want* to. If I ever felt like he was watching me during our shifts, I made sure to avoid meeting his eye.

"Where's Jackson?" I asked, turning down the radio.

Julie kept bopping her head along to the music as she answered, "He's home sick today."

"Oh, is he okay?" For the six months that I had been working at the restaurant, Jackson had never called out sick. Even when he had a cold so bad that he was sneezing every five minutes and sweating from what was probably a fever, he never went home. A small rush of anxiety slithered through my stomach.

"He's fine," Julie said nonchalantly. "He had surgery this morning, so he's been sleeping."

My eyes widened. "Oh my god, what happened?" I was overcome with worry. Surgery? And why was Julie acting like it wasn't a big deal?

She looked over at me and smirked. "Seriously, it's no big deal. He didn't want you to worry."

I couldn't focus at all during my shift. Jackson had surgery, and he didn't tell me about it. He didn't even text me to tell me he wasn't coming into work. My mind was racing with a million different thoughts, and after Julie dropped me back at home that night, I didn't sleep for the rest of the weekend.

On Monday morning, Jackson finally sent me a text to say he wasn't coming to school, and I went into full panic-mode. I was so sick with concern I couldn't even eat my lunch. I didn't even sit in the cafeteria, partially because I had no idea who to sit with if Jackson wasn't there to pick what group of people to join.

After school, I walked around to each of Jackson's classes and collected his homework for the day, even though he didn't ask me to, and I hadn't texted him to ask if I could come over.

I rode my bike to his house, ringing the doorbell as I anxiously bopped from side to side on his porch.

Julie answered the door, a surprised look flashing across her face before she said, "Hey."

I held Jackson's homework papers to my chest. "I uh, brought Jackson his homework."

Julie shook her head with a laugh, but motioned for me to come in. I followed her to the couch, where Jackson was laying under a blanket, watching TV. He didn't look pale or sweaty, just like he hadn't showered in a couple days. I was so relieved to see he looked okay.

"Surprise visitor," Julie said as we walked into the room.

When Jackson saw me, his eyes widened a bit before he muted the TV. He stayed laying down, not attempting to sit up.

"Hey, I brought you your homework. How are you feeling? Julie said you had surgery."

Jackson narrowed his eyes at Julie, and she let out a laugh. I looked back and forth between the two of them.

"Julie, I told you to keep your big mouth shut." Jackson looked pissed. "Addie, it wasn't a big deal. Seriously, I'm fine."

He looked embarrassed now; splotches of red crept up his neck.

"What happened?" I tried asking.

Jackson opened his mouth to answer, but Julie cut him off. "His balls got twisted and he had to get them fixed."

"Julie!" Jackson shouted.

At the same time, I let out a horrified, "What!?"

Julie laughed and made a motion in front of her crotch. "Jerking off too much."

My jaw dropped and Jackson whipped the remote at Julie. "It's called testicular torsion, you bitch! And no, it's not—it just happens!"

Julie looked over at me. "He's so grumpy since he hasn't been able to masturbate all weekend. He almost lost a ball."

"Get the fuck out of here, Julie!" Jackson screamed. I was the one that was flushing red now, and Jackson being angry made me feel embarrassed about coming here. I definitely should have asked first.

Julie put her hands up in surrender, covering half her mouth with a palm to hide her laugh. "I'm leaving for work, do you want me to drop you off at home, Addie?"

I set Jackson's homework on the coffee table, slinging my backpack over my arm to leave.

"Can you stay for a bit?" Jackson asked me. "I've been bored out of my mind all weekend, and my parents have been at the restaurant all day. Julie can drop you off later."

"Are you sure?" I asked. I looked over at Julie and she just shrugged before putting on her work shoes.

"Please," Jackson begged. He was still laying on the couch, hair mussed, looking helpless. The blanket slipped down his chest, revealing that he wasn't wearing a shirt. One glimpse of that freckle on his collarbone, and my decision was made.

"Okay." I took off my backpack and sat back in the recliner, pulling the lever and swinging out the footrest with a clunk.

Julie was nice enough to hand the remote back to Jackson from where it landed on the floor when he threw it at her. Then she refilled his water and set it on the coffee table.

"Anything else I can get before I go?" Julie asked with her hands on her hips.

Jackson ignored her, putting his full attention back on the TV.

"I'm good," I answered over the awkward silence.

"Later," Julie said before walking out the front door. I heard the music blaring from her truck before it faded away as she drove down the street.

I started cracking my knuckles, not knowing what to say. I didn't want Jackson to feel any more uncomfortable than he already did.

Jackson cleared his throat. "Sorry Jules is so annoying. Don't act weird, I'm seriously fine."

"I should have texted you before I came over. I didn't mean to embarrass you," I said bashfully.

Jackson let out a small laugh. "I'm not embarrassed. I was just pissed at Julie for telling you my business without asking me first."

I looked over at him, and he was smiling at me. He fixed a piece of his hair then pulled the blanket up to his neck. "Seriously, I had like, a million different people look at my nuts this weekend. I don't even think I *can* be embarrassed anymore."

A nervous laugh burst out of me, and all the weird tension left the room. I quirked an eyebrow at Jackson, glancing down to where his groin was beneath the covers, then looking back at his face.

"Did you really almost lose a ball?"

Jackson let out a small chuckle. "I really did. You have to have the surgery within six hours or else you could lose it. 'But don't worry,' they said, 'We can give you a prosthetic!'" He shivered. "I do not want a fake nut."

I laughed again, rocking back in the recliner and leaning my head to the side to face him fully.

"How did you know something was wrong? Was Julie right about the . . . ?" I made the same motion Julie did earlier.

Jackson rolled his eyes and scoffed at me. "Jesus, no, I'm not some freaky chronic masturbater. I woke up in the middle of the night with such intense pain"—he pointed down there—"that I started puking. I had to wake up my mom and explain that my package felt like it was being ripped to shreds." He shuddered. "I could puke again just thinking about it. They had to take an ultrasound at the hospital."

"I'm so glad I'm a girl." I made the sign of the cross.

Jackson smiled at me again, eyes traveling over every inch of my face. "Thanks for bringing my homework. You didn't have to do that."

My whole face felt hot. "No problem, Jackson."

His eyes flickered toward the TV. "How was work without me on Saturday?"

"It was fine, it just took Julie and I longer to close because she was on the phone half the time, arguing with someone."

Jackson rolled his eyes. "Lesbians are so dramatic."

I raised an eyebrow. "Huh?"

He looked at me again and smiled with one side of his mouth. "You are so sheltered, Addie. Julie—she's a lesbian. She's always got a new girl she's arguing with. She loves the drama."

"Oh," I said stupidly. Apparently I was sheltered, because I had never heard of anything like testicular torsion before, or how to tell if someone was gay. "Do your parents know?"

Jackson raised his eyebrows now. "Yeah," he said confused. "They're pretty old-fashioned, but they don't care that she likes girls; they're not assholes."

"I know!" I said quickly. I felt like an idiot for even insinuating they would care. "Your parents are cool." I snuggled back into the chair, feeling like a little kid who got yelled at for accidentally cursing.

"I didn't mean to get defensive," Jackson added. "Jules drives me insane, but she's still my sister."

I wished I cared about Peter the way Jackson cared for Julie. Or that Peter cared about me the way Julie cared for Jackson. She messed with him a lot, but it was out of love. She picked up the remote for him even though he hit her with it, got him a glass of water even though he didn't ask, and she drove us around after work with no complaints even though she was nineteen and in college. What was it like for someone to stick up for you and defend you? To want to protect you even when you weren't around?

Jackson turned on a movie, and we both fell asleep before it finished. I woke up later that evening to Phil and Marie coming home from the restaurant, and they fed Jackson and I pizza for dinner. I helped Jackson with his homework before Julie got home, and then she drove me back to my house. I got my bike out of the truck bed myself, and walked it to the side of the house.

Jackson didn't come to school for the rest of the week while he recovered, and everyday I rode my bike over after school with his homework, ate dinner with the Delvecchios, and had Julie drop me off after.

When Jackson came back to school the next week, I was almost disappointed because I wouldn't have an excuse to come over every day after school anymore.

Chapter 11

NOW

June

Wren called me the next day, and our phone call quickly turned into a FaceTime. Mia's smile filled the screen as she showed off her adorable smile. "Do you think they'll say I need braces?" she asked as she pulled back one side of her lips to show me a side view. As if I hadn't seen the girl twenty four hours ago, and forgot what her teeth looked like. "Only the orthodontist can give you an answer," I said with a smile. Most of the time Mia felt like a little sister, and Wren like my older sister, or a mother figure. She was thirty-four when she had Mia, so she was almost fifty now. I swear she still didn't look a day over thirty.

Wren stole the phone back from Mia. "It's been such a drag without you," Wren said dramatically.

"How will you ever survive?" I teased as I opened a bag of Chex Mix. Jackson's snacks from yesterday were still on the table. I'd had a bag of sour gummy worms for dinner last night.

"Mia has never been to Michigan, so we're planning a trip because we miss you so much."

I rolled my eyes. "Don't get me excited!"

"We're serious!" Mia squealed. "We're flying up tomorrow; we rented a lake house. Dad already took off work!"

"George actually requested off work?" I said in disbelief.

Wren stole the phone back. "You better believe it. We land at nine tomorrow morning. We'll pick you up on our way. I'll send you the address. It's somewhere on Lake Huron."

The thought of already getting a break from being at the house, plus getting to spend time with Wren, George, and Mia sounded fantastic. "How many days?"

"Just three—it's all George could get off. We're renting a car so you don't have to pick us up or anything."

"You guys are insane. I can't wait, though," I added excitedly. It felt good to know it had barely been two days, and this family missed me just as much as I missed them. *See, this is what people who love you do.*

"We have to see if the sunrises are better up there," Wren said with a wink. "Alright, I gotta help this toothy girl finish packing before her ortho appointment. See you tomorrow!" We said our goodbyes, and I sunk back into the couch. The rest of the house could wait.

***

The next morning, the Wilsons picked me up in their rental car and we drove for an hour and a half to Port Huron. The cabin they rented was less than a block from the waterfront, and we could see the Blue Water Bridge from our window.

"Let's get coffee first. George hasn't had a drop yet, and he's about to get cranky," Wren said when we finished taking our bags inside.

"I already have a café saved in Google Maps," George said good-naturedly. He picked up Mia with one arm, swinging her in a circle as she giggled.

We got coffees downtown, then walked along the waterfront on Lake Huron. We found a sunny spot to rest, and Mia and George played behind us on the grass while Wren and I sat on a bench together, staring out at the water.

"So, how was the house?" Wren asked.

I took a sip from my iced coffee, swatting away a mayfly in the process. "Exactly as I expected—a dump."

"Have you decided what you're going to do about it?"

A cloud covered the sun, and I lifted my sunglasses to the top of my head. "Probably fix it up a bit and sell it."

"All by yourself? I hate that you're alone," Wren said with an over-exaggerated pout.

I lowered my sunglasses to perch back on my nose, averting my eyes. "Someone offered to help me."

I could feel Wren staring at me. "Yeah?"

I kicked my feet back and forth, feeling like a little kid about to admit they had a crush. Except this wasn't a crush. I didn't even know exactly *what* it was I was feeling, but I was feeling something, alright.

Like a sick joke from the universe, my phone vibrated on the bench between us, and Wren bent down to read the text. "I'll bet his name is Jackson," Wren said in a sing-song voice.

I snatched my phone up, reading a text from Jackson that said, *I came by the house but you didn't answer. Is everything okay?*

"God, he's so annoying," I mumbled. "I never even gave him my number. He must've texted himself from my phone when he added himself to my contacts." I texted Jackson back that I was out of town for a few days, taking a break from the house.

"Okay, I'm waiting. Explain," Wren said.

In the ten years I had known her, I had never told her about Jackson. I gave her pieces here and there about Peter and my mom, but even that took literal years for me to finally share. It wasn't something I liked to talk about—or remember, for that matter.

I let out a long breath of air. "Some guy I worked with in high school. He owns the restaurant we used to work at. I ran into him in town and he offered to help. I don't know how I feel about it yet."

Wren smiled at me. "Well, it's about time you started dating again. You and Phoenix have been broken up for almost two years now." Phoenix and I dated for almost a year, and it wasn't a pretty year. We had a lot of ups and downs, a continuous cycle of harmony and chaos. He was an addict, and having lived with one growing up, I thought it was my duty to fix him. I couldn't, and he reminded me way too much of Peter in his reactions to conflict. Finally, I let him go, because his behavior was exactly what I'd run from in the first place.

I let out an exaggerated laugh. "Well, *this* guy is engaged. So dating is a no."

"Buggers," Wren said with another frown. "How well did you know Jackson back then?"

I paused for a while. *Well, I've seen him naked.*

"I mean, pretty well. I was close with his family." I couldn't meet her eyes, thankful I still had my sunglasses on to block my face.

Wren was still staring at me, waiting for me to go on. Her eyes were boring into me like a spotlight. "Okay! Fine! I was in love with the guy. Can you just stop looking at me like that?"

Wren let out a laugh and patted my knee. "Love isn't a bad word." She stood up from the bench. "Come on, let's play tag with George and Mia, burn off that sexual energy."

I shook my head, but a laugh escaped me. "You're sick."

***

We spent the next three days visiting the lighthouse on the water, roaming antique shops, and swimming in the water when we weren't being attacked by mayflies. On our way back home we were all starving, and Wren suggested we stop at Delvecchios', to see where I worked before moving to North Carolina. Their flight wasn't until later, and it would be better than an airport dinner, so I agreed.

Jackson had told me he was rarely at the restaurant, so I wasn't nervous about bumping into him. I was, however, worried I might run into Sophie, but I figured she'd rather ignore me than force a conversation. We walked into Delvecchios', that typical blast of A/C hitting us as we approached the hostess stand.

"Well, if it isn't Addison Bianchi." I squinted at the face in front of me until recognition hit.

"Rami!" I wrapped my arms around his neck and he swung me around in a circle.

"It's so good to see you!" we both said at the same time.

"You've hardly aged a day. You look exactly the same," Rami said as he looked me up and down.

"And you're looking bulkier than ever." I squeezed one of his biceps and he flexed.

"I'm half-manager, half-security here." He winked before turning toward the Wilsons. I introduced him to the family, and Rami grabbed four menus. I noticed Mia staring longingly at the stack of coloring sheets beside the hostess stand, and I grabbed one for her, along with a box of crayons. When I was her age, I'd already lost all semblance of a childhood; if Mia wanted to cling to hers for a little bit longer, I'd happily help her do so.

"These are new," I said, holding the coloring sheet up to Rami as we followed him to a booth.

"We got them after Sam had kids. We let them pick out the sheets. It's the first thing they ask for whenever they visit." I wondered how much Sam had actually come to visit, especially after he got married and had kids. He was the Delvecchio I knew the least, since he had lived in New York the entire time I knew them.

Rami asked for our drink orders, then motioned for me to follow him. "Let me show you around—we've made some good changes." I slid out the booth to follow him around the restaurant. Not much was different until we got to the kitchen. Most of the appliances had been updated, and everything looked so sleek and modern.

The corkboard of Polaroids was still on the far wall, and I slowly walked over. There were plenty of new pictures, and Rami pointed out one that had Sam's kids in it. They looked about four and six in the photo, with gap-toothed grins, and slices of pizza in their hands. There was a photo of Julie and a woman who I assumed to be her wife, and next to it, one of Phil with his arms draped over Marie, his chin resting on her head.

The photo beneath it was of Jackson and Sophie kissing. I averted my eyes.

Rami reached forward and tapped one of the photos. It was the picture of me, Julie, and Jackson from that first Christmas party. I smiled, taking out my phone and snapping a picture of it. My gaze drifted down to the photo directly beneath it, and I gasped. It was the

Polaroid of me and Jackson; the one where he was looking down at me, smiling while he made me laugh. Why hadn't he ever taken it down? Why didn't Sophie at least throw it away? Jackson probably wouldn't have even noticed if it went missing.

That wasn't even the picture that rocked me the most—I continued scanning the board, and one picture made my heart completely stop. There was a photo of me and Jackson from our high school graduation, tacked to the board in the lower left-hand corner. I was on his back, both our diplomas in my hands as I held them over my head. I couldn't remember a time I had smiled that large since then. It was the last picture we had ever taken together, because it was the last day I had seen him. I would've burned that picture if I was Sophie. I cleared my throat and turned back to Rami.

"You guys did really great with the place. You should be proud," I said.

"Thanks, Addie." I walked back to the table, burying the feelings of nostalgia back into my chest.

***

I split a pizza with Mia, and I hardly ate more than three bites. My stomach was a mess after seeing those pictures in the kitchen.

George was signing the check when three cannoli were dropped off at our table.

"Oh, we didn't order these." I looked up to see Jackson, a smile on his face with his hands clasped in front of him. My stomach knotted even tighter.

"Gift from the owner." He winked at Mia, and she giggled. *Oh Mia, you little traitor. Don't fall for his charm!*

He introduced himself to George and Wren since I had been rendered mute, the shock of seeing him leaving me feeling like I had been tased.

"Jackson? The famous Jackson Delvecchio?" Wren said with a Cheshire cat grin. I kicked her under the table.

"It's very nice to meet you. I've heard great things about you guys," Jackson added. *Bitch! I told you about them ONE time, don't act like we're best friends!*

"I thought you were never here," I blurted. Everyone at the table laughed at my outburst, and it took everything in me not to kick George and Wren simultaneously.

"Special visit," Jackson teased. Fucking Rami probably texted him.

"We have to get to the airport; we were just leaving." I scrambled out of the booth, not waiting for the Wilsons as I ran out onto the sidewalk. Stupid Jackson. Stupid fiancée-having Jackson. I placed a hand over my stomach, sure I was about to puke up my three bites of pizza. I should've ripped those photos off the corkboard myself, and burned them to a crisp along with Peter's house.

After a few minutes, Wren, George, and Mia walked out of the restaurant with the three cannoli in a takeout box.

"Addie, that was crazy! I've never seen you act so weird," Mia said as she grabbed my hand to cross the street.

"I'm just not feeling well," I said as we got in the car.

Wren met my eyes in the rearview mirror, giving me a sad smile. "He was cuter than I expected," she admitted.

I groaned and leaned my head against the window, letting the cold pane cool down my overheated body.

"He was nice. I love cannoli," Mia added.

I ran a hand through her hair, untangling one of her curls, which was knotted by her ear.

"It's tough when they're cute *and* nice," Wren said as she grabbed George's hand to kiss it before setting it down in her lap.

"I'm really gonna miss you guys when you leave," I said sarcastically, but they knew I meant it. It wasn't enough time. I hardly ever spent multiple days away from them. Their good-natured humor and teasing were my favorite things about them.

When we got to Peter's house, we all hugged goodbye, Wren promising to call me as soon as they landed. I watched as they backed out the driveway, then I slipped into the house and fell asleep on the couch.

Chapter 12

BEFORE

August, Thirteen Years Ago

The August before sophomore year, Jackson turned sixteen. Julie's truck became Jackson's since it was a family car, and Julie bought a new car for herself. Jackson said he could start picking me up for school in the mornings even though it was out of his way, and instead of walking to the restaurant on Fridays, we'd drive.

He usually drove Julie and I home after work now, with Julie sitting in the middle so we no longer had a chance to touch in the car. Even when he picked me up for a shift, we acted completely normal—singing along to our favorite music like always, or talking about something that happened at the restaurant.

The weekend before school started, Marie and Phil went to New York to visit Sam, and Julie was also away, visiting Lake Michigan with one of her friends. The Saturday they were gone was surprisingly slow, and at nine thirty I was sitting on the kitchen counter, eating a slice of pizza and playing a game on my phone.

Jackson came flying through the kitchen doors, grabbing a rag from one of the bins. "There's some belligerent asshole sitting at the bar. He came in drunk, and is getting pissed that nobody will serve him."

I shoved the last bite of pizza into my mouth before jumping off the counter. Jackson held out the rag so I could wipe my fingers on it before we both walked out the swinging doors.

"Which guy?" I asked as we looked over at the bar.

"The tool in the green shirt."

I moved to the right so I could see where Jackson was pointing. I almost passed out when I saw who it was. Peter was at the bar, his chestnut-brown hair plastered to his forehead with sweat. He was talking animatedly, and swaying where he was sitting on one of the barstools, clearly both drunk and high.

Peter had gotten worse this year; he was still drinking like it was his day job, but now he was also experimenting with harder drugs. After visiting Mom at Christmas, something darkened in him. I don't know what happened while he was there—he never told me about it—but there was a dramatic change in him. We had just been ignoring each other for the most part, but now here he was, causing trouble at my job.

"I want to whip him with this rag." Jackson started to walk toward him, and I grabbed his arm.

"Jackson, that's my fucking brother," I said horrified.

Jackson's head snapped toward me, his mouth dropping wide open. "*That's* Peter."

I nodded, embarrassed that this was the first time Jackson was seeing my brother. I'd never told him or his family about Peter's drinking problem, but now I didn't have to. It was apparent.

"I'll go talk to him, get him to leave," I said as I let go of the death grip I had on Jackson's arm.

Jackson watched me as I approached my brother. I tapped him on the shoulder and waited for him to turn around.

When Peter's eyes met mine, it took him a second to realize who I even was before a sloppy smile spread across his face. "Ah, there's my little sister. Can you help me out? Get them to give me a drink?"

"Peter," I said slowly, "why are you here?"

He threw his arms out wide, looking back and forth across the restaurant like it was obvious. "I came to see my sister at her job."

I shook my head at him. "You have to leave, Peter. You're making a scene."

He reared his head back. "Me? You're the one making it a big deal."

I gaped at him. I could see Jackson watching us out of the corner of my eye, and I felt my face getting hot. My other coworkers were starting to watch now, too. I just needed him to leave—this was *my* place. He was ruining it, and embarrassing me in front of my coworkers.

I grabbed his left bicep with both hands. "Please, follow me," I said, keeping my tone as calm as I could manage.

Reluctantly, he got off of the stool, and I pulled him toward the front door while heads turned to watch us. I focused on the door, trying my hardest not to look at anyone as we passed.

As soon as we were outside, I let go of Peter, my heart racing in my chest.

"Okay, how did you even get here?" I looked toward the street parking zone, wondering if his car was there.

"I drove, obviously," Peter shouted. I took a step back. He looked pissed now. "What the fuck is your problem, Addie?"

"Me? You're the one who showed up to my job drunk!"

He raised a hand and for a second, I thought he was going to slap me. I flinched, covering my face with my hands. Instead, he grabbed my right forearm so tight I cried out.

"You're hurting me!"

"If you're making me leave, then you have to leave, too," Peter spat at me as he tugged me toward him.

I dug my feet into the concrete, trying to pry his fingers off me. "Stop!" I was trying to catch my breath as Peter began dragging me down the street. I couldn't fight the fat, hot tears running down my face. A sob escaped me when I felt one of his nails pierce my skin. Peter had never hurt me before; sure, he yelled at me half the time, and the other half he acted like I didn't exist. But he had *never* put his hands on me.

I felt a rush of instant relief as Peter let go of my arm, and I pulled it to my chest protectively. All I could hear was yelling, and when I looked up, someone was clinging to Peter's back, trying to choke him out as he fought to get their fingers off his neck.

I watched as Peter swung the person off, throwing them to the ground and straddling them as he punched them in the face over and over. When I realized it was Jackson on the sidewalk, I couldn't make myself move. What the hell was he doing? Jackson was a sixteen-year-old kid, and even though he had grown a few inches over the summer and was starting to get bulkier, he wasn't a match for my stocky twenty-three-year-old brother, inebriated or not.

"Peter, stop!" I cried. He wasn't listening to me, and Jackson wasn't giving up on fighting him off. I didn't know what to do; I felt helpless standing there, watching Jackson take hit after hit from my brother.

Peter looked like he was getting tired at least, and eventually Jackson was able to stop his fists from connecting with his jaw another time.

"What the fuck!?" I turned around to find Rami running outside. He pulled Peter off Jackson in an instant, tossing him to the side like a rag doll. I kneeled down to inspect the damage to Jackson's face. He wiped blood from his nose, and I hoped it wasn't broken. He had splotches of red on either side of his jaw that would turn to bruises later, and a split top lip.

I was scared to touch him—to hurt him anymore. We both turned to watch Rami push Peter down the street. I don't know what he said to Peter, but whatever it was, it worked. He was leaving. I shivered.

Rami walked back to us, helping Jackson stand. "You're fucking crazy, kid," Rami said as he pulled Jackson up, patting him on the back.

"He was about to rip her fucking arm out of its socket," Jackson scoffed, holding an arm out toward me.

My cheeks got hot. Jackson had protected me, taking a beating in the process.

"We should really call the cops. And your parents," Rami said.

"I'm so sorry. This is all my fault." I was crying again, and Rami put an arm around me, attempting to soothe me.

Jackson reached forward and lightly touched his hand to mine. It didn't linger—he pulled it back quickly, and shoved his hands into the pockets of his work pants. "It's not your fault, Addie." Blood was still running down his face, and I had to suppress another sob.

He looked up at Rami. "Please don't tell my parents. Let's just let it go. We don't need to cause an issue for anybody."

I let out a long, shaky breath, praying Rami would agree. What would happen if we called the cops and they showed up to my house? I was only fifteen, and Mom was gone. Could they take me away? Would Marie fire me for bringing trouble to the restaurant? I felt like trash—a pathetic piece of garbage who was ruining a nice family's restaurant.

Rami stared at Jackson for a long time before shaking his head and dropping his arm from my shoulder.

"Next time I'm calling the police," Rami sighed.

"Thank you, thank you so much." I threw my arms around Rami, feeling like I could finally take a full breath.

"Why don't you guys get out of here? I'll handle closing tonight." He patted my back awkwardly.

We didn't fight him on the suggestion, and Jackson and I walked around the block to the truck in the back alley.

When we got in the truck, Jackson didn't start it right away, and we sat in a pained silence. He was staring down at his hands, picking at some of the now-dried blood from when he wiped his split lip with the back of his hand.

"I, uh . . . really don't want to go home to Peter tonight," I said quietly.

Jackson turned on the car without a word, and I let him take me to his house. "Look After You" by The Fray started playing, and I forced myself not to cry, telling myself that the song didn't mean anything.

We walked through the dark garage and into the kitchen. It would just be the two of us here tonight, since everyone was out of town.

"I'll grab you some of Julie's clothes," Jackson said before sprinting upstairs.

I sat on the couch, stretching my legs out in front of me. I felt exhausted, and entirely depleted.

When he came back downstairs, he had a pair of Julie's leggings and an old T-shirt in his hands.

"You're bleeding too, Addie," Jackson said as he dropped the clothes to reach for my arm. He gently flipped it so my forearm was facing up.

I pulled it back sharply. "It's just a scratch; it's not a big deal."

Jackson let out a sigh. "At least let me get you a Band-Aid." He left the room before I could argue.

When he came back, he motioned for my arm again, and I slowly lifted it toward him. He held onto my wrist while he carefully placed the Band-Aid over the cut. It felt dramatic. It was just a small scratch from Peter's nails—nowhere near the injuries Jackson had on his face.

He didn't drop my arm right away, and his grasp tightened as he stared at my forearm before leaning down and pressing a soft kiss to my wrist. I had to bite my cheek to stop myself from reacting. His eyes met mine briefly, then he disappeared to go shower like nothing had happened.

I changed into Julie's clothes, and was cuddled up on the couch when he came back into the room without a shirt on, his hair still dripping wet. His face was clear of any trace of blood, but he still looked awful. The split in his lip was raw and red like it had split back open during his shower.

"Don't look at me like that," Jackson said as he sat down on the opposite side of the couch.

"I can't help it; you're hurt," I said with a scratchy throat.

"You should see the other guy," Jackson said with a smirk as he grabbed the remote. We both knew he was the one who lost that fight, and I didn't like that he was joking about it. He positioned himself so his head was resting on the opposite armrest, then he stretched out his legs so they rested up against mine.

"I really don't want to see the other guy ever again," I said softly. Hopefully Peter was at home cooling off, and maybe—if I was lucky—he'd be too drunk to remember anything by tomorrow.

"Yeah, fuck that guy," Jackson said. His jaw was clenched, and I could already see a bruise forming where his jaw connected to his neck. He clicked something on the TV, then tossed the remote between us. "It's time you watched *Never Back Down*. Best movie ever."

I faced the television, watching as his favorite movie started. He positioned his legs so one of mine was between both of his. I was hit by that familiar jolt in my heart, and I tried to tamp it down.

"Thank you, Jackson," I whispered. There was so much to thank him for. For making Peter let go of me, for getting punched for me, for convincing Rami not to call his parents or the cops, and for letting me stay here and taking care of me.

He stayed silent for so long that I thought maybe he didn't hear me.

"That's what friends do, Addie. They protect each other." He let out a long breath before facing me for a brief moment. His brown eyes were so sincere I wanted to burst into tears. "I'll always protect you."

I wanted to say something back—to admit that he was my favorite person, that I didn't know what I would do without him. That regardless of what Julie said, I wanted to touch him. I wanted to kiss him to show my gratitude—to kiss his split lip, his hands, the bruises on his jaw. Instead, I stayed silent, and didn't move a single muscle.

When the credits of the movie played, Jackson was already asleep.

And when we woke up in the morning, our legs were still intertwined.

Chapter 13

NOW

June

On Saturday afternoon, Jackson reappeared at my door with a bag of food. I opened the door and stared at him for a moment, trying to look intimidating. He burst out laughing, squeezing right past me and into the house like he owned the place.

"Why do you do that?" I asked as I crossed my arms.

"Do what?" he asked with a lazy smile as he set the food on the kitchen table. He opened a box filled with eggs, hashbrowns, and bacon, placing it in front of the chair closest to me. He sat down in the other chair, opening the other box and cutting into a pancake.

"Walk into the place like you've been here a hundred times. Sit at my table like this isn't your first meal here."

He squinted his eyes and moved his head from side to side like he was thinking. "I had a smoothie here on Monday, so technically this isn't my first time sitting at this table."

I let out a frustrated growl then threw myself down in the chair across from him. I couldn't fight the smell of the breakfast; my stomach was begging me to give in. I hadn't had anything to eat since my three bites of pizza last night.

"Why are you so hostile toward me?" Jackson asked with a curious smile.

Hmmm, maybe because you ghosted me ten years ago? Because you still flirt with me like you aren't engaged?

And why was he always smiling!? By the time he turned eighteen, he wore a near-permanent scowl. I wasn't used to this cheeriness he constantly seemed to have now.

"Can you stop smiling all the time? It's seriously creeping me out," I said as I inhaled a forkful of eggs.

"Are you cranky because you didn't eat the cannoli last night?"

"You only brought three to the table," I said, deadpan. "Looks like someone can't count."

I knew that comment would hurt him. Jackson never got good grades in school, and his siblings always teased him for failing kindergarten. From what I knew, he never bothered trying to attend college, either. I regretted it as soon as I said it.

"You've gotten mean," Jackson said, with a fucking smile STILL plastered on his face. "I only brought three because I know you can't take more than a bite without getting sick of the ricotta cheese. I thought you could share it with the kid."

I threw my fork down. Why!? Why did he have to remember all these details about me? Why did he have to bring me breakfast? Why was he being so *nice*!?

"Why are you like this?" I shouted as I stood up.

His smile finally slipped, and he held his hands up in surrender.

"Like what? What am I doing?"

"Just stop! Why are you being so nice? Why are you like, obsessed with me? It's exhausting."

I was acting insane. I felt like I was quite literally losing my mind. I put my hands in my hair, piling it up in a bun before realizing I didn't have a hair tie and letting it flop back down.

"Obsessed with you? Get over yourself, Addison," Jackson said softly.

I hated that he used my full name. I *loved* it. Fuck!

"Why didn't you get rid of the Polaroids?" I asked without looking at him.

"What?" Jackson asked. The question was out of left field for him, but not for me. I had been obsessing over it all night, and it was still fucking with my head.

"The pictures of us, on the bulletin board at the restaurant." I sounded so whiney, I wanted to stab myself in the foot with the plastic knife.

"Why would I get rid of them?"

I turned to look at him, and he was watching me with his brows pinched in confusion.

"Because . . ." I let the sentence trail off, gesturing between us as if to say, *Because of our ending, because of what happened between us. Because you have a fiancée! You fucking idiot!*

He chewed the inside of his lip, shrugging one shoulder. "They remind me of a time when I was happy."

I stared at him. "But you have one from graduation. That was put up after I left," I said sharply.

He swallowed thickly, then added, "It was all I had left of you." He said it so softly I wasn't sure if he meant for me to hear him or not.

He was getting *married*. He'd had an engagement party just last weekend. How could he say he *was* happy—past tense?

"So what?" I shot back, because I was mad now. How could he just say things like that? Make my feelings rise back up when there was nothing I could do about them? I wanted to know what changed between then and now; why he hurt me, why he even still cared. Instead, I said, "Where's Sophie anyways, while you're here bothering me?"

"Her sister is in labor with her first baby, so she's visiting her in Connecticut. I took her to the airport this morning. She's staying out there for two weeks."

I crossed my arms. "And you think helping me out is a good idea?"

Jackson let out an exasperated breath. "Sophie can't tell me who I can and can't be friends with."

"Right, 'cause she never could," I shot back.

"Can we just stop with the bullshit?" Jackson said, almost yelling now. I dropped my arms. "Just—just stop, okay? Can we just be friends? I want to help you with the house. Peter sucked, and this house sucks, and I just want to do something for you for once. Is that too much to ask?"

My heart squeezed in my chest. I just wanted to yell at him to go fuck himself. But I also wanted him here, because no matter what had transpired between us, he was still *here*, and he wanted to help me.

"Fine," I said quietly.

He nodded at me. "Now sit and eat your breakfast. Damn, you're a brat when you're hungry," Jackson said in a low voice.

A laugh escaped me, and Jackson started laughing, too. This felt ridiculous.

"Truce?" he asked as he reached his hand across the table for me to shake.

I shook my head. "Julie's first rule: no touching."

I swear to god Jackson blushed as he cackled. He pulled his arm back. "That never stopped us before, did it?"

"You're an asshole," I whispered. I turned back to eat my breakfast, avoiding his gaze to prevent my stomach from flipping.

***

We decided to tackle the rest of Peter's room after breakfast. There wasn't much left to go through, and I was actually thankful Jackson was here, because I didn't want to have to go through the drawers myself. Who knew what I would find in there? I hated Peter, but he was still my brother. I didn't want to find something like a sex toy that would haunt me for the rest of my life.

Jackson handed his phone to me so we could make another playlist. I was choosing my songs for the task with angst. Even though we had called a truce, we didn't shake on it, so was it actually sound? And then he had to make that comment about how Julie could never stop us from touching; I was still in disbelief he was ballsy enough to say something like that.

I had just chosen "Silver Springs" by Fleetwood Mac because, well, fuck him, and was tapping "Red" by Taylor Swift when a text from Sophie popped up on his phone. *Just got to Amanda's. We'll talk again when I get back.* Oh shit. That sounded like a *We* won't *talk again until I get back*. Were they fighting?

I finished picking songs with shaky fingers and pretended to ignore the text until Jackson lifted his watch to read a notification. I knew it had to be the text message appearing on his watch, and his eyes lifted to meet mine. We both knew I saw the text. It was pointless to lie.

"So, you guys in a fight or something?" I said as I handed his phone back to him.

"Or something," Jackson said, letting out an irritated huff.

"What'd you do to piss her off?" I added as I crossed my arms.

He met my eyes again. "Take a wild guess."

My heart started to flutter. They were fighting over me; I was sure of it. It was like high school all over again. "You're an idiot," I mumbled before turning around.

The first song started playing; Jackson had chosen "moody" by Royel Otis. I couldn't tell if it was about me or Sophie.

Jackson started clearing out the bottom dresser drawer, and I held out a trash bag as he pulled out random knickknacks. I either nodded yes for keep, or shook my head no for throw away. So far, everything had been thrown away.

"So," I started lightly, trying to play nice. "How long have you and Sophie been engaged?"

"Three years," he said as he held up a package of Post-It notes. Half the notes were filled with random scribbles.

"Toss," I said. "That's a long engagement. Why make the poor girl wait so long?"

Jackson held up a pile of birthday cards and I motioned for him to throw them in the bag. I doubted there would be any leftover cash.

"Busy. Never had the time," Jackson said without looking at me.

God, he was being cagey. "When's the wedding?"

"Don't have a date yet."

Jackson held up a stack of pictures next.

"Ugh, just fucking toss," I said without looking at the photos. "How did you have an engagement party without an official date set?"

"Well, aren't you just full of questions?" Jackson said as he tied the garbage bag. It was already full.

"I'm playing nice!" I said with a hand on my hip. "This was what you wanted, wasn't it?"

Jackson smiled at me, nodding. "Sophie wanted new stuff for the house, so we had the party."

I grabbed a new bag and we started another dresser drawer. When the playlist ended, we just let it repeat until we'd finished the basement. We were on a roll, and we both figured we should get it done while we had the energy.

Time slipped past, and when I lifted my arms to crack my back, I realized how sore my muscles were. A glance at my phone showed that it was already well past midnight.

"We should call it a night," I said as I plopped down on the floor.

Jackson was staring at me from where he was standing by the staircase, leaning his back against the wall. And guess what—he had that dumb smile on his face again!

"What?" I asked as I leaned back to balance on my palms.

"You're acting like yourself again," Jackson said.

After the third time the playlist had played I had let my guard down, and Jackson and I had slipped into that feeling of routine we'd had while closing at the restaurant. We'd both been singing along to the songs while we cleaned the basement, and it had almost felt like we'd slipped back in time. It was the closest I'd felt so far to how things were before.

I shrugged at him. "Thank you for helping me."

He nodded before pushing himself off the wall. "That's what friends do," he said sincerely. *They protect each other.*

I pushed myself off the floor. "I'll walk you out."

I followed him up the stairs, and Jackson grabbed the trash bags to put on the curb. I didn't even try to fight him on it.

"I'll text you," Jackson said before stepping out onto the porch.

I wanted to make a smart-ass comment. To pretend like I didn't want him to come back, or to keep helping me. But I knew it was pointless.

"I'll answer," I promised. He smiled one last time before walking down the driveway. This time I waited until he got in his car before I locked the dead bolt.

Chapter 14

BEFORE

October, Thirteen Years Ago

Marie and Phil's thirtieth wedding anniversary was on October 30th, which fell on a Tuesday this year. The weekend before, Sam flew in from New York and he, Julie, and Jackson threw a costume party at the restaurant to celebrate.

The restaurant was filled with a bunch of their extended family that I had never met before. Phil had two brothers, Marie had three sisters, and there were too many nieces and nephews for me to keep track of. Marie and Phil were both the youngest in their families, so all their siblings' kids were significantly older than Sam, Julie, and Jackson. Some of Jackson's cousins were already married with kids of their own. I had never been surrounded by so many Italians before. It was *awesome*.

Jackson and I were wearing matching Peeta and Katniss costumes from The Hunger Games—a movie Julie had taken us to see earlier this year. She and Jackson had massive crushes on Jennifer Lawrence, and I'd admitted that I had been obsessed with Josh Hutcherson since

I saw the movie Bridge to Terabithia. Jackson and I looked nothing like the characters, with his hair so dark it was basically black, and my hair as light as snow, but Julie braided my hair for me so I had a perfect Katniss braid. Jackson brought me an old plastic bow and arrow toy set he had from when he was younger—it was lime green and bright orange, and the child-size quiver barely fit on my shoulder, but it got the costume across. Jackson was carrying around a bread roll from the kitchen, and half his family didn't get his costume, which just made it a million times funnier than it had to be.

Marie and Phil were dressed as a zombie bride and groom, with fake blood painted on their faces. Julie was wearing a lime-green shirt with a sparkly silver skirt and an alien antenna headband, her long brown hair crimped down her back. Sam was dressed as Clark Kent, in an unbuttoned suit with sunglasses, and a red S on his undershirt.

There were bottles of wine at every booth, and someone had filled a punch bowl with a bright-orange mixed drink, which sat on the hostess stand. Jackson was sneaking us cups throughout the night, but I didn't have enough to get drunk—unlike Jackson, who had a steady buzz going.

Julie was somewhere in the dining room with her cousins playing a game of Twister, and Phil and Marie were still doing their rounds, playing host and saying hi to family while Jackson and I hid in the kitchen, drinking more of the orange mixed drink and eating slices of pizza. Halloween music was playing in the background, and even with the kitchen doors closed, I could hear the laughter and loud talking of his relatives out in the dining room, speaking a mixture of English and Italian.

"You have a really big family," I told Jackson as we swung our legs back and forth from where we sat on the countertop. "Your uncle

Tony scared the shit out of me; he told me some story that I'm almost positive was about his time in the mafia."

Jackson let out a low laugh. "Don't worry, you're Italian, too. You're safe. But yeah, my family is huge. Half of them forget my name most of the time."

"Are you serious?"

"Yeah, or they accidentally call me Sam." He rolled his eyes as he shoved the rest of his pizza in his mouth. "Do you have a big Italian family, too?"

I shrugged. "I don't know. I've never met any of my relatives."

Jackson stared at me with sad eyes before looking away and studying the food containers on the wall. I was desperate to change the subject—I didn't want him to pity me. He had no idea how much fun I was having here tonight.

"I can't believe your parents have been married for thirty years. That's a really long time," I said.

Jackson nodded. I tried to do the math in my head. Sam was somewhere around Peter's age, so he was probably twenty-four or twenty-five. I squinted my eyes for a second, realizing I had no idea how old Marie and Phil were.

"Wait, how old are your parents?"

Jackson squinted his own eyes, and I watched his lips move as he figured it out. "Well, my mom had me when she was forty, so she's like fifty-six or something."

I had to hold my lips together to keep my jaw from dropping. His parents were in their mid-fifties? I didn't think they looked a day over forty-five. My own mom was more than ten years younger than his parents. She was only twenty when she had Peter, and twenty-eight when she had me.

"Oh, that makes sense now; why you're so much younger than your other cousins, I mean," I said.

Jackson made a sound from the back of his throat before chugging the rest of his drink.

"I'm so much younger because I was an accident," Jackson said.

An accident? "What do you mean?"

Jackson looked up at me. "An accident. Like, a mistake. My parents didn't plan on having more children after Julie."

I furrowed my eyebrows as my eyes traveled over his face. I refused to believe that was true. His parents loved him—he was their baby. "Why would you say that, Jackson?"

He looked me dead in the eyes. "I'm serious. My dad got a vasectomy after they had Julie. They didn't want another baby. But somehow, they ended up with me." He started playing with the zipper of his costume so he didn't have to look at me anymore.

"What's a vasectomy?"

Jackson started laughing, placing his hands over his face as he shook from his chuckles.

"You really are sheltered. Did you not pay attention in health class?" he asked with a goofy grin.

I felt my cheeks grow warm. "I'm not taking health until next trimester." It was my turn to avoid eye contact. I spun the ladles and spatulas around on their hangers behind me, refusing to meet Jackson's gaze.

"It's a surgery guys get so they're like, infertile. They can still come and stuff, but there's no sperm in it to get a girl pregnant."

I was sure my entire body flushed red. I didn't understand how Jackson could just talk about this stuff so freely without being embarrassed.

"Oh, I see," I said quietly.

"Yep," he said. "So that's why my parents didn't expect me. Sam and Julie used to tease me about it all the time when I was younger."

It hurt my heart to see Jackson act like he was a mistake in his family, or like they didn't want him. He was such an essential part of his family, and such an essential part of *my* life. I couldn't imagine him not being around.

"Well, if it makes you feel better, I was a mistake, too. I was the product of a one-night stand. My mom cheated on Peter's dad. That's why Peter hates me so much; I destroyed their family by being born," I said.

Jackson's nostrils flared as he met my eyes. I thought the statement would make him feel like we had a mutual connection, but he was looking at me with anger now.

"Why would that make me feel better?" he asked with an expression that read, *Are you an idiot?*

"I—" He held up a hand to stop me before I could say more.

"You're not a mistake. Don't ever say that about yourself. And don't say *you* destroyed a family by being born. Your mom cheated, not you," Jackson said adamantly.

My heart was slapping against the inside of my chest. I didn't know how to respond. It wasn't like he was making some grand statement, but after being made to feel like an inconvenience by Peter my entire life, it felt so, so good to have someone like Jackson tell me that my situation wasn't my fault.

I chewed on the inside of my lip. "Thanks, Jackson," I said quietly. "Don't say you're a mistake, either."

I could feel him staring at me, then he tapped a finger against my kneecap. "Come on, let's get back to the party. I think they're playing bingo in a few."

I followed Jackson back into the dining room, and we sat at a booth with his family and got ready to play bingo. Throughout the rest of the party, I kept catching Jackson watching me, looking at me like I mattered.

I kept staring back, hoping he knew my look was telling him that he mattered, too.

Chapter 15

BEFORE

February, Twelve Years Ago

I spent most of my sixteenth birthday hiding in my room. I hadn't gotten so much as a text from Julie or Jackson all day, and I kept checking my phone to see if I just hadn't heard it ring.

When my phone finally vibrated under my sheets, I dove head-first for it. The moment I read Julie's name, I answered with a flustered, "Hello?"

"Hey Addie, what are you up to?" Julie said cheerily.

I tried not to sound disappointed. "Good, just hanging around." I shouldn't care that she and Jackson forgot my birthday. My birthday had never been important to anyone in my family, so I don't know why I was expecting so much from them.

"Do you want to come with me to the restaurant? I was going to help Marie with inventory."

I hadn't done a single thing all day, so even though it wasn't about me, I said yes. When Julie picked me up half an hour later, I was wearing a pair of dark jeans and a blue oversized sweater I got from

Goodwill, which I paired with my black high-top Converse. I left my blonde hair in its natural pin-straight style down my back.

When I got into the truck, Julie had on a full face of make up, her hair was curled in long waves, and she was wearing a long-sleeve dress with black tights.

"You look nice for inventory," I said as she turned up her CD so we could sing along.

"Oh, I was dressed nice for church this morning," Julie said.

I raised an eyebrow. I had never once heard Julie say she went to church on Sunday mornings, but I didn't press her.

She parked in the front of the restaurant on Main Street, which she'd also never done before. I started to ask her why we were going through the front when she pushed open the door and a loud bundle of voices screamed, "SURPRISE!" I jumped back at the sound, looking over at Julie as she clasped her hands together and jumped up and down.

I was trying not to cry as I looked around the room. A banner hung from the ceiling, a hand painted "Happy Birthday Addie". Jackson was standing beneath it with his hands in his front pockets, grinning at me with Marie and Phil next to him, smiles plastered on their faces. Behind them were half the employees from the restaurant. Everyone started to hug me one by one, and when I got to Jackson, I squeezed him tighter than everyone else.

"Were you surprised?" he asked against my ear.

"Yeah, this was the last thing I expected," I said with a huge smile on my face. "I thought everyone forgot about my birthday."

Jackson nudged his shoulder against mine. "We'd never forget your birthday, you fool." Nothing could ruin the happiness that was radiating from me.

Julie had created a game of *Jeopardy!* with questions about me in different categories. There were four different categories with four questions in each one. I couldn't believe she knew enough random facts about me to make this game.

Marie chose a category first: Addie for 300.

"Okay Marie, lucky for you it's an easy one. What brand of shoes is Addie always wearing?" Julie asked.

Marie crinkled her eyebrows, trying to think. "Vans, right?"

Everyone in the room started cracking up, including me.

"Marie, you're joking, right? She's literally wearing them right now," Jackson said with a shake of his head. "It's Converse."

"I don't know brand names! I'm old!" Marie said with a laugh.

"They have literally been around since like, the 1900s," Jackson said, exasperated. I couldn't stop laughing.

"That's 300 for Jackson!" Julie called out, writing down the numbers under his name on a dry-erase board.

The questions continued, Julie asking things like "What is Addie's go-to meal at the restaurant?" (pepperoni pizza), "What topping can't she stand?" (mushrooms), and "Who is her favorite singer?" (I'm currently on a Miley Cyrus kick since watching the movie *The Last Song*). Every time someone answered a question wrong, Jackson spoke up and got it right. It made my heart skip a beat every single time.

The final question in the Double Jeopardy! round was "What's Addie's middle name?" I was surprised Julie even knew what it was to write the question, and she admitted to me later that she had to sneak into the restaurant's office and look at my paperwork to find out.

I assumed Marie would be the only one to get it right since she helped me fill out my paperwork two years ago. But when everyone flipped over their papers, Jackson was the only one who had the name Maria written down. He even fully wrote it out: *Addison Maria*

Bianchi. I stared at his block handwriting with my lips parted. How did *he* know my middle name?

Jackson ended up winning the game, trying to play it off that we worked together the most out of everyone, and that's why he knew all the answers. But it meant more to me than he would ever know that he remembered so many things about me.

***

We all played karaoke, with Jackson and Julie hogging the microphone for most of the night. Phil drank until he was feeling goofy enough to sing a song, and Julie made him sing "When I Look At You" by Miley Cyrus. Marie even let me and Jackson dance on top of the bar while he performed, and we had to keep grabbing each other's hands to keep from sliding off the wet countertop.

After we had cake and ice cream, Marie handed me a bundle of presents. Julie helped me unwrap them, claiming she was too excited to wait for me to slowly remove the wrapping paper. I couldn't help it—I'd never had so many presents before, and I wanted to savor the experience. The first gift was money to buy more minutes for my cellphone. The next bag was three different shirts, which Julie animatedly explained she picked out, and that they would make my brown eyes pop. Rami got me a new backpack for school filled with new notebooks and supplies.

Jackson pushed the last gift toward me, and when I opened it, I found a new pair of high-top Converse. They were black high-tops like my current pair, which I'd been running into the ground for the past few years, except these had a piece of pizza embroidered onto the outside of the ankle.

"We custom ordered those online," Jackson said, his ears turning pink.

I smiled up at him, already untying my laces and putting on the new pair. "They're perfect!" I squealed as I stood up, bending my feet to break them in. "Thank you everyone!" I went around the circle and gave everyone a hug again.

"Jackson designed those himself. He was adamant you absolutely *needed* those," Marie said in my ear. I smiled down at the shoes. Jackson had gone out of his way to gift these to me.

We ended the night by eating pizza—obviously—and lounging around the restaurant, talking about anything and everything. I was the happiest I had probably ever been in my life, and nothing could bring me down. These people had become my family; they did more for me than my own brother and mom. Peter didn't get me anything, and Mom didn't so much as call me to wish me a happy sixteenth. I hadn't even heard from her since Christmas. She was living it up with her boyfriend in Traverse City, probably making snow angels or some ridiculous shit like that.

I couldn't believe how significantly my life had improved since Marie gave me this job. I caught Jackson smiling at me from across the room as we cleaned up, and I smiled back. This was the best birthday I had ever had. All because of the Delvecchios.

***

Jackson drove me home after the party by himself, and we sang along to "Bitch, Don't Kill My Vibe" by Kendrick Lamar at an ear-splitting volume. I was still on a high from the party, and even though it was

February, we had the windows cracked, a soft stream of wind blowing our hair around in the car.

When we got to my house, Peter's car was gone. Jackson restarted the song, and we rapped through it together for a second time. I could barely get the words out this time because of how hard I was laughing. When it finished, I sat back against the seat and looked over at Jackson as I caught my breath.

"Your family is amazing. Thank you guys so much for the party. No one has ever done something like that for me before." My entire face split into a smile, and Jackson turned toward me to match it.

"You deserve it, Addie, and so much more." He swallowed deeply, his eyes never leaving mine.

"How did you know my middle name?" I asked him.

He looked at me timidly, then said, "Because I pay attention to you." He leaned forward slightly, and my heart raced.

Don't mess it up by screwing around with Jackson.

I didn't care about what Julie said. No one was around, and I was craving Jackson's touch. Nothing had happened since the time we got caught, and I didn't want to wait another second. I closed my eyes, but felt him kiss the side of my cheek. I opened my eyes and found him an inch away from me. He licked his lips before looking down at mine. He was so close. So, so close. I could smell the frosting from my birthday cake on his breath. I wanted to taste it, to relive the kiss from the closet.

I leaned forward but he backed up before we could connect. We stared at each other, one of Jackson's hands gripping the steering wheel so tightly his knuckles were turning white, the other one sliding to the headrest behind me. I rested my head against his arm, and he positioned his hand so he was cradling my head.

"I'm not supposed to touch you," Jackson whispered. At least he sounded as disappointed as I felt.

"What if I want you to?" I admitted.

He pulled his arm back slowly, rubbing his hands up and down his face before staring out the windshield. "We can't," he said with finality.

I stared at him for a while, wondering if he would change his mind. A muscle kept popping in his jaw from how hard he was clenching it.

I reached a hand toward him, for just one touch, but he pushed himself against the window and closed his eyes like I was about to burn him.

I put my hair behind my ears before grabbing my gifts and hopping out of the truck.

"Happy birthday, Addison," he said without looking at me.

I knew he was fighting his feelings, because Jackson would've carried my presents to the door for me if we weren't alone. That meant he didn't trust himself to follow me to my front door. I shouldn't have felt happy about that, but I did. At least it meant he wanted me, too.

Chapter 16

NOW

June

On Sunday morning, I drove out to a bookstore to pick out some summer reads. Then I went to the mall and walked around for hours, letting myself buy some new clothes since I still hadn't attempted to clean my old bedroom, or even stepped inside it. I had been sleeping on the couch, instead. I also bought some more cleaning supplies for the bathroom, which was next on my list to tackle.

The next day, I Facetimed Mia again before starting in on the bathroom. She had just gotten an expander put on the roof on her mouth that Wren had to turn with a key every night. She had her head tilted back, trying to get a good view of it for me.

"Wow, that's a lot of metal," I told Mia.

She nodded her head so dramatically I was sure it would roll right off her neck. "Right! Did you ever have orthodontics?"

"Nope, couldn't afford it. How are my teeth, anyways?" I smiled brightly into the camera, fluttering my lashes as I did. I never had braces, but I lucked out and had straight teeth anyways.

Mia giggled. "You're so lucky! I keep scratching my tongue on this thing."

The phone moved, and suddenly Wren was on the screen, telling Mia to go brush her teeth. They went back and forth for a little until Mia finally agreed and stomped off.

"So, how's it going there Miss Fixer-Upper?" Wren asked me.

"Jackson and I finished the basement, so that makes me feel better. I'm about to tackle the bathroom next." I was perched on the sink, both of my feet dangling off. I moved the phone around to give her a full three-sixty view. "These rust stains are going to suck so bad. My biceps will be huge by the time I'm done with it."

"How are things with Jackson?" Wren gave me a waggle of her eyebrows.

"Still engaged."

She laughed at me and I sighed. "It's complicated. My head keeps telling me to be mad at him over everything that happened between us, but another part is just really attracted to him still."

"I don't blame you. The boy is handsome."

"It's so annoying, right? He's absolutely gorgeous." I frowned, missing how easy it was to talk to Wren. "I already miss you guys again. Two weeks, and I promise I'll be back. I want to finish this stuff ASAP."

Wren pulled in her lips to hide a laugh and pointed like there was something behind me. I raised my eyebrow before turning around and letting out an ear-piercing scream, my phone falling to the floor.

Jackson was in the doorway of the bathroom, arms crossed and smirking at me. Why the hell didn't I lock the front door!?

I scrambled to pick my phone up off the floor. "Gotta go, Wren. Love you, bye." I shoved my phone in my back pocket and whipped around. How much of that conversation did he hear? I could tell my cheeks were red from how hot my face felt.

"What the fuck, Jackson?"

He was trying not to laugh, and failing miserably. I wanted to smack the smirk right off his face. "I texted you that I was coming over."

"I was Facetiming Wren and Mia, I didn't see it." I pulled my phone back out my pocket. Sure enough, Jackson sent me a message fifteen minutes ago.

"So, you think I'm absolutely gorgeous?" Jackson asked as he cocked his head to the side with a smug look on his face.

"Can you just shut up, actually?" I covered my cheeks with my hands. I hated him. "We're working on the bathroom today. Make yourself useful and start cleaning the tub." I threw the rust remover into his hands, and a wand brush directly at his chest.

He laughed at me again. I swear the guy got off on getting me flustered. I picked some songs for a playlist, starting with Royel Otis's cover of "Linger" before handing my phone to Jackson. "She Calls Me Back" by Noah Kahan started to play, and I rolled my eyes at the smirk Jackson gave me. He was so irritating.

***

I scrubbed the toilet for almost an hour while Jackson worked on the tub. The stains were awful, and my back was starting to ache. I had probably sprayed rust remover fifty times, and we were both so focused we hadn't talked. "Heat Waves" by Glass Animals was just finishing the last verse when I paused my scrubbing to watch Jackson. He was on his knees in the tub while he scrubbed around the drain.

There was sweat on his hairline, and I watched as it trickled down the side of his temple and dripped into the tub. His lips were parted as he focused on the task, his biceps straining as he scrubbed back and forth. I started to picture myself under him, his body moving back and forth in the same way, our bodies connected, him looking into my eyes with that same concentration. A shiver ran through me. I was probably just getting high from all the fumes in this small bathroom.

I tried to get a view of the tattoos on his arm instead to refocus my attention away from the dirty thoughts. "So, what are all the tattoos?"

He looked up at me and sat on the edge of the tub, setting down the brush. I closed the toilet seat and sat on it as he held out his arm.

"Well, you know Delvecchio." He ran a finger across his last name, written in black ink across his right forearm. I went with him when he got it on his eighteenth birthday.

He bent his arm to point at the back of his bicep. "A cannoli, obviously, for Jules." I laughed. While I could only take one bite of cannoli, Julie could easily eat ten in one sitting. He moved to the inside of his bicep, where the outline of Italy sat. "This one was for Mom and Dad, because of our heritage."

There was a drumstick, too, and next to it, a broken wine bottle. I stared at him, waiting for him to explain the broken bottle.

He ran a thumb over the wine bottle. "This is to remind me of the mistakes I've made while drinking."

I chewed on the inside of my lip. I had been there for plenty of those mistakes. He cleared his throat and flipped his arm to show the inside of his forearm. "And, of course, a piece of pizza."

I laughed when I saw it, shaking my head. "No way."

He looked up at me with that ridiculously cute smile, a question in his eye. *And, of course, a piece of pizza.* He said it so easily, like I *should* know why.

It couldn't be, though. Right? It couldn't be because of me. That would be crazy to assume. So instead of questioning him, I said something else.

"I actually have a tattoo that looks just like it."

"Nuh-uh," Jackson said, his mouth hanging open. "You said you would never get a tattoo."

I laughed and shrugged. "My twenty-first birthday. I was feeling silly."

Jackson laughed at me. "Show me."

I shook my head. "I don't want to. It's not good."

Jackson let out another laugh, "So you don't just have a tattoo, but you have a *bad* tattoo." His eyes started to roam my body. I was wearing denim cut-offs and a short-sleeve Columbia T-shirt, but he wouldn't be able to see it, no matter how hard he looked.

"Seriously, it's awful. I went to some sketchy shop and the guy did a terrible job. The lines are wonky, and it scarred my skin, so the ink is raised—it never set," I said as I crossed my arms.

"That all just makes me want to see it more! Come on, how bad can a slice of pizza be?" Jackson asked.

"You'd be surprised," I mumbled. The poor quality of the tattoo wasn't the only reason I didn't want to show him. It was also because we both had the same tattoo—for most likely the same reason.

He returned his gaze to mine, and those big brown eyes pulled me in. They were like drops of chocolate that I couldn't say no to. I rolled my eyes and finally stood up, lifting my shirt to show him the left side of my ribs.

He leaned forward from his spot on the side of the tub, his face level with my rib cage to inspect the botched outline of black ink. I watched him as he lifted his right hand to place on my side, rubbing the raised ink with his thumb. The tip of his finger briefly passed over the band of my bra, and I shut my eyes.

His hand felt so good—warm and tentative across my sweaty skin. I let myself enjoy it for a moment, imagining him pressing his lips to the spot, dragging them down my side, and stopping at my waistband. Unbuttoning my shorts, and . . .

I was definitely high off the fumes in the bathroom. My eyes shot open and I smacked his hand away in a flash. "No touching," I said before leaving the bathroom and slamming the door shut with him inside. I ran outside to get some air.

I was down the block before I stopped running. I was breathing heavily, and I pulled my hair up into a ponytail. How could one small touch do so much to me? I didn't need this. I shouldn't want this. He's engaged for christ's sake!

The memory of running down this street ten years ago flashed through my mind, and I had to put a hand to my chest and breathe deeply to avoid the panic attack I could feel rising up. It was too much—the coincidental matching tattoos paired with the thought of the last time I was here was fucking with my head. I had to get it together.

I walked up and down the block for a while before finally feeling like I could go back inside. Jackson never came to find me, and I was glad. I needed to clear my head and put it back on straight.

When I got back to the house, Jackson wasn't on the couch or in the kitchen. I walked down the hallway, and the bathroom door was still closed. I could hear music coming from his phone, and I opened the door without knocking. He apparently didn't care to knock, so why should I?

I regretted not knocking immediately, because Jackson was standing in the tub, cleaning the tiles . . . without a shirt on. His back muscles flexed as he cleaned a spot above his head. Every inch of skin was glistening with sweat. "I Can See You" by Taylor Swift was playing on his phone, and man did I want to strangle him—and straddle him at the same time.

I cleared my throat, and he turned around. I let myself look at his body, because, well, it was my house and I could do what I wanted! His tanned skin was so toned, just like it had been in high school from playing the drums. Except he was such a man now; bulkier, and with more deeply carved muscles. My eyes wandered to his left collarbone, where I knew I'd find a freckle. It had been so long since I had seen it. Since I had touched it.

No touching!

"Can you put your shirt back on?" I said with as much annoyance as I could muster.

"Can you knock before you open the door?" Jackson said as he threw his shirt back over his head.

"I will when you learn how to," I shot back.

Jackson held up a hand and nodded. "Fair. I'll stop doing that."

"Thank you." I cleared my throat again. "I think we should call it a day. This bathroom doesn't have a window, so you should probably head out before the chemicals start messing with you."

I wanted to take a break anyways, and start reading one of the books I bought. Anything to not think about the free view I just got of him, or how there was once a time when that view had been above me.

"You sure?" he asked.

"Yep, the bathroom looks great. I'm gonna clean the floor and be done. I'm not going to redo anything."

He let the brush fall into the bucket on the floor. "I think we should do the kitchen next. It'll be easy since it's small. I'll bring some boxes."

"Sounds good. Thanks for the help today."

Jackson dragged a hand through his hair before grabbing his phone off the counter. "See you later."

I didn't walk him to the door this time.

Chapter 17

BEFORE

August, Twelve Years Ago

The summer before our junior year, Julie got into Stanford and moved to California. She left a week after we celebrated Jackson's seventeenth birthday. The weeks building up to her departure, I was filled with an uncomfortable sense of dread. It reminded me of when Mom left—like I didn't know for sure if Julie would come back.

An underlying patch of anxiety sat beneath my chest for weeks until the day she left. Julie and I both cried as I helped her pack her bags. She was closer than a friend; she was like my sister now. I couldn't imagine being at the restaurant without her. Would Jackson and I still sing happily without her? It didn't seem possible. We were a trio. Jackson and I hardly spent any time alone together outside the restaurant or school these days, and he'd stopped looking at me like he wanted to touch me, too.

When it was time for Marie and Phil to take Julie to the airport, Jackson and I sat in the backseat of the car with her, Julie in the middle seat between us. After we said our goodbyes, the three of us stayed connected in a group hug for a good ten minutes. Other cars started honking at Marie's SUV to get a move on, but it did nothing to break us apart. Julie promised she'd be back for Christmas, and I tried to believe her.

She wasn't my mom. She would come back for us.

I noticed a drastic shift in Jackson after she left. The typical rap songs we used to listen to while closing the restaurant transitioned into heavy, sad songs. We started listening to things like "I'm Not Okay" by My Chemical Romance, and the glasses of wine we used to drink behind the bar turned into stolen bottles.

A few weeks later, we were sitting against the wall in the dining room, a new routine we had started after Julie left. Jackson and I would close by ourselves, clock out, then drink.

"It's so weird that Julie's gone," I said with a sigh.

Jackson took a long pull from the bottle. "I'm like an only child now. It's so weird. Is this what it feels like for you at home?"

I shrugged. "I guess so. Peter's left me alone since last summer. I think even he knows he was acting insane. At least you have your parents."

He let out a groan. "They've been so far up my ass. My grades have been shit these past two years. If I don't raise them, there's no way I'll be able to get into a good college. The last thing I want to do is get stuck with this restaurant."

"What? Why?"

"I'm not smart like Sam or Julie. I could never get into law school." He rubbed a hand down his face. "My family would never sell this place to anyone that's not family, either. It's not fair that my siblings left and I can't."

I didn't know what to say. I loved this place. Being stuck with the restaurant and the Delvecchio family sounded like a dream to me. And

Jackson wasn't stupid, so I hated that he constantly compared himself to his siblings.

"Just because you might not become a lawyer doesn't mean you can't do something just as successful," I encouraged.

Jackson shook his head. "Didn't you hear me? My grades are trash."

I itched the tip of my nose, trying to think of a way to make him feel better. "Well, junior year is important. Just study hard for the ACTs."

Jackson rolled his eyes. "I'm stupid. I fucking failed kindergarten. I doubt attempting to study will help."

"We could study together," I offered.

"No thanks," he added quickly. "I've already accepted my fate." I hated how much he had started talking down on himself. He used to be so confident—the life of the party wherever we went. Even though he wore a near-permanent scowl now, he was still popular at school.

We sat for a little longer until my stomach started to hurt. I rubbed my hand against it, figuring it was probably just the wine. "I'm gonna go to the bathroom before we go, my stomach is acting up."

When I got into the bathroom another wave of pain hit my stomach, almost doubling me over. Maybe the fettuccine we had earlier was bad.

I pulled down my pants and screamed. My underwear was drenched in blood. I took off my pants to check if any had transferred to the back of them. They were ruined. Shit, shit, shit! Of course *this* was when my body would decide to give me my period for the first time; at the restaurant, with just Jackson here. I needed Julie.

I heard a knock at the door. "Did you fall in? What was that scream about?"

I couldn't even laugh. I didn't know what to do.

"It's a warzone!" I yelled out. I wasn't even trying to be funny—I was freaking out. My underwear and pants were literally drenched in blood. I couldn't even put my clothes back on.

I heard Jackson laughing from the other side of the door. Tears prickled at my eyes. Why did my mom have to abandon me and Peter? This was the worst possible time for Julie to move to California, too. Jackson's laughter quieted, and I tried to brainstorm what to do.

"Are you crying in there? Addie, are you sick?" Jackson said softly through the door.

"Sick of my stupid life," I mumbled to myself. "Jackson, I um . . . This is really embarrassing, but something happened."

He was silent for a second, then said, "Oh god, did you shit your pants?"

A laugh escaped me. "No, you idiot, I didn't shit myself. I started my period. And it's like, everywhere. I can't put my clothes back on. I don't know what to do."

Jackson was quiet for another moment, then started trying to open the door. I screamed at the top of my lungs and threw my arms over my body to block myself, even though I knew the door was locked.

"Relax! I just wanted to open it a crack so we could hear each other better," Jackson said. Hesitantly, I reached up and flipped the lock. Jackson, true to his word, cracked it open only slightly before saying, "Do you have like, feminine supplies in your backpack?"

I groaned. I hated that he said "feminine supplies" like he was a health teacher. "No Jackson, this is my first period. This fucking sucks."

I stared at my work pants on the floor. I could live with one less pair of underwear, but having to get new work pants irritated me.

"Listen, I'll run down the street to the store and get you some pads," Jackson offered.

"Okay, but my pants are gross, I can't put them back on. Jesus, what if it got on the carpet out there?" The tears that had been blurring my vision finally started to fall.

"If it's on the carpet, we can get it out. I'm sure it's the same as red wine. I'll be back in five minutes." The door clicked shut, and I rested my elbows on my knees. Blood was still dripping into the toilet, and I managed to stretch my arms far enough to throw away my underwear without getting up. I started wiping at the blood on my pants with toilet paper; I would have no choice but to put them back on. Shit, I had just thrown my underwear away. What was I going to put the pad on?

Jackson came back five minutes later, as promised. He knocked on the door before opening it a sliver again. "I got a box of pads. I also took off my boxers so you can wear them. They're in the bag. Can I hand this to you? I'll keep my eyes closed."

I guffawed. "Your boxers! That your sweaty nuts have touched?"

He shoved his arm through the crack, holding the bag up. "What other choice do we have? You just have to wear them home."

He was right. It would be easier to put the pad on his boxers rather than try to stick it to my ruined pants. The drive home was hardly ten minutes, and I could change into something else immediately. I was kind of impressed that he'd even thought of it. "Okay, bring in the bag, but don't you dare open your eyes."

"No offense Addie, but I really don't want to open them."

I let myself laugh as he pushed his way through the door. He stayed facing the door as he backed his way to me, eyes closed as promised. I grabbed the bag from him, and he ran out the bathroom, shutting the door behind him.

I looked inside the bag. There was a bottle of ibuprofen, his navy-blue boxer briefs, a box of pads, and a bag of sour gummy worms. I wanted to cry—Jackson was the best.

I took the boxers out of the bag, placing a pad inside them before cleaning myself up as best I could and pulling them up. I folded up the pants and put them in the bag, then I took three ibuprofen, washing them down with water from the sink.

When I left the bathroom, Jackson already had my backpack on his arm, ready to take me home.

We stood staring at each other for a second. His eyes dropped to look at me standing in his boxers, while I was looking at him like he was my entire world. He held my backpack out for me.

"Can you see if there's a jacket in the back I can tie around my waist?" I asked. "I will die of mortification if you see how bulky this pad is in the back."

Jackson laughed and ran back toward the kitchen. I followed him through the swinging doors and he got me an old jacket of Julie's from the coat hook. I tied it around my waist and we headed outside for the truck.

"Are you going commando right now?" I asked Jackson as we got in the truck.

He shook his head with a smile. "Obviously. Do you think I just go around wearing two pairs of underwear in case of an emergency?"

We broke out into laughter, and Jackson turned on the radio for our drive to my house. I ate the gummy worms as the cramps started to fade away. When he pulled into my driveway, I grabbed the door handle, not turning to look at Jackson while I spoke.

"Thanks, Jackson. For uh . . . everything. I'll wash these and give them back."

He didn't respond, and I turned my head to face him. He was watching me with an expression I couldn't decipher. His brown eyes looked so beautiful in the darkness; I wished I could reach over and touch him. Finally, he gave me a small smile. "That's what friends do for each other." *They protect each other.*

"You're the best," I said quickly. I hopped out of the truck and walked up the path to the front porch, making sure not to turn around to see if he was still watching me.

Chapter 18

NOW

July

Jackson helped me for the next two days with the kitchen. We boxed up old dishes and silverware, and threw out stained and burnt pans, and cutting boards that were unusable. We ended up taking the kitchen table out to the curb to throw away. We scrubbed the fridge out, and wiped the walls and counters from top to bottom. We even ripped out all the wallpaper that was inside the cabinets.

On the Fourth of July, Jackson invited me to come to the restaurant to sit inside and watch the parade that went down Main Street every year. He picked me up in that clunker of a truck that we drove around in high school. The only difference I could spot was a new front bumper. I hopped up into the passenger seat, the sweet feeling of nostalgia covering me.

We drove with the windows down, listening to one of Julie's old Taylor Swift CDs. I love that he never got rid of them; her music was the soundtrack to our youth. "You Belong With Me" was playing, and

I ran my hand across the worn seat, reliving a million little memories of squeezing in here with Julie and Jackson.

"How is this truck even still running? It's like, a million years old," I said when we pulled into the alley behind the restaurant.

"This truck is like a damn heirloom in this family. It can't die."

"How often do you drive it?" I asked.

"Hardly ever, honestly. I usually drive my SUV. But this was a special occasion."

I refused to meet the smile I knew he was wearing.

We walked through the back door into the kitchen, then through the swinging doors and into the dining room as we switched on the lights. He motioned for me to sit at one of the barstools as he slid behind the bar.

"What would you like to drink?" he asked as he settled his forearms on the counter in front of me.

"Just water is fine," I said as I swiveled on the seat.

"You don't want a glass of wine?"

I shook my head, crossing my hands on the counter. My finger grazed against his forearm and I inched my hand away. "If you can't drink, I'm not drinking."

He smiled at me before grabbing a glass and filling it with water. "Just because I don't drink doesn't mean you can't."

"I don't want to. Seriously," I added. *Unlike your future wife, apparently.* He slid the glass across the bar to me while he poured his own.

"So, what's your family doing? Didn't you guys always get together for the Fourth?"

He walked around the bar to sit next to me, his knee bumping against mine in the process. "Everyone usually flies in for the holiday, but they were just out here for the engagement party, so we decided to skip a family party this year. We're all going to FaceTime later."

I only got that one quick hug from Julie, and never even got to see Marie when she was here since they flew back the same day I ran into Jackson and Julie at the restaurant. I was so close to being with all of them again.

"You guys seem closer now?" I questioned.

He nodded. "Yeah, Julie and I are best buddies, even with her living farther away. Sam and I are the same as always—I'm really close with his kids, though." He took a sip of his water, then wiped his mouth. "Marie and I are better, too, now that I'm sober."

I traced my finger up and down the condensation on his glass, remembering the one and only time I heard Marie yell at Jackson.

"What about your mom?" Jackson asked.

I let out a self-deprecating laugh. "Denise? The only time she managed to get a hold of me was to tell me the house had been left to me. She never gave a shit about me."

Jackson's fists were clenching and unclenching. He was staring straight ahead at the bottles of wine, and I wondered if he was thinking about a drink. About how good it would feel to taste a drop, let the fuzziness overcome his body, and forget about everything. If he could fight the feeling, then so could I.

We changed the subject, and he gave me his phone to choose music to play softly over the speakers. He left to go to the ice cream shop to get something to hold us over through the parade.

We were drinking peanut butter banana smoothies and sitting on the floor in the lobby, cross-legged against the front windows like little kids. Every time someone threw candy into the street, Jackson sprinted out to grab some and hand it to the kids who were sitting on the curb. It was adorable, and I wanted to hate it.

When the parade ended, we moved to the dining room, still seated on the floor with our backs up against the wall like we did in high school. Except this time, we weren't passing a bottle back and forth.

"So, are you seeing anyone?" Jackson asked.

I pulled my knees up to rest under my chin. "Nah. I haven't dated in a while. I haven't had the best of luck."

"No?" he questioned.

I ran my hands up and down my legs. "I mean, I've been a live-in nanny for ten years. It's kinda hard to meet people unless I use a dating app. Every time I try dating, the guy has some underlying issue. Apparently, I can only attract addicts. You'd think I'd know how to stay away from them after being surrounded by them growing up." I said it jokingly, but as soon as it came out, I wished I could take it back. I didn't mean to make a jab at him specifically. My eyes met his apologetically.

"I'm sorry," Jackson said.

I raised an eyebrow. Was he sorry I had a bad experience with dating? Or was he sorry he had been one of the previous addicts in my life?

I knocked my elbow into his. "I'm proud of you, ya know," I told him sincerely.

He looked away, staring at the bottles of wine on the wall. So many nights we had stolen from that bar and gotten drunk together.

"Thanks, Addie." He didn't sound like he believed me, and it tugged something in my heart.

"I'm serious, Jackson. I know how hard it is to get sober, and it's even harder to *stay* sober. I mean, look at Peter. He always claimed he wouldn't be like his dad. Then ended up exactly like him."

Jackson rubbed a hand over his mouth, letting out a deep, shaky breath. This was probably the nicest I had been to him in the time we'd spent together so far. And it felt . . . *good*. Jackson wasn't a bad guy. He never really was, he just hadn't known how to handle his problems.

"What did Peter do to you that night?" Jackson whispered the question, like he was scared to know the answer. I looked down at my arms. I couldn't believe he'd brought it up—that we were going to talk about that night. I wasn't ready.

When I didn't answer, he grabbed my right arm, extending it so he could see the inside of my right bicep.

"Is this from him?" he managed to ask.

It wasn't a huge scar; maybe two inches long, and it was the only mark Peter had ever left on me. I pulled my arm back, tucking it between my thighs. "It really wasn't that bad."

Jackson flared his nostrils, looking away and shaking his head. His fists were clenching and unclenching again, and I felt uncomfortable. I would do anything to change the subject, because it all just led back to me needing Jackson and him not being there for me.

"Hey, why don't we go make a pizza?" I offered.

He looked over at me, and I could tell he wanted to say more, wanted to ask more questions. He must've decided against it, because he stood up then, reaching down to help me stand. We headed for the kitchen and dropped the subject, but I didn't let go of his hand until we passed the kitchen doors.

***

At one o'clock, Jackson joined a family FaceTime, and I stayed out of view on the other side of him. We were sitting at the bar now, and had each finished our third piece of pizza.

I could hear Julie and Marie's voices in the background, a male voice that I assumed was Sam, and little kids giggling.

"I have a surprise visitor here with me," Jackson said. He swiveled in his chair to face me. "Hold up your middle fingers so I can turn the camera to you."

I laughed, covering my face. "I'm not going to do that, it's disrespectful."

I heard Julie's scream. "I already know who it is by the voice! Britt, get over here!" I assumed Britt was her wife.

Then I heard Marie ask, "Surprise visitor?"

"I'm not turning the camera around until you double-flip the bird," Jackson encouraged.

"There's children," I argued.

"And Julie is their aunt. They've seen a middle finger," Jackson said with an eye roll. "Come on, it's funny!"

I let out a groan before holding up two middle fingers. Screams erupted from the phone, and I heard Julie tell Britt that I'm like a little sister to her. She didn't say "used to be"—she spoke in the present tense. My heart ached, because I missed her just as much as I had missed Jackson.

"Oh, is that Addison? Let me see you," Marie said.

Jackson let me take the phone from him, and when I did, I couldn't help the tear that fell from my eye. Marie's hair was almost fully gray now—I knew she'd had Jackson later in life, so she must be almost seventy now. I had missed out on her aging, and something about that fact hurt so deeply. I had been so close to her for years, and lost so much time I could've had with her. At the same time, it felt like I had just seen her yesterday; like I was still a fourteen-year-old girl, standing in this lobby, asking for a job.

She was crying, covering her mouth with her hand. "You're radiant, honey," Marie said, trying to get control of her tears.

"It's so good to see you," I said quietly.

I waved to Julie's wife, and Sam gave an awkward wave. I hadn't ever really talked to him, so this was anticlimactic for him. His two sons were sitting on either side of him, and they looked like carbon copies of Jackson and Sam. They were watching me with confused looks on their faces, and suddenly I got the feeling this was a bad idea.

It was like the kids read my thoughts. "Where's Aunt Sophie?" one of them asked.

I shoved the phone back into Jackson's hands and heard him say, "She's visiting her sister." I swung through the kitchen doors before I could hear anything else.

I put my hand over my chest to calm my heart. I was sure I was having a heart attack. What was I doing? What the actual *fuck* was I doing?

I turned around and came face-to-face with the bulletin board. The picture of me and Jackson from graduation stared back at me. I stormed toward it, ripping it from the corkboard and sending the tac flying across the room. I ripped it in half perfectly, so that I was disconnected from Jackson. My smiling face with the diplomas on one half, him with my legs around his hips on the other. I threw both halves in the trash and walked out the back door.

***

I had walked for thirty minutes by the time Jackson pulled the truck up beside me.

He rolled down the window and called out to me, "Jesus Addie, don't just leave like that. I couldn't find you anywhere."

A part of me felt bad for worrying him, but another part didn't care. Because I shouldn't care. Because what I do shouldn't matter to him.

I didn't say a word as I opened the passenger door and got in. It was humid as fuck today, and I was drenched in sweat. It was soaked through my shirt already, and the truck's A/C felt heavenly.

"Can you take me home, please? I'm not feeling well," I mumbled.

"Yeah, you probably gave yourself heatstroke," Jackson said. He wasn't fighting me on it, because he probably also knew that me joining the FaceTime was a bad idea. It made him look like a cheater, and that made *me* look bad. I was brought into this world as a product of my own mother's infidelity, so why was I playing with fire?

"Don't act like you care," I muttered.

"Stop acting like I don't," he shot back.

Don't let him affect you.

He handed me a cold bottle of water, and I ripped it out of his hands to chug shamelessly. "Big Blind" by The Story So Far was playing, but neither of us sang along. I was irritated by how well the lyrics fit with our situation.

When we pulled into the driveway, Jackson covered his mouth while balancing his elbow on the window ledge like he was thinking.

"Hey, Addie?" His voice was laced with emotion. I turned away, staring through the windshield at my house. When I didn't respond, he talked anyways. "Please don't just leave me like that again."

His sentence rocked me. I was falling down a cliff, rolling and tumbling and getting scratched from every side. He sounded like he was talking to eighteen-year-old Addison—the Addison who got in her car without telling him where she was going, and without saying goodbye.

Not the Addison now, who left the restaurant without telling him first half an hour ago.

"You can't disappear again," he whispered. I couldn't respond even if I wanted to, because my throat was on fire from how hard I was fighting back the tears.

I grabbed the door handle to leave, and Jackson said, "I'll text you."

I nodded my head, but didn't promise I'd answer.

Chapter 19

BEFORE

December, Twelve Years Ago

Julie didn't fly back for Christmas like she said she would. She was too overwhelmed with school, and didn't want to travel. She was also thriving in the California sun, her skin more tanned than when she left, and her dark-brown hair looking a shade or two lighter.

Julie knew how upset I was over her promising to come home and then bailing, so she triple-swore she'd be back for Jackson's eighteenth birthday next summer. That meant it would almost be a full year before I saw her in person. I had to keep telling myself she wasn't my mom—she would come back.

Since Julie wasn't going to attend Christmas, Sam decided he would stay in New York, so Christmas Eve ended up just being me, Jackson, Marie, and Phil. This year they were going to one of Marie's sister's houses, and Jackson had already given me a heads up that it was going to be just as chaotic as his parent's anniversary party. I seriously couldn't wait.

Julie told me I could pick out an outfit from her closet—her way of sliding back into my good graces—and I felt like I was shopping at the mall as I went through her closet.

Jackson was laying on his back on her bed as I perused, totally uninterested as he scrolled through his phone.

"I don't think Julie has even worn half this stuff," I said as I pulled out a black denim jacket that still had the tags on it.

"No wonder she has no money to fly back home; she wastes all her money on clothes," Jackson said bitterly from where he was laying.

Jackson was just as upset as I was that Julie wasn't coming home, and even more aggravated because he bombed his classes this trimester. He wasn't studying for the ACT in the spring, and for the first time ever, he had actually *failed* a class.

"She didn't stay in California because of money. She stayed because she's stressed over her classes."

"Keep on telling yourself that, Addie," Jackson quipped. "It's winter break; she doesn't have classes till January."

God, he was so grumpy these days. Argumentative with the entire world.

"What are you wearing to the party?" I asked as I put my hands on my hips to face him.

"A pair of sweats and a hoodie. I'm not dressing up for these people who are just going to call me Sam a hundred times tonight."

I tried to think of something to say to pull him out of his black mood. "I don't think you have to worry. Your hair covers half your face these days; they won't know who you are at all."

This was the longest Jackson had ever gone without a haircut, and his dark hair was so long now he had to constantly push his bangs behind his ears on one side, and it had started to flip up at the back of his neck. It didn't look bad—it made him look like he belonged at a heavy rock show. I just missed seeing the entirety of his face all the time.

He propped himself up on his elbows and gave me a wicked grin.

"You don't like my long hair?" He sprung up from the bed, shaking his head in my face so his bangs brushed against my cheeks. I laughed and pushed him away from me, wiping a hand down my face to scratch the tickle.

"Oh my god, I bet it would fit in braids." I put a hand over my mouth, stifling the giggle that tried to sneak its way out.

Jackson ran his hands through his hair, watching his reflection in the mirror of Julie's vanity. He met my eyes in the reflection. "Do it, my family would *hate* it."

"Okay, but I don't know how. I'd have to watch a YouTube tutorial. Go brush it out and let me finish picking an outfit."

Jackson left the room to go use his hairbrush, and I turned around and quickly went through Julie's closet again, picking out a brown long-sleeve top and the black denim jacket that still had the tags on it.

I switched out my leggings for a pair of her dark jeans, and had just slipped off my shirt when Jackson walked back into the room. I gasped and my arms flew to cover my stomach instead of my chest.

He stopped in his tracks with his hand still on the doorknob, cheeks reddening and eyes growing wide as they dropped down to my chest.

I was too stunned to move. Jackson watched me standing there in my cream-colored push-up bra that I was way too excited to buy when I found it at Goodwill.

Jackson's eyes slammed shut, and his other hand flew to his crotch. Oh my god, was he . . . *reacting* to seeing me like this?

"Jesus, I'm so sorry. It's just like, a natural reaction. I'm not trying to be a freak. Fuck, I'll give you a minute," he strangled out as he backed out the room, slamming the door behind him.

I was still standing there, heart racing in embarrassment. I finally snapped out of it, grabbing Julie's shirt off the bed and pulling it on in a flash, then ripping off the tag from the denim jacket and throwing it on. Now my body had a double-layer of protection from Jackson's eyes.

My cheeks still felt hot as I heard him start to play the drums in his room. I waited until the song was finished, then I counted another minute in my head before heading down the hallway to his bedroom.

I knocked twice, waiting for him to give me a signal that it was safe. I had my ear against the door, waiting for him to call me in when he pulled it open, causing me to fall into his chest. We pushed apart from each other faster than we fell together.

"Sorry!" we both said at the same time.

Jackson cleared his throat. "Can we like, not be weird about what happened?"

My words spewed out like vomit. "Absolutely. We never speak of it again. Just like when I started my period at the restaurant—it's wiped from our memories."

Or, ya know, the time we kissed at a party, and dry humped each other at the restaurant.

Jackson started laughing, covering his face and rubbing his hands up and down.

"We can blame Julie. Everything is her fault for leaving," he said good-naturedly.

"Alright, now that that's settled, do you still want me to do your hair?" I asked, dying to change the subject.

He looked at my hands, then over at the staircase. "Probably not. We have to leave soon." I was actually grateful he changed his mind, because my hands were still shaking. I wasn't sure if I would be able to properly use them right now. And touching Jackson would not be a good idea, either. For him or me, I couldn't tell.

***

Jackson's family's Christmas party was just as bustling as he predicted. I recognized a lot of the family from the anniversary party, but his aunt had invited her husband's family, too, who were *also* Italian. I didn't even know who was actually related to the Delvecchios and who wasn't.

Some of Jackson's uncle's nephews were around our age, and we were hanging out with them in the basement of his aunt's house, hiding away from the adults with a bottle of vodka that one of the older cousins sneaked for us.

We were playing a card game called spoons, and these guys went *hard*. I wished Julie was here, because all the cousins were boys, and they were obnoxious and rough while we played. Someone had the idea to put the spoons halfway up the staircase, so we had to run across the entire basement to grab them. A guy named Luca suggested that whoever got to the spoons first got to take a shot. The game turned super competitive after that because there were five of us and only one bottle of alcohol.

I had lost every game so far, so I was stone-cold sober in a room with four annoying teenage boys. Jackson was trying his hardest, and he was hands down the drunkest out of all the other guys.

Once everyone had a steady buzz going, I started to actually try during the game. I wanted at least *one* shot, but some dick named Brian was being a stickler for the rules, and hogging the bottle.

Someone got up sneakily to tiptoe to the stairs for spoons, and when I noticed, I sprung up from the floor, throwing my cards down in a panic. I ran for the stairs, but someone grabbed my waist from behind and pulled me back. I toppled backward, falling to the floor and hitting my tailbone.

All the boys passed me, each grabbing a spoon and waving it in my face before joining the circle again. Jackson walked up to me slowly, throwing the spoon in his hand down to the floor with a clink and helping me stand.

"Which one of them pushed you?" Jackson asked.

I rubbed my tailbone, sure there would be a bruise later. I turned around and pointed. "That asshole, Brian. Is it really too much to ask for one sip?"

Jackson didn't answer me. Instead, he stormed past me and shoved Brian in the shoulder as he was taking a drink, causing him to stumble and hit his tooth on the lip of the bottle.

"What the fuck, man?" Brian said as he covered his mouth.

"You hurt Addie," Jackson said, his fists clenched at his sides.

Brian's eyes flicked toward me. "I was playing the game; it's not that serious."

"You're right, it's not that serious. So, you didn't have to push her down," Jackson quipped.

Brian shrugged a shoulder like he couldn't care less. "Okay, and she's standing. She's fine."

"That's not the point," Jackson argued. "Just give her one fucking sip of the vodka. You're being a dick."

Everyone in the basement was watching the interaction. I didn't want Jackson to defend my honor—mostly because he had the same look in his eye that he'd had when he fought Peter. The last thing we needed was a fight with some kid we had just met, especially over something as stupid as spoons.

"Everything is good," I said nervously. "Let's go, Jackson. It's almost time to go anyways."

Jackson turned around and looked at me like he agreed. Brian dropped his defenses—then Jackson stunned us all by turning around and punching Brian directly in the nose.

I gasped and covered my own face while Brian let out a yelp. Everyone else's jaws dropped.

"Don't touch her again," Jackson said before turning around and running up the stairs. I whipped around just as fast, running up after him.

When we made it to the top of the stairs, he grabbed my arm, and we slithered through the throngs of people until he found the front door and we slipped outside into the December air.

Jackson started laughing, putting a hand over his abdomen as he hunched over.

"What the hell was that?" I asked, breathless from our run.

Jackson shook his head, standing up straight and catching his breath. "That guy was so fucking annoying. He's not gonna do anything about it; his parents would find out about the alcohol and kill him. My uncle's side of the family is way stricter than mine." Jackson ran his hands through his hair, leaving them clasped around the back of his neck.

I stared at him, still in disbelief over what he just did.

"Do I thank you?" I asked with a small chuckle.

"If I'm being honest, that was more about me than you. I wanted to deck him from the moment he opened his mouth."

I shook my head. "You're a lunatic. Don't make that a habit."

His hands dropped from his neck. "Let's take a walk. I need to sober up a little before we find my parents."

We walked down the block, finding a playground and sitting on the swings. Jackson was trying to see how high he could swing, while I just pushed myself back and forth lightly with my foot on the ground.

"So, what bothered you so much about Brian that you wanted to, in your words, '*deck him from the moment he opened his mouth*'?"

Jackson slowed himself down on the swing, turning to face me. "He was such a creep—didn't you notice the way he was staring at you?"

I reared my head back, suppressing a laugh. "I don't think he was staring at me as much as he was staring at that bottle of vodka."

Jackson scoffed. "Trust me, he was trying to undress you with his eyes."

"Oh, was he?" I joked. "And how would you know that?"

Jackson looked away. I couldn't tell why he was being so weird. "I heard him say something to one of the guys when you went to the bathroom."

I raised an eyebrow. "What'd he say?"

Jackson stood up from the swing, motioning for me to follow. "It doesn't matter; he got what he deserved."

I followed Jackson back to the house, trying to keep up with his quick stride. "Just tell me, I won't get upset. I'm sure I've heard worse."

"He . . . He was just talking about how good you looked, and said that he was thinking about asking you out," Jackson finally said.

My lips parted and I furrowed my eyebrows. "And that's bad because . . . ?"

"Because he was an asshole!" Jackson's voice started to rise. "And you deserve better than that."

"Okaaay," I said. "I guess, thanks again?"

"Yeah," Jackson said with a slight nod. "That's what friends do."

They protect each other. If Jackson thought keeping Brian away from me was protecting me, then I trusted his judgment.

I gave him another nod, wondering why it bothered him so much. But I didn't question him anymore. I was just happy to finally leave the party.

Chapter 20

BEFORE

December, Twelve years ago

Mr. and Mrs. Delvecchio let me spend the night on Christmas Eve this year since Peter went to go see our mom again. This would be my third Christmas with the Delvecchios, but the first time I ever woke up with them on Christmas morning.

I slept in Julie's old room, and in the morning, I padded my way down to the kitchen to get a glass of orange juice. When I entered the kitchen, Marie was making a pot of coffee and sniffling. At first I thought she was blowing her nose, until I got closer and realized she was crying.

I stopped in my tracks, and when she noticed me, she plastered on a smile, wiping at her eyes.

"Good morning, honey. How did you sleep?"

"Pretty good." I put my hair behind my ears nervously. "Are you okay?"

Her smile got wobbly, and her eyes glassy. "Oh, just emotional that my kids are growing up. I miss Sam and Julie. I always braid Julie's hair on Christmas morning, and she's not here for me to do it this year."

Her coffee finished brewing, and she turned around to fill a mug. I grabbed the orange juice from the fridge, and she handed me a glass to fill. I leaned back against the counter as I took a sip.

"You can braid my hair if you want," I said with a shrug. My mom had never braided my hair—I didn't even know if she knew how. Nobody had ever even taught me how to do a simple braid before; just last night I was about to watch a tutorial to learn how to do Jackson's.

Marie smiled. "Yeah?"

I nodded, feeling bashful over how excited I was about the thought of my hair in two French braids.

She guided me to the family room, where she sat on the couch with me on the floor in front of her, my body between her legs. She ran her fingers through my hair to untangle the knots, then divided it into two sections, putting one side over my shoulder to separate it.

"You have such beautiful long hair, Addie," Marie said as she grabbed three strands and started the process.

"Thank you." My mom and Peter had brown hair, so I assumed I got my white-blonde hair from my dad. I didn't even know his name, or what nationality he was. I knew I was half Italian from my mom's side, but I would never know what the other half was.

I hadn't seen my mom since I was fourteen, and she had never mothered me like this even when she was here. She didn't do the things Marie did with her children. She'd never given me the type of attention this family gave me. For the first time since my mom left, I realized how shitty of a mom she had been, and how unfair it was. Did she even love me? Mr. and Mrs. Delvecchio showed me more affection than my own mom ever did.

When Marie finished braiding my hair she asked, "What do you think?"

I started to cry—I couldn't help it. How had my mom never embraced me like this? I put my hands over my face to hide my tears, trying to control the sobs.

"Oh Addie . . . What's wrong, honey?"

Being called honey just sent me over the edge, and I couldn't hold back the full-on sobs, my entire being shaking with each cry. Marie pulled me up from the ground and right into her lap, my face buried under her chin. She wrapped her arms around me and I held onto her like I was a child. I would be seventeen in just two months, but I was crying like a fucking baby.

"My mom never did anything like that for me." I didn't even know if Marie could understand me with how watery my voice sounded. "I barely even have a mom; I don't even think she loves me." It was so easy for Mom to leave me, to move away with her boyfriend and abandon me and Peter.

Marie kissed the top of my head, pulling me closer to her chest. Her voice was serious when she said, "Addie, you are such a special girl. You've been dealt a shitty hand in this life, but you are growing into such a lovely person."

It felt so good to hear—to hear how much she cared about me, and that my life mattered.

"You are so important to this family. We all love you, so much," Marie added.

They loved me? I knew they liked me, but love? My heart felt like it grew one hundred sizes. This family *loved* me. I loved this family, too. It was the closest thing I'd ever had to an actual family, and it settled something in me to know they felt the same.

"Even Jackson?" I don't know why I asked, or why I needed the confirmation. He had been my best friend since I was fourteen years old, but we didn't tell each other that we loved each other. I had never really told anyone, not even Julie.

Marie was rubbing smooth circles on my back that made me want to fall asleep. "Yes, honey, especially Jackson."

What did that mean? Especially Jackson? I couldn't think about it for too long, because I heard him say, "Hey."

I leapt out of Marie's lap, running my hands under my nose and wiping my eyes with the neckline of my pajama top. "Hey," I said as I forced a smile. "Merry Christmas!"

Jackson stood in the doorway to the family room, looking from Marie to me with a question in his eyes.

"Your mom braided my hair for me," I said, trying to steer the conversation away from my crying.

Marie gave me a small smile, seeming to understand how self-conscious I felt about my meltdown.

"What'd she do? Braid it so tight it made you cry?" I could tell he was trying to make a joke to ease the tension, but I was desperate to change the subject.

"Why don't we open presents, yeah?" Marie asked as she stood from the couch, squeezing my shoulder as she passed me. The woman even knew how to read me.

Jackson walked up to me, his hair still in disarray from sleep. "You good?" he said, quietly enough so that his mom couldn't hear him from where she was grabbing the gifts under the tree.

"Yep, I'm great." I gave him two lame thumbs up.

He gave me a wary look, but he left it alone.

Phil came into the family room five minutes later, and Jackson and I opened our presents while sitting on the floor. He got a new pair of drumsticks, clothes, and a pair of high-top black Converse to match mine—although his didn't have the embroidered pizza slice.

I was gifted two new sweaters that Marie said Julie picked out, a new purse (also courtesy of Julie), and three books that Marie said were trending right now at Barnes & Noble.

After gifts we ate breakfast, which consisted of a massive stack of blueberry pancakes with bacon and eggs. Then we sat around the family room and played our usual game of Monopoly. It was different with just the four of us, but it was one of the best Christmases I'd had with them.

Later in the day we Facetimed Julie, and then I followed Jackson to his room to watch him play the drums. After he played two songs, he took a break to give me a quick lesson, which mostly consisted of me not listening to anything he said. I couldn't remember how to read the music, so I just hit the bass drum as fast as I could while freestyling with the cymbal and the other parts that I couldn't remember the names of.

At the end of the night, Marie and Phil said I could sleep over again, and after Jackson and I watched a movie, we went upstairs to get ready for bed. We were in the upstairs bathroom, both brushing our teeth in tandem at the double-sink vanity, and Jackson kept looking over at me in the mirror. I knew he wanted to ask me something, and after I spit and rinsed my mouth, I asked him what was up.

"Are you going to tell me why you were crying earlier?"

I wiped my mouth with the bath towel, then handed it to him. I didn't want to tell him, partially because I was humiliated that he watched me weep like a little kid while sitting on his mom's lap.

"It was stupid," I said.

He looked at me like he didn't believe me, then looked away.

"It hurts me to see you cry," Jackson said in a low voice. He was pretending to fix his hair in the mirror, avoiding the way I was searching his face. Then he added, "If there is something I can do to fix what's wrong, I want to know."

My heart squeezed in my chest. Because that was the kind of friend Jackson was; he had always been a protector toward me in his own way.

I pretended to fix my hair in the mirror now, too, just so I didn't have to look directly at him. "Nothing was really wrong. It's just that your family is really important to me."

He didn't even skip a beat when he replied with, "And you're really important to my family."

I loved hearing it from his mouth just as much as I'd loved hearing it from Marie's. I wanted to tell him that his mom said the family loved me—that *he especially* loved me, too. I wanted to tell him I loved him, and that he was the most important thing to me.

I got that weird feeling in my chest then, as I noticed how much he had changed since freshman year; how much he was turning into a man. I squished it down quickly though, because Jackson was my best friend. This family meant everything to me, and I wasn't going to mess it up just because of how much I wanted their son. So instead, I said, "Thanks, Jackson. Good night." Then I walked past him and shut the door to Julie's room, locking it before crawling into bed.

***

The Delvecchios ended up letting me stay over for the rest of the week, and on New Year's Eve, Jackson and I stayed home to hang out with his parents instead of going to a party. The holiday always made my stomach feel weird, because it was the first time I watched Jackson kiss someone else.

That evening Marie and Phil let us drink champagne with them, and we spent the night playing Monopoly before Jackson and I dug out the old game of *Jeopardy!* that Julie made for my sixteenth birthday. This time there wasn't a single question that got answered wrong.

All of us had flushed cheeks and were a bit tipsy by the end of the night. When "Happy New Year" flashed across the screen and fireworks began exploding outside, Phil and Marie kissed while Jackson and I just stared at each other with awkward smiles while he rolled his eyes at his parents.

There was a split second where Jackson leaned toward me, and I thought he was about to kiss me right then and there in front of his parents. He hugged me instead, and it was so tight that I could feel his heart beating right against my own heart in a perfect rhythm. "Happy New Year, Addie," he whispered into my ear. I couldn't help the way my body leaned into him.

"Happy New Year, Jackson," I said with my mouth pressed against his neck. A strangled sound escaped the back of his throat.

We separated without making eye contact.

Marie gave each of us a hug next, pressing a kiss to my cheek and then his.

"Happy New Year, my lovely children! May this new year bring you adventure, and life-long memories," Marie announced dramatically. She didn't drink often, and I could tell she was feeling the champagne by how she accidentally called me her child—but a part of me wondered if it *wasn't* an accident.

This would be an important year. We would take the ACTs in the spring, finish junior year, Jackson would turn eighteen, and we would start senior year.

I never planned on it being the year that things started to fall apart.

Chapter 21

BEFORE

August, Eleven Years Ago

On Jackson's eighteenth birthday, Marie and Phil planned to throw him a giant party to celebrate. Julie and her new girlfriend flew in from California, and most of the people invited were either about to start senior year like us, or had graduated in previous years. Everyone would be between the ages of seventeen and twenty-one, so there was going to be alcohol. It would be too hard to keep track of who was actually legally allowed to drink and who wasn't, so the Delvecchios made a rule that if someone was driving home, they would have to check in with them to prove that they were sober first. Anyone could stay the night, and I already knew I'd be sleeping over since everyone I knew who could drive me home would be drinking.

Before the party, I went with Jackson to a tattoo parlor. I sat on a chair and watched the tattoo artist begin to write the D for Delvecchio on his forearm.

"I could never get a tattoo," I said over the buzzing of the gun.

Jackson turned his head to face me.

"You don't think so? Not even on your birthday?" he asked.

I shook my head. "It's crazy how permanent it is. And your skin is so red—it looks like it hurts," I added. I watched as the artist rubbed the ink with a paper towel before he continued spelling out Jackson's last name. His arm looked even redder now.

"It really doesn't. It's more annoying than anything," Jackson said.

The appointment was no more than thirty minutes. The tattoo looked good—he picked a nice cursive font that wasn't too curly, so it was easy to read.

"Do I look tough?" Jackson asked as he held up his arm and pretended to kiss his bicep.

"You look *very* Italian," I said as we got in his truck to drive to the party.

He chuckled. "I'm not supposed to swim with this. Jules is gonna be pissed. She set up a pool this morning."

I let out a small laugh. "She's so obsessed with her girlfriend I doubt she'll care if you don't swim with her."

"True. You'll have to hang around them, get the 411 on this chick. If she's the reason Jules didn't come home during Christmas, then it's game over."

I gave Jackson a small salute. "I'm on it."

When we got back to the house, we helped Phil and Marie finish setting everything up for the party. Kids started arriving, and it was a huge mix of different groups. Julie had invited people she graduated with, and the booze was flying.

It was another hot August, and the last thing I wanted was to get sick from drinking, so I took it easy. Jackson, however, was not taking it easy; the last time I talked to him, he was at a beer pong table inside, completely intoxicated. He was laughing and goofing around, and I was so happy to see him like that. The last trimester of junior year had gone worse than the first, and just like Jackson had predicted, he didn't do well on the ACT. He had already said he didn't plan on going to college. He was in a weird head space right now, but today he was acting like his old self—something I'd barely seen in the past six months.

I hung around with Phil and Marie for a little while, setting out hamburgers and hot dogs as Phil grilled them. Marie had made a cake, and she let me decorate it; I covered it with sprinkles and made a horrible attempt at writing "Happy 18th Birthday Jackson" in scribbled frosting.

Julie and her girlfriend were in the pool, so I changed into a swimsuit before joining them. One of Julie's old friends, Jeremy, jumped in and we played a few rounds of chicken. Julie's girlfriend, Laney, was tough, and she knocked me off Jeremy's shoulders every time. I liked Laney; she was goofy and carefree like Julie was. They were a good match. I was only a little bitter I didn't get her all to myself, considering I hadn't seen her in a year. But she looked so happy today that I let it go.

Jeremy got out of the pool after a couple rounds, and I swam with Julie and Laney for a long time before I got tired of playing third wheel. We were the only three in the pool now, and I figured I should give them some time to themselves.

I lifted myself out of the pool, squeezing the water out of my hair. When I turned around, Jackson was leaning against the side of the house, watching me. He was only wearing a pair of black athletic shorts and a red pair of Vans. I was wearing one of Julie's old bikinis, an orange triangle top with matching bottoms. I suddenly felt exposed—the bottoms only covered half my butt. Jackson had never seen this much of my body before, not even when he walked in on me in Julie's room, and I felt the need to hide it. I walked over to the lawn chair I'd left my clothes on, and slipped on my denim shorts without clasping them. They were warm from the sun, and I already felt like they were drying the soaked bikini.

I grabbed a water bottle from a cooler, walking over to Jackson to give it to him. He had been drinking for over four hours straight; he definitely needed the hydration. "Settle Down" by The 1975 was playing softly from a speaker, and I mouthed along to the words.

As soon as I was directly in front of him, his eyes dragged down to my chest. I was about to call him a perv for staring at my boobs when he reached up to grab the bottom of the orange triangle, his knuckle brushing against the curve of my breast. I gasped at the pinprick sensation under my skin as his warm fingers adjusted the triangle so it was sitting more securely over my chest. He had *never* touched me like this before.

"Fixed it," he said in a low voice. My legs were tingling, slithers of need coursing through me. I wanted more, and I bit the inside of my lip to tamp down the desire.

He let his fingers skim down my side until they landed at the waistband of my shorts, then he grabbed my belt loops and tugged me toward him until our hip bones smacked together. We were outside, and I worried that someone would see us. Julie was only ten feet away in the pool, and his parents could be anywhere.

He buttoned and zipped up my shorts for me as he leaned forward. My knees locked, and the spot just below my zipper started to pulse. "You're distracting everyone here, Addison," he whispered against my ear.

The way he said my full name and the heat I felt from his breath against my ear almost made me lose my mind. I pushed him back suddenly, slamming him into the wall. "You're not supposed to touch me," I whisper-yelled. I was off-kilter, my entire equilibrium thrown off by what he was doing. It had been a long time since Jackson acted like this, but he also had never been this drunk before. Did he even mean what he was doing? He hadn't so much as looked at me like he wanted me since my sixteenth birthday.

He wasn't wearing a shirt, and my hand was still pressed against the hard planes of his chest. I had seen Jackson shirtless before, but never this close, and I had *never* touched him like this. That freckle on his collarbone taunted me to move my hand over and touch it. The feelings for Jackson that I had buried in my chest started to sprint to the surface. I wanted to touch more of him—but I couldn't.

"But it's my birthday," Jackson said in a flirty tone. "And I really like your hip bones." I took a step back from him, bringing my arm with me in the process. He put his hand back on my waist, and his thumb brushed against the protrusion of my hip. My swim bottoms were soaked, and not just from the pool. I wasn't strong enough to tell him no this time.

His gaze traveled over every inch of my body, like he was deciding which part of me he wanted to start with. His brown eyes finally settled on my mouth, and my lips parted against my will. If he leaned in to kiss me, I wouldn't stop him—I physically *couldn't*.

"Hey!" someone called out to us. I flinched, feeling like I'd been caught doing something I wasn't supposed to, ready to get reprimanded. My heart was thumping aggressively in my chest, and I was convinced everyone could see it. I put a finger to my neck to check my pulse; was I too young to have a heart attack?

"Do you guys want to play badminton?" There was a blonde-haired guy and a redheaded girl holding up rackets in the grass, standing on opposite sides of the net.

"Yeah!" I said quickly. I shoved the water bottle into Jackson's hands before turning around.

I didn't look back at Jackson to see if he was following me, but I heard his shoes hitting against the pavement behind me as I wobbled over to the grass on bare feet.

Jackson and the blonde guy, Chris, situated themselves on one side of the net, and I joined the girl, whose name was Sophie, on the other side. I'd had a few classes with her in the past, and we had gone to some of the same parties before.

Sophie and I both sucked at badminton, and we lost the first two games before she suggested one of us switch teams with the boys. I didn't want to be close to Jackson again—I was having a hard enough time just playing across from him. His chest was glistening with sweat, and I was addicted to the way his chest heaved when he lunged for the birdie. Every time he ran a hand through his dark hair, I almost groaned. A frickin' high five from him would be enough to turn me on at this point.

"You go play on Jackson's team, I'll take Chris," I told Sophie. They switched spots and we continued the game.

All of a sudden, Sophie was a pro at badminton, and she and Jackson beat us in the first game. They were high-fiving, and after every good play, she would find a reason to touch his bicep. Halfway through the second game they were hugging, and by the third win he was picking her up and spinning her around. It was hard to watch after his hands had just been on me.

Chris wanted to be done after the fourth game, so I followed him to play cornhole. I stayed there for as long as I could, playing with new sets of people until my arm ached.

By the end of the night I was exhausted, and almost everyone who was staying the night had secured a spot to sleep. All the Delvecchios were in their rooms, and Jackson had said his good-nights to everyone an hour ago with a drunken smile on his face.

I was laying on the couch with Sophie, our heads at opposite sides of the couch. We were both small enough that our legs weren't touching. Two guys were on the floor, and someone else was in the recliner, lightly snoring.

I was half awake when a light flicked on in the kitchen. I rolled the other way on the couch, finding that Sophie was gone. I sat up, rubbing my eyes as I looked to see who was in the kitchen. Only one small light was on, and I saw Sophie sitting on the counter with her back to me. Someone was on the other side of her, standing between her legs with their hands on her hips. I could tell they were kissing, and before I could lay back down on the couch, the person took a step back. My heart stopped when I saw it was Jackson. The second our eyes met, his expression changed.

He probably thought I was a freak, watching him make out with someone in his kitchen. His jaw clenched, and he almost looked apologetic. I watched as he helped Sophie off the counter, and I slid back down on the couch before I could see what happened next. The light in the kitchen turned off, and I listened as Sophie and Jackson walked upstairs, their feet padding across the carpet. I looked up at the balcony as their figures passed in the dark down the hall to his bedroom.

I felt sick. I'd hardly had anything to drink, but I felt like someone had dropped an entire house on my stomach.

I rolled over and saw Julie's friend Jeremy from the pool, asleep beside the couch. He was lying closest to me on the floor, facing me with his hands tucked under his head. I reached my hand out, rubbing his forearm until he opened his eyes. His eyes roamed my face until they adjusted in the dark.

"Hey," he whispered softly.

I slid down to the floor and pressed my lips to his. He kissed me back in a half-sleep daze. All we did was make out slowly, because I didn't want to do more than kiss. I didn't care that his hair was sandy blonde instead of being so dark it looked black, and I didn't wonder if he had a freckle on his collarbone. I felt nothing when he placed his hand on my jaw and rubbed it with his thumb. I didn't feel the need to press my hips into his. It wasn't a bad kiss, but it was nothing like kissing Jackson.

Chapter 22

NOW

July

Jackson didn't come over once during the weekend, which was probably a good thing. The restaurant was probably busy for the holiday weekend, and with Sophie being out of town, Jackson would've had to step in. I didn't go in once, even though I was craving pizza. I had to get my head back on straight.

I spent the weekend moving the family room around, pushing all the furniture into the middle so that I could start prepping the walls for paint. I washed the walls and filled in the holes, then I sanded every surface. Everything was ready to paint by the time Jackson came over on Monday.

When Jackson stepped into the family room, he took one look at my blanket and pillow on the couch and quirked his eyebrow. "Have you been sleeping on the couch?"

"Yeah," I said without looking up at him. I had to fight the urge to cringe. The couch usually faced away from the front door, so he hadn't seen the bedding until today. I'd meant to move it all before he got here, but I got so caught up in preparing the walls that it slipped my mind.

"Why? Did Peter get rid of your bed?" He leaned over and tore a loose strip of leather off the couch. Every morning when I woke up, I had to peel pieces of that faux leather off my arms and legs.

I shrugged one shoulder. "I haven't been in my old room yet." I finally met his eyes.

He looked at me like I was insane. "Maybe we should do that today instead? You shouldn't sleep in here tonight with the paint drying."

A lump appeared in my throat. I wasn't ready to look inside that room. The last time I had been in there, it was a whirlwind of grabbing what I could and running. For all I knew, Peter had destroyed what was left of it, and being in there with Jackson might force me to finally discuss the past—something I *still* wasn't ready for.

"Why don't we tackle it tomorrow? We'll just do the trim in here today," I said as I picked up the paintbrushes and handed him one. Jackson didn't argue, and instead of us picking songs off his phone, he put on a random playlist.

We were being nice, making small talk, and working on different sides of the room. Jackson told me about his nephews, Sammy and Nico, who were six and seven now. Sam had a wife named Emma who was also a lawyer, and every summer, Jackson and their boys stayed with Julie and Britt for two weeks in California.

Julie became a lawyer like she'd always planned, and her wife owned a coffee shop in downtown LA. Jackson told me that every time he flies out there with his nephews, it's like a big sleepover for two weeks straight. Sophie has never gone with him because of the restaurant. I was surprised he shared that with me, but it was clear that the restaurant was more important to Sophie than it was Jackson. It didn't escape my notice that she was gone for two weeks right now, though.

Was this the first time she'd been gone for this long? It wasn't my business though, and I didn't want to ask him.

I told Jackson story after story about Mia. I had watched her grow up since she was two, and my entire life had revolved around her for the past decade. "I can't wait to see her again; I miss that girl. She's about to be a teenager now, and Wren and I are in denial."

"Time flies, doesn't it?" Jackson said with a small smile.

Ten years had gone by in a flash. So much had happened in our lives that the other wasn't a part of. There was so much to catch up on between graduation and now. Even though I wanted to know more about what Jackson had been doing all this time, that could lead to a conversation about why he never tried to find me. I couldn't ask—I wasn't strong enough to know.

We fell back into a comfortable silence, refocusing on painting. I turned the music up, letting the sound fill the room. "Paper Rings" by Taylor Swift started playing, and I couldn't help myself from shaking my hips from side to side as I sang along to the song. It was too catchy not to, and I could hear Jackson start to sing, too. I felt like we were teenagers again, closing at the restaurant together.

When I turned around, Jackson was singing into his paintbrush like it was a microphone, so of course I had to follow suit. We danced around the family room, jumping on the couch and coffee table as we belted out the lyrics. Jackson looked ridiculous, and he almost fell off the couch when he tried to spin in a circle. I leapt from the coffee table to the couch, and I felt winded from how much I was exerting myself. I missed this side of us, acting like idiots together.

He started to sing into my face, and I leaned back, laughing as I pushed against his chest. He gave me a devious grin, then flipped his paintbrush to swipe it across the skin above my tank top. I gasped and tried to get him back but he ducked, and my paintbrush skimmed the side of his head.

We laughed as we attempted to paint the other, wrestling with each other's hands until we fell off the couch and onto the floor. I landed on top, my hips pinning him down as I tried to paint his face again. He abandoned his own brush to hold both of my wrists. I was crying from how hard I was laughing, trying to break free from his grip.

The song ended, and "That's So True" by Gracie Abrams started playing like a warning. Both our smiles slowly faded as the lyrics basically screamed at us. My thighs tightened around his hips anyways, and Jackson pressed his lips together to keep from making a sound. I was breathing so heavily I felt like my breasts were about to fall out of my tank top with each inhale. The paint on my chest was dripping down into my cleavage, but the only thing I could concentrate on was the feeling of Jackson beneath me. The way he was *enjoying* me on top of him.

The paintbrush fell from my hands, and paint splattered against Jackson's side. Neither of us reacted to the mess. *He has a fiancée. Get off.* His lips parted, and for a second I thought he was going to pull me down to kiss him. I wasn't sure if I would be strong enough to fight it. At least I didn't rock my hips against him—that had to count for something, right?

Suddenly, Jackson flipped us so I was on my back and he was holding himself up between my legs. He was still holding my wrists even though I had already dropped the paintbrush. Our hands hovered over my chest, and I wriggled my hips slightly. As if he'd sensed my thoughts, Jackson leaned forward, pinning my wrists to the floor above my head. Our chests connected, and I felt a rush of heat run through my center at the hardness of his chest against the softness of mine.

This time I was the one pressing my lips together to keep from reacting. Paint was transferring from my chest to his T-shirt with each breath I took, but we still didn't move away. His brown eyes bored into mine, filled with want. It was like he was daring *me* to make the first move. I averted my gaze to stare at his lips, because I'll admit it, I *wanted* to kiss him.

I saw a faint scar right above his mouth, and the memory of his split lip at sixteen years old rocked me back in time. Suddenly, I remembered the rules.

"No touching," I whispered.

He slammed his eyes shut and took in a huge breath of air.

"I'm so sorry. I should go," Jackson said as he let go of my wrists and scrambled to get up.

I sat up just as quick, fixing my hair and picking up the paintbrushes.

"No, no. I'm sorry. That was..." I couldn't even finish the sentence. *Highly inappropriate.*

Jackson looked at me with apologetic eyes. I knew that look; he'd looked at me like that plenty of times when we were teenagers. That look meant he was fighting something inside—that he wanted me, too. The past started rolling over me in unwanted waves. I hated this. I hated everything about this.

"I'm sorry," he whispered again before flying out the front door.

I dropped one of the paintbrushes, then returned to the wall to keep painting. I had to give up when I couldn't get my hand to stop shaking.

Chapter 23

BEFORE

December, Eleven Years Ago

After Jackson's birthday party, he started dating Sophie Waters. For the first couple months she was cordial with me, then when she realized how close Jackson and I were, it felt like everything she said to me became passive-aggressive. She started coming to the restaurant on days Jackson and I worked together, sitting at the bar and flirting with him during his shift. She would even sometimes stay while we closed, which irritated me because Jackson and I couldn't sing obnoxiously, or sit up against the wall with a bottle of wine like we used to. He would still drop me off at home after, but with Sophie sitting between us in the middle seat.

The Delvecchios invited me over for Christmas Eve again, but for the first time, I was nervous to attend because Sophie would be there, too.

I knew it bothered her, how often I was with the family, but I couldn't help it. They were *my* family. I couldn't give up Christmas just to make her more comfortable. I would probably hang out with

Julie the whole time anyways, because Sam was bringing a girl he had been seeing and Julie had broken up with Laney a few weeks ago.

I was letting Julie curl my blonde hair in long waves down my back, and she'd let me borrow one of her nice sweaters that fell off one shoulder. I'd paired it with black leggings and my high-top Converse with the embroidered pizza slice. They were getting worn out by now; the bottom flap was coming apart when I walked, but they were still my favorite pair of shoes. They meant so much to me.

"So, why did you break up with Laney?" I asked as Julie wrapped a section of my hair around the wand, tapping it a few times to feel the heat before releasing the curl.

"She had been flirting with this other girl for a while. It bugged me, so I ended it." She didn't even look upset, and my jaw dropped open slightly.

"Just like that? You thought she was being flirty with someone else so you dumped her?" I couldn't believe how fast she had decided she was done.

Julie looked at me like I was crazy. "Uh, yeah," she said like it was obvious. "Why would I want to be with someone who doesn't give me their full attention? I deserve someone who cares about my feelings."

"Wow," I said breathlessly. If only it was that easy for me. "Did it break your heart? Were you in love with her?"

Julie released a puff of air that sounded like a laugh. "I liked her a lot, but no, I wasn't in love. I don't think I could've broken up with her like that if I was."

I thought about this with an uneasy feeling in my stomach. What did it say about me that Jackson was with Sophie, and I still had all these feelings for him, even after the way he'd treated me? Could I be in love with him? Was that why it was so hard? Was that the reason I couldn't just walk away?

Julie finished curling my hair and tied half of it up for me, leaving the other half loose to frame my face. As she finished securing the elastic, she let out a frustrated huff at the sound of Jackson in his room, absolutely obliterating his drum set.

"Will you go tell Jackson to shut up?" Julie asked. "I thought he'd stop half an hour ago, but he just keeps getting louder and louder."

We switched places so she could sit at her vanity. I hadn't seen Jackson since I got here earlier this afternoon. He had been holed up in his room all day.

"Sure. Wish me luck," I said as I leaned over her shoulder to look at my hair from all angles in the vanity mirror.

"He's gotten really mopey lately, right?" Julie asked as her brown eyes met mine in the mirror. She looked concerned. Jackson had been different this school year—even worse than junior year. We mostly went to stoner parties these days, and when we went out, he drank way more than he probably should. When we went to a party, Sophie always drove since I still didn't have my license, so he was able to drink as much as he wanted.

"He just had a tough time this past year," I said, trying to convince her he was fine. We had just finished our first trimester of senior year, and Jackson got terrible grades again on his report card. It's like he wasn't even trying anymore since deciding he wasn't going to college. Half the time I'd walk into the lunch room only to get a text from him saying he had slipped out to smoke in the parking lot.

I walked down the hall to Jackson's room, listening to see if he'd stop playing. I could hear muffled lyrics from behind the door, but I knocked anyways. I waited twenty seconds before I realized he probably couldn't hear me, so I let myself in.

When I opened the door, Jackson was drenched in sweat. He was shirtless, every muscle in his body contracting as he played his drum set with what I could only describe as hostility. His arms were flying from piece to piece, aggressively smacking each drum so hard with his sticks that I worried they might crack in two. It was so loud I could feel the beat of the bass drum rattling my bones. He didn't notice me watching him, and he continued playing with his jaw clenched, completely in the zone.

It was mesmerizing, watching him. He was in his own world, throwing his body into the music. When the song ended, he flipped his sweaty bangs off his forehead. His chest was heaving up and down as he caught his breath. He finally noticed me then, and motioned for me to hand him the water bottle on his dresser.

I walked it over to him and he gulped half of it down. I couldn't take my eyes away from his throat, and the way his Adam's apple bobbed with his swallows. He wiped his mouth with the back of his hand.

"What's up?" he asked.

"What song were you playing?" I sat down on his bed as I watched the muscles of his abdomen flex and relax with his breathing.

"'The Lines' by Beartooth." He set a hand over his chest, like he was trying to slow down his heart rate. His index finger grazed against the freckle on his collarbone, and I made myself look away.

"Sounded heavy," I added.

He shrugged a shoulder. "Is it almost time for the party?"

"Yeah, we're just about ready to head downstairs."

Jackson rubbed a hand down his face, wiping off more sweat. "Your hair looks good like that," he said, lifting his chin in my direction.

I fiddled with the back of it, ignoring the butterflies in my stomach. "Thanks. Julie did it." I cleared my throat and stood up. "What time will Sophie be here?"

He averted his eyes. "I don't know, probably soon. I'm gonna go take a quick shower."

He stood up from his seat and I froze when he slipped off his basketball shorts right in front of me, showcasing the bulge in his boxers. He walked across the room, grabbing a towel from behind his door and leaving his room in a flash.

I stood stunned for a moment, my brain taking a second to register that I did still have the ability to move my legs. I ran down the steps with Bambi legs, walking into the kitchen to join Marie and Phil just as Sophie walked through the front door. I tried to slow my heart rate as I gave her a fake smile, burying the guilt in my chest.

***

The thing that I knew bothered Sophie the most was that Jackson wouldn't touch her around me. If I was in close proximity, he'd let go of her hand, or move his head when she tried to kiss him on the mouth. He thought I didn't notice, and he claimed he thought PDA was stupid, but I knew it was a lie. He just didn't want to make me feel uncomfortable. A part of me was grateful, because it was tough seeing him with Sophie, but it just made her hate me more. She was smart enough to know it was because of me.

Sophie looked beautiful today, and I told her as much. She was wearing a red sweater with a black-and-white plaid skirt over black tights. She took one look at my outfit and muttered a lousy, "Thanks."

When Jackson came downstairs, his hair still wet from his shower, he gave her a lame side-hug. Sam was over on the couch with his new girlfriend, and I was awkwardly sitting at the kitchen counter, silently begging Julie to finish getting ready so she could come downstairs and save me.

Phil made us grasshoppers—an alcoholic drink that contained ice cream, and who-knows-whatever-else. He allowed me, Sophie, and Jackson one glass, and I couldn't even tell there was alcohol in it thanks to the minty taste and vanilla ice cream.

We started the night by playing a game of Monopoly. Every time Jackson got up to "get a snack" or "use the bathroom", I knew he was secretly drinking more of whatever alcohol he could find. As the game progressed, he got more and more drunk. He thought he was being sly, but if I had figured it out, I was sure everyone else had, too.

At one point, Phil slapped Jackson on the back playfully and said, "Slow down on the drinking, son. I know it's Christmas, but it's not even dinner time yet, and you're tipsy." Jackson brushed him off with a playful shoulder bump, but I was nervous. I could tell Sophie was annoyed with him. Jackson got too risky when he drank. There was no telling what he would do or say.

After the game finished, I stuck to Julie's side like glue. It didn't help that when we ate dinner, I was seated between Julie and Jackson, with Sophie on Jackson's other side. I'd tried to avoid sitting beside Jackson, but he purposely chose the seat next to me so he could be between me and Sophie.

During the meal, Jackson reached over to put a lock of my hair behind my back, dragging his fingers against the exposed skin of my shoulder in the process. I tensed, trying not to react to how good his delicate fingertips felt against my smooth skin. I had to press my nails into my palm to distract myself.

I looked at him in my peripheral vision, mouthing the words, *No touching*.

"Your hair almost got in the gravy on your plate," Jackson said, loudly enough for everyone to hear before turning back to his food, like that was an excuse for doing what he did.

I glanced up and Sam's girlfriend was watching me with her eyebrows furrowed, like she was trying to figure me out. She looked at Jackson next, then Sophie, before returning her eyes to me. My whole body went hot, and I could feel my back starting to sweat. It was so embarrassing to feel like I'd been caught having feelings for Jackson; like I was doing something wrong. It was him that had the girlfriend—him who was touching me when he shouldn't be.

I took out the hair tie that was holding half my hair up, and put everything up in a high ponytail so I didn't have to risk him fixing my hair again. I knew Sophie had seen him touch me by the way I could physically feel her eyes burning my skin like laser beams. He had to stop drinking; he couldn't do things like this. I could barely finish eating because of all the nerves bubbling in my stomach.

As soon as dinner was over, I made up an excuse that my stomach hurt (which was honestly a half-truth) and went up to Julie's room to lay down on her bed. I dug through Julie's bookshelf before finding something that looked appealing and began reading. I dozed off for a bit, and an hour later Julie came to check on me.

"How are you feeling?" she asked as she lay down next to me on the bed.

"Better. I think it was from the grasshopper," I lied.

She started pulling out one of the threads on her sweater. "So, what do we think of Sophie?"

Was that a trick question? Julie flipped over to her stomach, positioning her fists under her chin to look at me head-on.

"She's cool. Really pretty, too," I said, attempting to sound as genuine as possible. The pretty part was true, at least. It just sucked to admit it.

Julie burst out laughing, covering her mouth with her fist.

"I haven't seen you in so long, but I can still tell when you're lying." Julie was smiling, and my cheeks flushed. At least she believed the lie about the grasshopper giving me a stomach ache.

"Jackson is kind of a dick to her," I said quietly. "It's awkward."

Julie nodded, her eyes wide. "I noticed that, too! I feel bad for her; why is he acting like that?"

I pretended not to have the slightest inclination as to why. The way Jackson acted around me wasn't right—not just because we weren't supposed to mess around, but because he had a girlfriend now.

"Like I said, he had a tough year. He hasn't really been himself," I said.

"I've also never seen him drink so much. Should we be worried?" Julie asked.

I didn't know what to say. Jackson was clearly dealing with a lot, mentally. "I think it's just a phase. He's eighteen now, and feeling lost or whatever."

"His music is so emo these days."

She said it like she was trying to be funny, but I couldn't make myself laugh. The music he listened to now was downright depressing.

"Can we just stay up here for the rest of the night? Change into our pj's and have a mini sleepover?" I asked.

Julie smiled and nodded. "I'm still used to California time, so I'm gonna be up all night. Let's watch a movie."

We switched our Christmas outfits for pajama pants and knit long-sleeve tops with fuzzy socks, then made a fort out of blankets on her bed. Julie turned on *Love, Actually* for us to watch on her laptop, and we cuddled up together with my head on her shoulder.

Even though Julie claimed she would be awake all night, she fell asleep before the credits played. I shut her laptop and gently untangled her limbs from mine before plugging it into the charger.

When I went to the bathroom to brush my teeth, I walked in on Jackson and Sophie making out in the bathroom against the sink.

"Fuck," I said as I stumbled back, hitting my head against the doorframe. My hands flew to the crown of my head, my eyes wide in horror.

Jackson flung back from between Sophie's legs like she had the plague, swaying as he did so. Thank god he was fully clothed. It wasn't lost on me that I saw more of his skin in his room earlier than I did now while he was hooking up with his girlfriend.

Jackson took a wobbly step toward me. "Are you okay?" he asked, looking at me with bloodshot eyes. His words were slurred, and Sophie crossed her arms against her chest like I was the biggest inconvenience in the world. It's not my fault they decided to do this in the bathroom and not his bedroom!

"I'm fine, sorry to interrupt," I choked out.

I realized Sophie's skirt was pushed up to her hips, her tights were down around her knees, and I could see her lacy white underwear. She didn't even try to hide it; she *wanted* me to see that he was touching her. My eyes flew up to her face, and she smirked at me. Jackson was *hers*. I was just the best friend that was obsessed with him.

I shut the door with a slam on accident, then rushed back to Julie's room. I slipped back under the covers, facing away from Julie and shoving her comforter against my face so she couldn't hear me cry.

Chapter 24

BEFORE

December, Eleven Years Ago

The next morning, I had Julie take me home as soon as I woke up. I couldn't even stay to let Marie French braid my hair with Julie. I didn't want to spend Christmas in my pajamas with the Delvecchios if it meant watching Sophie hang off Jackson's arm all day. It wouldn't feel like Christmas if I was miserable. I was glad to leave before either of them woke up.

Sophie was still asleep on the couch when we left, and something about her not sleeping in Jackson's bed with him made me happy, even though I wasn't supposed to care about things like that. They probably had sex last night, so them sleeping in the same bed should be the least of my worries. I thought about the time Jackson and I fell asleep on the couch together during sophomore year, our legs intertwined the entire night. He had slept with me on the couch then, but left his girlfriend to sleep alone on the couch on Christmas.

When Julie pulled into my driveway, I was surprised to see Peter's car there. He was supposed to leave last night to visit our mom. I walked inside hesitantly, finding him at the kitchen table already nursing a beer and what looked like a hangover from hell.

"Hey," I said as I bent down to untie my Converse. "I thought you would be at Mom's."

"She told me not to come at the last minute. She went on a trip with her boyfriend."

I wasn't shocked in the slightest; Mom did shit like this to Peter all the time. I'd stopped expecting anything from her. She had always been this way. I couldn't even remember the last time I'd talked to her on the phone. Peter looked sad though, and he took another swig of his beer. I felt bad for him—he kept giving Mom chance after chance, but she just kept letting him down.

"Sorry," I mumbled. I didn't know if that was what he needed to hear, or if it was even the right thing to say. I started walking down the hallway when I heard Peter's voice again.

"What are you doing today? I thought you were going to be at the Delvecchios' all day."

I stopped in the hallway, debating if I should turn around and walk back into the kitchen to talk to him. "No, I didn't feel good so I had them bring me home," I said.

"Oh, well I'm going to make dinner later if you want any."

I mouthed the words, *What the fuck*. When had Peter ever been nice like this to me? When had he ever acted like I was anything besides an annoyance in his life that he couldn't wait to get rid of?

"Maybe. I'll see how I'm feeling. Thanks, Peter."

I started heading for my room again, and I heard Peter call out, "Merry Christmas, Addie."

***

I read in my room all day, occasionally putting my ear to the door to listen to what Peter was doing. He kept going up and down the stairs, and I assumed he was spending the day in his room as well, only coming back upstairs to get a new drink.

At one point he left, and I watched his car drive away, then heard the door open and close an hour later.

I had a few texts pop up on my phone throughout the day. Marie and Phil wished me a Merry Christmas, and said they hoped I felt better soon. There were also a bunch of one-sentence texts in a row from Julie, giving me a play-by-play of her spying on Sam and his girlfriend while he tried to teach her how to play a video game.

She's acting like she doesn't know how to hold the controller so he can put his hands on hers

Ew she giggled and he tickled her, like right under the armpits, wtf

Sam kissed her neck, I saw tongue *gags*

It's like a cringey reality show, I just can't stop watching

Oh, Sophie is attempting to climb Jackson like a tree and he is NOT having it

She just told him the drum set is obnoxious ahhahahhha maybe I do like her?

I wished I had a smartphone like Jackson and Julie, because I didn't even know how to put my ancient phone on Do Not Disturb. I didn't even know if it had the option.

The whole point of not being there was to get Sophie and Jackson off my mind. I threw my phone into my bundle of sheets and walked toward the kitchen, the smell of spices hitting me before I even entered the room.

Peter was cooking chicken on the stove, there were potatoes boiling in a pot, and something was baking in the oven.

"Can you mash the potatoes for me? Milk is on the table," Peter asked.

He was talking to me so normally, so I acted completely normal in return as I drained the potatoes and poured in milk, mixing them around. He set the table with two plates and silverware, then pulled out the tray from the oven. It looked like glazed carrots.

I felt like I was in some alternate universe where Peter and I were a team; that we had a sibling relationship like Julie and Jackson did.

He turned off the burner, using tongs to place a piece of chicken on my plate. He joined me at the table and we filled our plates with the sides. We ate in silence, no words passing between us.

Peter was drinking what looked like a glass of coke, and as we ate, I assumed he was sober. We were almost done with our meal when he refilled his glass, pouring whiskey into the glass until it was almost full, and then topping it off with coke.

I stared at his glass as he sat back down at the table, and when he set it down it sloshed over the side, splattering against the table. I looked up at him, and he was staring at me. He didn't look nice anymore, and something dark flashed across his eyes. My defenses kicked up, getting ready to run if he started to yell at me.

He shook his head suddenly and scoffed. "You're starting to look so much like Mom."

It sounded like a bad thing. A very, *very* bad thing that caused goose bumps to raise across my skin.

I was wrong—Peter and I would never have a relationship like normal siblings. He still resented me, and I was dumb enough to let my guard down for this dinner. I didn't say anything in return as I cautiously got up to put my dishes in the dishwasher.

"Thanks for dinner, Peter," I said quietly before hurrying out the kitchen.

As soon as I closed the door to my bedroom, I heard Peter throwing things around the kitchen. It sounded like he threw his plate against the wall to shatter it, followed by the clang of silverware, pots, and pans being knocked to the floor. I covered my ears, trying to hide from the sound. All this, just because I looked like Mom and it set him off.

My phone started vibrating under my back, and I dug around under my sheets to find it. Jackson's name was on my screen, and I hit the side button to decline the call.

I sent him a text instead: *What's up?* I didn't want to risk answering and having him hear Peter's tantrum. He would freak out and drive over here in a second to pick a fight with my brother.

Sophie's gone and Julie and I are bored. Wanna hang with us?

My fingers flew across the keys. *Yes yes yes*

He responded that they'd be here in ten. I changed from my pj's into jeans and an old jacket of Julie's I still had from sophomore year. I smacked myself for leaving my shoes by the front door. I didn't want to risk passing Peter's freak-out in the kitchen.

I looked out my window when headlights flashed across my room. I heard something crash again in the kitchen and cursed. Julie and Jackson were idling in the truck in the driveway, and my heart started to race.

Be out in a sec, I texted Jackson. I could hear them singing along to the music in the car. I prayed for Peter to go downstairs, worried that he would hear the music and walk to the door. They had to have seen Peter's car in the driveway—they knew better than to be this loud. God, what if he approached them?

I looked out the window again just as Jackson was getting out the truck to walk up the front porch. A feeling in my gut alerted me that something really bad was going to happen if Jackson walked up to the door. He was a loose cannon these days, and if he saw Peter in this condition—or the mess he had caused in the kitchen—I knew he would throw down right there.

I felt a wave of panic crash over me, and I rushed to unlock my window and pull it up.

"Hey! Hey!" I whisper-yelled, waving frantically against the screen.

Jackson looked around until he spotted me, then he furrowed his eyebrows before walking toward my window.

"Uh, whatcha doing?" Jackson asked with a grin as he looked around. He had no idea what kind of situation was behind my door right now, and I wanted to slap the smile off his face and yell "Danger!"

"Peter's having an absolute meltdown right now, and the last thing I want to do is walk by him in the kitchen," I admitted.

Jackson's eyes narrowed, and he started to move for the front door.

"Jackson! Get your ass over here." My entire body was shaking now. I could barely hold myself together imagining an interaction between him and Peter. Sure, Jackson was bigger now, but it was not the fucking time to be a hero. He reluctantly turned around and walked back up to my window.

Julie was in the truck still, the music lowered now as she watched us. She was playing with one of her French braids, nervously twirling the end around her fingers.

"I'm just gonna come out the window. I don't have my shoes, though. Can you catch me?" The drop wasn't far—our house was only one story, but it was up on a slant, so I couldn't reach the ground from the ledge. Plus, I wasn't about to jump into the frozen bushes without shoes on.

"Addie this is insane. I'll go grab your shoes from the front door and come get you from your room."

"No, you are not coming in this house," I pleaded. I didn't give him time to counter. I pushed at the screen and it popped right out.

I swung one leg over the edge and Jackson jumped forward to catch me. He positioned us until I was piggyback riding him, and then he carried me to the truck. As soon as he set me down, he started walking for the house again instead of sliding into the seat next to me.

"Jackson!" I yelled out the window.

"What was up with the dramatic window escape?" Julie asked as she looked back and forth between me and Jackson.

"Peter. I didn't want to have to walk by him in the kitchen—he was breaking a ton of shit."

Julie's eyes widened, and we both turned toward Jackson just as he opened my front door, bent down, and then turned around with my Converse in his hands.

My jaw dropped, and Jackson slid into the truck, plopping my shoes on my lap like it was no big deal.

"Let's go," Jackson said in a low voice.

Julie backed up faster than I was ready for, and my shoulder smacked into Jackson's as I slid my feet into my shoes. I tucked in my laces, not even attempting to tie them.

"Did you see Peter?" I asked nervously.

Jackson's jaw was clenched, and he leaned forward to turn up the music.

"I didn't see anything, Addie. Just grabbed your shoes. I don't even think he noticed," Jackson said.

I let out a relieved sigh.

When we got to the restaurant, we parked in the alley and went through the back door, walking through the kitchen and turning on lights. The three of us sat at the bar in a row, me between the two of them. Julie picked out a white wine tonight, and we passed the bottle back and forth between us in a pattern.

"So, does Marie still have no idea we treat the wine like a free-for-all?" Julie asked as she slid the bottle past me to give Jackson his turn.

"Rami has been doing inventory on Sundays now to give Marie a break. I think she just assumes the bartender has a heavy hand," Jackson said.

Julie snickered behind her hand. "Sucker."

Julie was tipsy now, and got up to use the bathroom. She turned around before opening the bathroom door. "No dry-humping while I'm gone!" She let out an obnoxious laugh before opening the door and flipping the lock.

I covered my face with my hands. The three of us had never once acknowledged the time Julie walked in on Jackson and I in the kitchen our freshman year. We certainly didn't joke about it, either.

I sneaked a glance at Jackson, but he looked totally unfazed, like he was in his own head.

"Does Peter do stuff like that a lot?" Jackson asked. I reared my head back, taken off-guard by the subject change.

I put my hair behind my ears, remembering the sound of all the loud bangs in the kitchen earlier. "He hasn't done something like that in a while. I think he was fucked up over our mom telling him not to come for Christmas. I don't know why he still holds out hope she'll one day magically care about us," I told him.

Jackson took a long gulp of the wine before rubbing a hand down his mouth. "I'm really sorry that happened. I saw his car in the driveway; I'd just assumed maybe he'd rented a car this year to see her. That was stupid."

I waved a hand to let him know it was fine.

"I, um . . . I told you I didn't see anything, and I didn't. But I heard him. He sounded like he was crying, and he kept saying the name Denise," Jackson said.

"That's my mom," I said quietly. Damn, Peter truly was fucked up over our mom. "It was so weird, Jackson. He was so *normal* when I got home from your house this morning. He cooked us dinner, and then at the end of it he said I looked like our mom and it just flipped a switch in him."

Julie came out of the bathroom then, and I gave Jackson a look that said I didn't want to talk about this in front of her.

We spent the rest of the night listening to Julie's music—none of the sad, hardcore music that Jackson was into now. We jumped around the room, dancing on tables like the three of us used to before Julie left for California. We split some cannoli and chatted until Julie had sobered up enough to drive us home.

They were both reluctant to take me home, but I promised them that Peter would be asleep by now, and that I would even use the front door when I got home.

On the way, Jackson played the song "Sleep Well, Darling" by Secrets, singing along to the words as we drove. He was sitting in the middle this time, his hip pressed up against mine. It had been years since the three of us had squeezed into this truck like this. We were so much more grown now, and I couldn't even press myself to the door to prevent contact if I wanted to.

His phone vibrated on his lap, and I watched as he ignored a tenth text from Sophie.

At the house, Jackson followed me out of the truck against my wishes. I let him walk me to the front door, but I still wouldn't let him inside. All the lights were off when I opened the door, and I did a quick scan of the kitchen from where I stood. The mess was apparent, but no Peter in sight.

I turned around, giving him a thumbs up that it was safe. He nodded at me.

"Can't forget your present." He reached into his coat pocket and pressed a box into my hands. It was an iPod Nano. "I already loaded a bunch of songs onto it for you."

A firework burst in my chest; I was sure Jackson could feel it. I bit my lower lip to stop myself from smiling like an idiot. "You . . ." I was so focused on holding back the tears that were prickling the corners of my eyes that I didn't even know how to finish the sentence. He was still everything to me, and I wanted to tell him how much this meant.

He's still dating Sophie.

I shook my head at myself. I settled with, "Thank you so much, Jackson."

He quirked his lips to the side, giving me a nod before reaching out a hand to squeeze my arm. "Thanks for hanging with us, Addie. It wouldn't have felt like Christmas without you." My heart went into a sprint.

"Merry Christmas, Jackson," I said with a nod goodbye. I raised my arm to wave goodbye to Julie in the truck, then I turned around and went inside.

This time I didn't take off my shoes until I got to my room and locked the door.

Chapter 25

BEFORE

December, Eleven Years Ago

Julie flew back to California the day after Christmas, and I missed her even more than when she left for school that first summer. I understood why Jackson was so upset over her absence now. We needed her sunshine in our lives, and when she left, she took it with her. It started to feel like a black cloud was permanently hovering over us without her around.

On New Year's Eve, someone named Paul who graduated a couple years ago invited us to his party. He had been part of the stoner circle in high school, and I had a feeling the party would be filled with drugs.

I still had a weird animosity toward New Year's Eve ever since I watched Jackson kiss someone else for the first time our freshman year, and I'd probably have to watch him kiss Sophie tonight. So, I figured a party where I could get wasted was exactly what I needed.

Sophie was driving the three of us to the party, dressed in a skin-tight black dress that showed off her curves. Jackson was in a button-up black dress shirt and light jeans, while I was in a boring pair of leggings and a plain cream sweater.

On the way to the party, Jackson and I passed a bottle of wine back and forth that he had snagged earlier from the restaurant.

Every time he reached into the backseat to hand it to me, Sophie would make eye contact with me in the mirror, giving me a dirty look. I was so used to sharing a bottle with Jackson at the restaurant before they were dating that I didn't realize the reason she was so mad was because our lips were touching the same spot over and over again.

The next time Jackson handed the bottle to me, I declined.

The party was already in full swing when we got there, with multiple different blunt circles going around. I watched someone do a line of coke in the kitchen as I awkwardly reached around them for a beer.

Sophie kissed Jackson's cheek before saying she had to go to the bathroom, and I watched as Jackson rolled up a dollar bill and sniffed a line of cocaine. I had never seen him do anything more than drink or smoke weed, and I was taken off-guard by how easily he did it. He wiped his nose after, and when our eyes met, he put a finger to his lips as a signal to keep it a secret.

I gave him the middle finger before leaving the room.

***

Sophie was hanging off Jackson's arm all night as he drank beer after beer, and took shot after shot. I never saw him do another line, but I kept my distance, joining different blunt circles and smoking whatever I could get my hands on between beers.

I took a deep inhale of the blunt in my fingers, coughing roughly before handing it to the guy next to me, Charlie. He was a couple years older than us, and was a cousin of Paul's that had been at some of the same parties as us before.

"What's up with you and that guy, Jackson?" Charlie asked after he took a hit.

I started coughing even worse into my fist. Charlie raised his eyebrows at me.

"Sorry, what?" I responded, feigning ignorance.

He motioned his head behind me, to where I was sure Jackson and Sophie were. I sneaked a glance behind me, confirming they were on the other side of the room. Jackson was watching me, and I gave a small wave before I turned back around to Charlie.

"We're just friends. I've been working at his family's restaurant since freshman year."

Charlie gave me a look that screamed, *Bullshit*. I happily grabbed the blunt from the rotation, taking another deep hit.

"Does he know that?" Charlie said as he pinched what was left of the paper between his fingers. Was Charlie fucking with me? I felt like I had been caught doing something wrong, *again*.

"Of course he does, he's dating Sophie Waters," I said defensively.

Charlie made a *hmmm* sound, as if he didn't believe me, then gave me a wicked grin. "Then why does he keep looking at me like he wants to fucking murder me every time I start talking to you?"

My heart started to race, and it wasn't from the drugs.

"He's not," I argued.

"Watch this." Charlie leaned forward to whisper in my ear, and I felt his breath against my hair. "I'm pretending to tell you something of importance, now hurry and turn around."

I stood up so fast I almost toppled over. I couldn't handle whatever look Jackson might have on his face, and I couldn't handle this conversation with Charlie anymore. It was making me feel sick.

I left the house and walked outside into the falling snow, letting the cold air settle my nerves. There were a few people outside smoking cigarettes, huddling close together to stay warm. I stumbled to the front of the house, walking up and down the block until my toes were so numb I couldn't feel them anymore. I wasn't wearing a hat, and my hair was wet from the snow by the time I finally decided to go back inside.

I took another shot before sitting on the floor next to someone named Scott. We had Spanish class together, and we started talking about our teacher and how happy we were to not be taking it next trimester.

"Your nose is all red," he said before handing me a joint, and this time I didn't cough when I inhaled deeply.

I was forcing myself to be engaged in the conversation, because I could see Sophie and Jackson across the room on the couch in my peripheral vision. She was sitting on his lap, his hand cupping her ass. I hated that I kept checking to see if they were still there, because every time I glanced over his eyes were on *me,* not her.

Before midnight, I watched her grab his hand and lead him upstairs. I had to fight to swallow down the bile that was climbing up my throat.

I stood up with everyone else when there was a minute left until midnight, my arms crossed against my chest while everyone around me counted down. I couldn't stop thinking about what Jackson and Sophie were doing upstairs. I considered going up to see for myself, but when the bile threatened to rise up again, I thought better of it.

Someone handed us red plastic shot glasses, and Scott and I clinked the plastic together when the ball dropped. As soon as I swallowed, he leaned in to kiss me fast and hard, the smell of weed wafting around us as everyone sparked a celebratory blunt for the new year. These stoners did not mess around.

When he pulled back to look at me, I grabbed his hand and pulled him upstairs.

We found an open bedroom and fumbled into the dark. I imagined he was Jackson. My body was filled with liquor and weed, and my blood felt like it was coursing through me faster than it ever had before.

The darkness around us transported me back to the closet I made out with Jackson in during the game of seven minutes in heaven. All I could think about was Jackson's hand on my jaw and pulling my hips into his when I pulled Scott against me.

I needed to be touched; I needed someone to make me feel good.

"Will you touch me?" I asked as I fisted Scott's shirt and pulled him closer until his lips were pressed against mine again. I felt him nod against me. My hands found his hair, and I moved my fingers back and forth in the strands. It felt just like Jackson's, thick and textured. The perfect length. I could smell the whiskey on his breath as we kissed. He didn't try to slip his tongue in my mouth, and I was grateful because my body felt too loose. I wasn't sure I'd know how to French kiss properly right now.

I was pressed against the wall and his hands were everywhere, sliding under my shirt and grabbing at any piece of me he could. All I could picture was Jackson's face, his brown eyes looking at me like he could drown in me, yearning to be able to touch me. I let out a moan.

He started kissing down my stomach, pausing at my waist before sliding my leggings down.

"Are you sure this is okay?" he asked before sliding them to my ankles. His hands were hesitant, but I was impatient. I just needed Jackson to touch me—to give in to the want. I pushed my hips forward.

"Yes, Jackson, it feels good."

His hands stilled, and he stood up from where he was kneeling.

"Hey," he said softly, gently grabbing my face with his thumb and pointer finger to make me look him in the eyes. I couldn't even see his face clearly in the darkness. "My name is Scott." His voice was gentle, like he was talking to a skittish animal.

My brain was too fuzzy from the alcohol and the weed, and I started to giggle. I knew his name was Scott, but I wanted him to be Jackson so badly. I closed my eyes again, trying to push his head back down.

"I know it is. That's what I said." I was a gaslighter now, too, apparently.

He pushed my hand away from his head, holding it away from him. "How drunk are you? I don't know if we should be doing this." The one time I try to hook up with someone they have to be a decent guy? I could feel the blood moving through my body, pooling in every area that ached to be touched.

All I could think of was Sophie and Jackson in some room up here, too; how she was able to touch him in all the ways she wanted to, when it was me that should be touching him instead.

"I'm fine, I'm just a little high," I lied. I was a lot of high. "I don't want to have sex. I just want to fool around a little."

He leaned forward and peppered kisses along my neck. I bit my lip, preventing myself from calling him Jackson again.

"If you're sure," he reiterated.

I started to rub the outside of his jeans instead of answering, feeling him grow as he groaned against my skin. His fingers slipped into my underwear, rubbing back and forth.

"Keep doing that," I pleaded as I gripped onto his shoulder. I stuck my other hand in his boxers, moving my hand with the rock of his hips. I could faintly hear the music from downstairs; someone was playing "I Tried" by Balancing the Different, and a group of people were singing along. God, why were they listening to something so depressing? It sounded like something Jackson would listen to, and the thought of Jackson made me pick up my pace on the body in front of me.

I could tell he was close by the way he matched my rhythm, and I let him finish in my hand as I succumbed to the feeling of his fingers on me. I grabbed his wrist while I jerked my hips against his hand.

When we both stilled, Scott leaned away from me. "Shit, Addie," he whispered as he straightened.

I fixed my hair with my clean hand and pulled up my pants clumsily as he re-clasped his belt. He tried to give me another kiss but I turned my head so it was on my cheek. I couldn't pretend he was Jackson anymore once we stepped out of the dark.

We slid out of the room together, and I walked directly into Jackson's chest in the hall. We stepped back from each other, both staring at the other for a moment. Then his eyes moved down to my neck, his nostrils flaring.

Scott hovered behind me for a moment, then darted down the stairs. I'll give him credit, he didn't try to take advantage of me when he could have, and he was smart enough to realize that this was the man whose name I had called him by. I was the piece of shit in this equation.

"You have a hickey on your neck," Jackson said with narrowed eyes.

I placed my hand over the spot Scott had been sucking. A chill ran through me; all I'd seen was Jackson's face when he was doing it.

My mind was still a mess, and for some reason, I blurted out, "I need to go wash my hands." I held out the hand that had been touching Scott.

Jackson looked down, eyes widening when he saw the semen. He took a step back like I had slapped him, bumping into the wall behind him. He didn't look mad anymore—he looked absolutely destroyed.

I turned for the bathroom, acting unaffected by our interaction.

As soon as I closed the bathroom door, I dropped to my knees and couldn't hold back from puking everywhere.

***

I woke up to something cold under my cheek, and when I opened my eyes, I found myself on the floor of a bathroom. Jackson was sitting on the toilet, his dress shirt fully unbuttoned. I could see a sliver of the planes of his chest, and he was watching me with sad eyes. I groaned, closing my eyes to hide from the light . . . and the way he was looking at me.

"Where am I?" I asked as I put a hand to my head. It felt like someone was drilling into the side of my skull. My mouth was dry, and I could taste the remnants of the blunt I smoked earlier.

"You're fucked up, Addison," Jackson said with malice.

I covered my face. "Don't use my full name right now. Seriously, where are we?"

"We're at my house."

I peered above my fingers, eyes traveling around the space. We were in the upstairs bathroom of his parents' house, and I was laying on the cold, hard tile.

He handed me a water bottle, and I held it against my cheek. The condensation was soothing against my flushed skin.

"Where's Sophie?" I asked. How the fuck did we even get here? I couldn't remember leaving Paul's party. Where was Scott?

"At home, sleeping. Pissed I made her leave the party to take you home."

I rubbed my head again before sitting up. "What time is it?"

"Five am."

"Oh, shit. How long have I been asleep?" I asked.

"A few hours. You've been puking off and on. I found you in the bathroom at Paul's, and I seriously thought you were dead." Jackson's voice cracked then, and he quickly cleared his throat. "I had to carry you out."

"I'm sorry," I whispered. Jackson leaned down to help me stand up, and I felt like I was going to puke or pass out again. I gripped his arm, steadying myself.

I closed my eyes as I inhaled and exhaled, praying I could prevent myself from throwing up again.

When I opened my eyes, Jackson was staring at me, waiting to see what was about to happen. "You okay to walk?"

"Yeah," I squeaked out.

He slowly guided me to Julie's old bedroom, helping me get under the covers.

He faced away from me, one hand hovering by the bedside lamp.

"It really hurt to see you like that tonight," he said softly.

"I won't drink like that again. I'm sorry you had to take care of me."

"It's not that—that's what friends do. They protect each other." Jackson was such an asshole sometimes, but I knew he cared about me above all else. And he had always protected me.

I stared at his back, watching as he clenched and unclenched his fists.

He was silent for another moment, then clicked off the light. "What I meant was, it hurt to see you with someone else." He hovered there in the dark, and I wondered if he wanted me to say something.

My heart rate quickened, and I was sure I was about to puke again. I wanted to reach for him, to tell him the stuff I did with Scott didn't mean anything, that I called him Jackson, that I had to pretend Scott was Jackson to even enjoy it.

Before I could gain the courage, he walked out of the room, slamming the door shut behind him. It didn't matter anyways, because he had Sophie. And it wasn't fair for him to say things like that to me. He just continued to hurt me.

Chapter 26

NOW

July

I woke up to Jackson at the front door with breakfast in tow. We sat cross-legged on the floor of the family room, eating in silence together. We didn't acknowledge what happened while painting, and I was grateful, since I was still trying to erase it from my memory.

Instead, my focus was on the goal for the day. I still wasn't ready to open the door to my old bedroom, and I purposely took an exorbitantly long time to finish my food.

"You ready?" Jackson asked as we put the empty takeout boxes in a plastic bag.

I thought for a second. "It's just weird. What if we open the door and nothing is touched? Like, what does that mean?" I had already peeked in my mom's old bedroom last night, finding it as completely empty as the day she left us.

Jackson chewed on a fingernail as he thought about it. "Just like the locks not changing . . . Maybe he thought you'd come back."

Something about that possibility made me want to cry. I threw my head back and stared at the cracked ceiling. "But like, what would that *mean*? That he cared? I know Peter was an asshole, but he was still my brother. He had his demons; he was fucked up from our mom and his dad. I don't think he ever meant to take it out on me. I don't know, I have all these complicated feelings. Like, what does that say about me, that I might not actually hate him?" I covered my face with my hands, willing the tears not to fall.

Jackson reached forward and tapped my arm to make me look at him. "It means you're still the best person I know. Being able to forgive people is your best quality."

Did I forgive Jackson, too? I forgave him time and time again when we were younger. It was hard not to, when he was so sweet to me. I could fall in love with him again, now. I knew I could. But he was engaged, so what did that make me? A piece of shit with feelings I shouldn't be letting myself feel.

I let out an exasperated sigh. "Alright, let's do this."

Jackson followed me down the hall, and I shook out my hands nervously before turning the knob and opening the door.

Just like the rest of the house, my bedroom was exactly as I expected—a mess. But nothing had been touched.

My comforter was still in a messy heap from the last time I slept on it, and my dresser drawers were left open haphazardly from when I scrambled to pull belongings out ten years ago. My old work polo with "Delvecchios' Restaurant" printed on it was still on the floor.

"He really didn't touch anything," I said as I sat down on the bed. I took a moment to let my gaze drift around the room before finally noticing the one thing Peter *had* touched. My yearbook sat on my bedside table, covered by a thin layer of dust. I distinctly remembered leaving it by the door after graduation. Tears pricked at my eyes as I imagined Peter placing it here, making sure it was within easy reach for when I came home. I blinked the emotion away quickly, before Jackson could see it.

Jackson leaned against my dresser as he crossed his arms. "Well, should we start with the dresser?"

"Might as well."

He left to go get a trash bag. I never had many clothes to begin with, so after Jackson threw on a random playlist, we went through the first two drawers relatively quickly. "All Too Well" by Taylor Swift played at a low volume as we filled the bag.

Jackson broke out into laughter, and he turned around with a pair of navy-blue boxer briefs in his hands. "Hmmm, looks like you had a pair of my underwear, too."

I snatched them out of his hands, stuffing them in the trash bag. "Stop, you know that wasn't a sex thing." My cheeks were so hot they hurt.

Jackson reached for the bag and I moved it away. "You shouldn't get rid of those; you might start your period and need them again," he teased as he fought me for the bag.

A laugh escaped me, and I pressed a hand to his chest. "I would appreciate if you wiped that from your memory. Do you know how horrifying that was for sixteen-year-old me? It *still* haunts me."

Jackson lunged for the bag again, this time getting an arm inside and retrieving the boxers. He threw them in my face and I yelped.

I removed them from my face and shoved them under the comforter on the bed. "Okay, you've lost dresser privileges." I sat back on the bed as he picked up the Delvecchios' polo from the floor. He pressed it to his nose and grimaced.

"This smells like rotten marinara sauce," Jackson said with a gag.

"It hasn't been washed in ten years—that thing is an antique. Toss," I said as I batted a hand at it.

"We don't make them like this anymore. The font is different now," Jackson added as he traced the letters.

I stared at the shirt as he folded it and placed it delicately in the trash bag. I tied my hair up into a ponytail, thinking about how many times I'd worn that exact shirt. And then I remembered the *last* time I wore it. My last shift with Jackson. He had worn this shirt that night, too—his skin had touched it.

I put my fingers over one of my eyes as I shut them, internally shaking my head at myself. Why was I doing this to myself? "Who Knew" by P!nk began to play, and I almost groaned at how ironic it was.

Jackson went to open another drawer, but I stopped him. "I'm serious, you're done," I said from my spot on the bed.

He grinned at me before turning back around and grabbing my yearbook off the dresser, showing it to me before he leaned back. He flipped through the pages until he found my senior photo. "Honestly Addie, you look exactly the same."

I grabbed the book from him, flipping it around so I could see my photo. I hadn't even smiled with teeth for it. I remembered waiting in line to get my photo taken; Sophie and Jackson were behind me, and I'd watched her kiss him on the mouth before I sat for the picture. I couldn't even make myself smile—I'd just raised my lips at each corner, even though the photographer told me to smile wider.

"You think I still look eighteen? That's disturbing," I said deadpan.

"No, I meant you're still beautiful," he replied without missing a beat.

I couldn't meet his eyes, and I ignored the compliment, even though my stomach couldn't. It flipped about one hundred times.

I looked three rows down and found Jackson's name. I burst out laughing. "You do *not* look the same. You were deep in your emo phase." His dark hair was in a heap of waves over his forehead, his stone-cold stare into the camera making him look pissed off. I looked up at him now. "You know, I never knew what your forehead looked like until now."

Jackson chuckled. "Now *that* you should burn." He ran a hand through his short hair. "I was such a little asshole back then."

I swallowed deeply without meeting his eyes. For every time Jackson did something to hurt me, there was always something selfless he'd do to redeem himself.

"You had your good moments too," I whispered.

I heard him exhale, but he didn't say anything as I continued to flip through the pages. I read through the signatures left from friends, until I realized that I had never read what Jackson had written. The night we wrote in each other's yearbooks we were distracted, and I'd forgotten about it.

My eyes searched the page until I found Jackson's handwriting, block letters in all caps in the bottom left-hand corner. "You're my best friend, period. And I love you, period. -Jackson Delvecchio."

I dragged my thumb over the words. It was real, everything that happened between us. All of it was real. And now it was gone, with no hope of getting it back.

"What's wrong?" Jackson asked.

I don't know why, but I shoved the yearbook into his hands. I leaned back against my wall, staring out the window. I wanted him to realize how much it hurt me that he'd never found me—that he never even tried. I was gone for ten years, and he had been completely fine with it.

I could tell when he found his handwriting, because he turned off the music and the room filled with silence. I couldn't face him. I didn't want to see his reaction to the words he wrote so long ago.

"Addie, can you look at me?" His voice was strained, like he was actually hurt, too.

I bit my lip hard to distract myself from the pain in my chest. I wouldn't cry in front of him. I couldn't.

"Hmm," I said, continuing to look out the window.

"Addison . . ." That use of my full name pressed more salt into the wound.

I cut him off. "I'd prefer to finish my room by myself. Can you just go?"

"Are you upset? I meant what I wrote," Jackson started to say, like he needed me to believe it. But why? It didn't matter now. "I remember what you wrote in mine, too, Addie." Now *that* was what almost broke me.

"I don't care; it doesn't matter. It's history, all in the past. Now please, leave. Please, Jackson," I begged. I was so close to crying.

His footsteps sounded down the hallway, and I got off the bed to follow him to the door so I could lock it behind him.

"Can I just . . . ask you one thing?" Jackson said from the doorway. I didn't want to look at him, but he wouldn't talk until I did.

I finally looked up at him, my throat aching from holding back my tears. "What, Jackson?"

His gaze dropped to his feet before he met my eyes again. "Did you at least miss me when you left?"

How could he ask me that? Wasn't it obvious? He looked like a little kid standing there, waiting for a yes or no answer. No matter what I responded with, the answer would destroy us both.

I rubbed my finger under my nose, staring at him with glossy eyes. I wanted to be sassy and say, "What do you think?" But I didn't have the energy to play this game.

"Of course I did." I barely got the words out.

Jackson nodded, like he was processing this information. He reached in his back pocket and pressed something into my hand before turning to leave.

I waited until he pulled out of the driveway to look at what he put in my hands.

It was the photo from the restaurant—the picture from graduation that I had ripped in half on the Fourth of July and thrown away. There was a piece of tape holding it together. I choked on a sob, the tears free-falling now.

I went back to my room and put on the dirty polo from Delvecchios' and Jackson's old boxers. I laid down in my old bed and cried myself to sleep, holding the picture against my heart.

Chapter 27

BEFORE

February, Ten Years Ago

By the time my eighteenth birthday came around, Jackson and Sophie had been together for six months. Things had been chill between Jackson and I since New Year's, and we both acted like the conversation in Julie's room never happened. I mostly avoided him and Sophie when we got back to school after winter break, because I knew the girl hated me even more than she used to.

My mom hadn't so much as called me to wish me a happy birthday, and Peter . . . well, I honestly don't think he even remembered it was my birthday.

I woke up to see a voice mail from Julie, left at three am. She was drunkenly singing Happy Birthday to me, and I realized it must've been sent at midnight in California time. She mailed me a new pair of high-top Converse for my birthday; pristine and white, with red and blue stripes around the soles. I still liked my ratty black pair from my sixteenth birthday better.

After school I met Jackson at his truck in the parking lot, and he took me to the only place I requested we go for my birthday.

"You sure this is all you want for your birthday?" Jackson asked when we stepped into the shop.

"Yes, all I want is my nose pierced."

We looked through the cases, picking out a silver hoop and signing papers before I hopped up in the chair. My eyes watered as the needle went through my nose, but I loved how I looked after. I was officially an adult. It was so freeing to be able to make a decision like this for myself now.

"I can't believe you'll get a piercing, but you won't get a tattoo," Jackson said.

I shrugged. "Piercings are a fast process. Tattoos are slower. Plus, you can take out a piercing—you can't take off a tattoo."

Jackson pondered this for a moment, then said, "You know what? I want one now, too."

"Of course you do, copycat." I stuck my tongue out at him.

"Maybe I just want to match with you," he said with a bat of his eyelashes.

We ended up switching chairs, and the piercer started sterilizing another silver hoop for Jackson.

"What side should I get it done on?" Jackson asked as he looked back and forth at himself in a handheld mirror.

"You should get the left side, same as your girlfriend; that way they won't get snagged when you kiss," the piercer said. I almost choked on my spit.

"Oh, we're just—" I started to say before Jackson gave me a look that said, *Play along with it.* I hated him, but it also made my stomach flip that the piercer thought he was my boyfriend.

"That's a great idea. Left side it is," Jackson said with a giant smile. "Any other areas you suggest piercings?"

The piercer looked at me. "You know all jewelry is ten dollars off for your birthday. You could get your nipples done, too."

My hands flew over my chest as my face turned beet red. Jackson was hollering; he had tears in his eyes from how hard he was laughing.

"Babe, you should *definitely* get those done," Jackson said devilishly. I hated how the word "babe" coming from his mouth made my heart race.

"We're through," I said, deadpan, as I stood up from the bench. "I hope you cry when he pierces your nose."

I walked out the room to peer into the different glass cases while Jackson got his nose done. I didn't hear so much as a peep from him.

***

Even though I told Jackson all I wanted to do was get my nose pierced for my birthday, he took me to an indoor glow golf course.

"I haven't played mini-golf in forever. I think the last time we went was with Julie before she moved," I said.

Jackson handed me an orange ball while he grabbed a blue one. "Yeah, same. I wish she flew back for your birthday."

I sighed. "Yeah, me, too. But she called and left a voice mail."

Jackson started writing our names on the playing card as we stepped up to hole 1. "She's flying back for graduation, at least."

"It's coming up so fast." I balanced my putter between my legs while I tied my hair up into a ponytail. I crinkled my nose, and a little pinprick of pain radiated from where I'd just gotten it pierced.

"Don't remind me," Jackson said. Graduation was a sore subject right now, because neither of us had a plan for the fall.

Jackson took his turn first, the ball bouncing off the wall and ending up mere inches from the hole.

"Can you go easy on me? It is my birthday after all," I joked as I bent forward to swing at my ball.

"It's 'cause you always smack it too hard. Hit it lighter," Jackson said.

I took a deep breath and lightly tapped the ball. It hardly rolled a foot. Jackson burst out laughing. "Not *that* light. Here, let me show you."

Jackson stepped behind me to put his hands around mine on the club, but I whipped around and pushed him back. "Stop," I said firmly.

His eyebrows furrowed. "What?"

He never tried to touch me like this when he was sober, and as I gauged his reaction, I wondered if he even remembered the times he'd touched me when he was drunk. The *ways* he'd touched me.

I attempted to play it off. "I was trying to hustle you. I know what I'm doing."

He gave me a smile, and one of the overhead lights reflected off his nose ring, which was a reverse mirror image of mine. "You're a menace, Addie."

I waved him off before I hit the ball, firmly but with less pressure. It rolled down the course and bumped into his ball, pushing it farther away from the hole. I shivered at the metaphor that it represented between us; he got too close, and I pushed him away.

"Hey, you hit my ball!" Jackson whined.

"Which one? Your testicular torsion ball?" I teased.

Jackson gasped and shoved me in the shoulder, causing me to lose my balance as we walked to take our second turns. "Don't make jokes about the worst thing to ever happen to me."

"But it's my birthday," I said as I batted my eyelashes.

"Then stop *thinking* about my balls," Jackson said as he nudged me in the shoulder with his own.

"Trust me, that's the *last* thing on my mind," I shot back.

Jackson stared at me with an amused look before shaking his head. "You're lucky it's your birthday," he mumbled. We both broke into laughter.

***

After we played mini-golf, we swung by Delvecchios' for pizza, and everyone who was working sang Happy Birthday to me while I blew out the single candle that was placed in the cannoli in front of me. I took one bite before handing it to Jackson to finish off.

"Do you want to come over for a little? I picked up *The Hunger Games: Mockingjay - Part 1* from Redbox." Jackson wiggled his eyebrows. I smiled, thinking about our matching Peeta and Katniss costumes from his parents' anniversary party when we were sophomores.

"I heard Peeta is barely in the movie, but obviously yes," I said.

Jackson drove us back to his house, and we sat on opposite sides of the couch. Both of us got bored during the movie, and since his parents were at the restaurant, we each took a shot of whiskey from Phil's stash.

"Can I ask you something?" I couldn't stop thinking of the coke Jackson had done at the New Year's party, and I needed to know if it was something he did on the regular.

"Shoot."

He pulled himself up to sit on the counter. I took the bottle out of his hands and placed it back in the cabinet so he wouldn't take another shot before driving me home.

"What was up with the coke at the party? Is that like, a regular thing for you?" I asked with caution.

Jackson was chewing on the inside of his lip, like he felt regretful.

"I've done it a couple times, but no. It's not a regular thing. Sophie and I had a fight before we picked you up, and I just wanted to feel better," he admitted.

I nodded my head like I understood. "Well on that note, can you take me home? School tomorrow." I gave a thumbs down and protruded my lower lip.

On the way home we blasted the music, singing along to "Maybe Next May" by Secrets. When we pulled into the driveway, I was out of breath from our car concert. I looked over at Jackson, and he had a hand over his chest as he tried to even his own breathing after the exertion of singing.

This was one of the first times in a while we were in the truck alone without Sophie or Julie. I was having such a good time spending time with him by myself, and I wasn't ready to go inside, but I knew being alone with him in an enclosed space wasn't a good idea for my well-being.

"Thanks, Jackson. That was a good day. I needed that," I said.

Jackson smiled at me, then leaned forward to give me a hug. I hesitated before putting my arms around his neck. I tried to keep my breathing even, to not give away how much this was affecting me, being this close. The second he started rubbing his thumb against my back, I shot away without making eye contact.

"I'll see you at school tomorrow," I said as I grabbed my purse and hopped out the truck.

"Happy birthday, Addison," Jackson called out from the open window. I tried to ignore the way him saying my full name still made my blood feel as thick as maple syrup.

Chapter 28

BEFORE

April, Ten Years Ago

A little over a month after my birthday, Marie took me to take my driver's test. I had taken the written portion of the test the week of my eighteenth, and had been practicing driving around with Jackson since then.

My knee bounced up and down as I got ready for the parallel parking portion of the exam. Every time Jackson had taken me to practice driving in his truck, I had struggled the most with parking. I could never gauge how long the bed of the truck was. Now, in Marie's SUV, I had to readjust three times. I remembered Jackson telling me that each time you readjusted, you'd lose a point. How many points had I already lost on reverse parking before this?

When I decided I was centered between the cones as evenly as I could be, the instructor motioned for me to get out of the car. I took a deep breath, preparing to hear that I botched it and wouldn't even be able to take the driving portion of the exam.

"Alright, your mom can get in the backseat. I'll be in the passenger seat," the instructor said after walking around the car once. I had told him already that Marie wasn't my mom, but I didn't want to correct him a second time. I enjoyed hearing her referred to as my mom; she basically had been for the past four years, anyways.

I assumed if I was able to get back in the car, that meant I had passed the parking portion. Marie gave me a wink before opening the back door to get in. I suppressed an excited squeal before getting back in the driver's seat.

Once I pulled out of the parking lot, the instructor started asking me questions like, "What would be the safest thing to hit if you swerved off the road?" and "What does a blinking yellow light mean?" I answered the first question by saying that hitting a fence with the side of the car was safest, and he nodded like I was correct. The question about a blinking yellow light I got wrong, saying it should be treated like a yield sign. When he said that I was wrong, I was convinced he would fail me. He asked me to turn the radio on and off, and I fiddled with the knob with shaky fingers.

If I failed this test, I was fucked. We were graduating high school next month; I couldn't keep expecting Jackson to drive me around, and I hated when Sophie had to take us somewhere. I didn't know if I would be starting college in the fall or not, but if I was, I couldn't just ride my bike to campus like I was twelve years old.

When the test was over and we pulled back into the lot, Marie and I sat in silence while the instructor scribbled on his stupid clipboard with his scratchy pen. I almost asked Marie to step out of the car; I was ashamed by the thought of her hearing the instructor say the words, "You failed."

When he finally looked over at me and told me I passed, I almost cried from happiness. I could get my license now. Thank you, universe!

Marie even took a picture of me smiling with the certificate to send to Julie in California.

We immediately went to the Secretary of State so I could get a temporary license. Marie took me to lunch after, and then surprised me by taking me to a used auto dealer. I used a huge chunk of my savings to buy an old Buick. It wasn't pretty—it was actually a really shitty car. It had a lot of miles, and kind of looked like a boat. But I could drive it to work and school, and best of all, it was *mine*. I no longer had to feel trapped in the house with Peter. I could barely contain my excitement. When Jackson texted me that night to invite me to a party with him, I couldn't believe I had the ability to text back and say, *I'll drive.*

***

The party was another bonfire at Paul's house, the same house we celebrated New Year's at. When I picked up Jackson without Sophie, I didn't question him.

We went our separate ways as soon as we entered the party, Jackson heading straight for the kitchen, and me moving toward the already burning bonfire pit.

Two hours later, Jackson was still throwing back shot after shot with the guys while I sat around the fire, watching the group around me share a blunt. I knew better than to take a drag tonight.

Neither Charlie nor Scott were present, and I was glad I didn't have them here as a reminder of how I acted at the last party.

Jackson wobbled over, falling into the chair next to me. His beer splashed over his cup onto his hand, and he licked it off with a quick swipe of his tongue before turning to face me. I squeezed my thighs together, pretending I didn't find it sexy.

"We have to go to prom," Jackson said adamantly.

"Sorry, what?" It sounded like he was asking *me* to prom. Which I knew couldn't be possible.

He pursed his lips and nodded. "I know we don't go to dances, but Sophie has been begging me for weeks. But I don't want to go if you won't."

Of course this was about Sophie. Why was I getting dragged into it?

"No."

"Addie—"

"I'm not spending a fortune on a dress I'll only wear once. Pass," I said angrily.

He made a *pssh* sound. "You can wear an old one of Julie's. Please Addison, please, please, *please*." He clasped his hands together and gave a puppy-dog pout. I almost fell into the temptation of those deep-brown eyes.

I said no again, and he genuinely looked sad. I had to look away.

"Addison," he whispered in a plea again.

Ugh, he was using my full name, and I hated how much I *loved* the way he said it. I lost the battle.

"Fine, I'll go. But you have to buy my ticket *and* help me pick out a dress of Julie's," I said.

"God, you're the best!" He threw himself toward me, wrapping me in a tight hug around my neck.

"Jesus, I can't breathe, Jackson." I pushed him off me, acting like the feel of his body pressed against mine didn't stir something up in my stomach.

"This calls for another shot!" Jackson hopped up, almost losing his balance before running back inside to the drinks.

I spent the rest of the party glued to my seat at the fire. The smokers around me switched the weed for cigarettes, and I took three puffs before coughing my lungs out and throwing it into the fire. We started playing a game of never have I ever, and when it hit midnight, Jackson came and found me again, asking me to take him to Sophie's.

He dragged his feet across the pavement on the way to my car, off-balance and zig-zagging down the block. I had to help Jackson get in my car. He was swaying so much I was sure he was going to face-plant right there on the cement.

"I don't think I've ever seen you so drunk, Jackson. Are you okay?" I said as I buckled his seat belt for him. I thought I'd seen Jackson at his drunkest before, but nothing compared to tonight.

"I'm grand!" he said sarcastically before clicking a song on his phone and throwing it in the center consol. I walked around to the driver's seat, looking at Jackson warily.

"I Have a Problem" by Beartooth was blaring, and Jackson was angrily singing the lyrics. I could feel the bass in my skull, and the entire car was shaking from the pulse of it. I didn't like the song—how heavy it was, or the lyrics he was screaming. He was tapping his hands against his thighs, like he was playing his drum set.

"Are you and Sophie fighting?" I asked tentatively as I lowered the music.

"Yeah, 'cause what else is new?" Jackson lifted his feet onto the dashboard, running a frustrated hand through his hair, leaving it in disarray. We were just talking about prom two hours ago; he'd finally agreed to go with her, so what could they possibly be mad at each other about?

I let out an annoyed breath. "What this time?"

"Because you're at the party and she's not." He sang along to the song for a second, turning it up and then turning it back down so I could hear him talking. "You know what, fuck it. Don't take me to Sophie's. I don't want to go. I want to stay with you."

I stared out the windshield, gripping the steering wheel tighter. I didn't know what to do. A part of me liked that he wanted to stay with me, and he probably needed to go home instead of to Sophie's, but I didn't want to make Sophie any more pissed off than she already was.

"That's not a good idea. You already told her you were coming, so we're going," I told him.

Jackson groaned and stomped his foot against the dash like a little kid. "I just want to be with you, Addie."

My eyes snapped to his, and I wished I hadn't looked at him, because he looked so sincere. It didn't sound like he wanted to just be *here* with me right now; it sounded like he actually wanted to *be* with me.

"You shouldn't say things like that to me," I whispered.

He threw his arms out. "Why not, hmmm?"

I scoffed at him. "If I was your girlfriend and you said that behind my back, I'd be really hurt."

He's just drunk—he probably didn't even mean any of it. He's always acting like this when he's drinking.

"If *you* were my girlfriend, I wouldn't *have* to say things like that." He said it so adamantly, and my heart jammed against my rib cage. *If you were my girlfriend.* Does that mean he thought about it?

I had to remind myself to keep breathing.

When I looked at Jackson, he just looked sad, and I felt bad for Sophie. But in a way, another part of me lit up, because when had he ever admitted it like this?

"Stop, Jackson." I couldn't take it. It started to hurt. It hurt so badly that he was with her and not me. She could touch him and I couldn't.

"What!?" Jackson was yelling now, and I startled, flinching in my seat. "I can't touch you, I can't hangout with you, and now I can't even tell you how I fucking feel? So what exactly can I do with you, huh?"

I slammed my foot on the breaks, causing both of us to jolt against our seat belts as they locked. "Linger" by The Cranberries started playing, a giant contrast to the song that was playing before. I'd almost missed the turn onto Sophie's street because of how badly this conversation had fucked with my brain. My heart was beating even harder than before. *So what exactly can I do with you?* My entire body was on high alert, frazzled sparks fraying and sizzling at each of my nerve endings.

"You're hurting me," I whispered, so quietly I wasn't even sure he could hear me. "And you need to stop." I couldn't even look at him.

My fingers were shaking, and I took a deep breath before putting my foot back on the gas and turning onto Sophie's street.

"You think I'm not hurting, too?" he mumbled. I didn't even respond. I couldn't do this anymore.

I pulled into her driveway, the gears squeaking as I put the Buick in park. Jackson didn't move to leave, and when I turned to face him, his arms were crossed and he was staring me down. He looked mad—madder than I had ever seen him. It pissed me off, because he couldn't possibly be as mad as I was, or as hurt.

"Jackson, we're here. Get out," I said firmly.

His eyes didn't move from my face. "No."

I sucked in a large breath of air through my nose. I was losing my patience with him. "Jackson, please, get out of my car."

"No," he said again with his teeth clenched.

"Get the fuck out of my car, Jackson!" I wasn't sure I had ever yelled at him before, or if I had ever been so angry with him. He was hurting me; I couldn't look at his face for a second longer.

His jaw dropped open at my outburst. "Leave!" I screamed in his face again, before reaching across him and opening the passenger door by myself, unbuckling his seat belt for him.

We stared each other down until he finally gave up and got out of my car, slamming the door as hard as he could before putting his hood over his head and walking up to Sophie's front door.

When I looked up at Sophie's house, I saw her standing in the front window, watching me. I knew, somehow, that she had seen our entire interaction. Fuck.

I backed out the driveway as quickly as I could.

Chapter 29

NOW

July

The day after Jackson and I went through my bedroom, I was still reeling. I spent the entire day on the couch, watching movies on my laptop, crying on and off. I even called Wren to vent. I was an absolute mess. The more time I spent with Jackson, the more fucked up my heart felt. I didn't know how much longer I could keep doing this.

Jackson had called and texted throughout the day, but I ignored every message. I needed space.

I had bottles of wine DoorDashed to the house, and I pushed myself to finish my room while listening to the song "Remembering Sunday" by All Time Low and blowing my nose every two seconds.

After I was done, I laid down on the couch, drinking as much as my body could handle. I had barely eaten anything all day, and it was hitting me hard.

I was half asleep on the couch, nodding off when I thought I heard a rap of knocks on the front door. "Vodka Cranberry" by Conan Gray had been playing on my laptop on repeat for at least the past two hours. The clock on my screen read ten thirty pm. The music was so loud I was almost positive I imagined the knocking. I took another quick drink from the bottle on the coffee table before closing my eyes and ignoring it.

Tap tap tap. Definitely didn't imagine it.

I groaned and pushed myself up off the couch, literally dragging my feet to the front door. I pushed the curtain aside to see who was there, raising an eyebrow before pushing the door open. "Jackson?"

He had a hand in his pocket, and the other was holding a bag. He let out a relieved breath of air when he saw me. "You weren't answering your phone all day. I was worried."

"I'm fine. Just busy," I lied. My words were slurred, and I tried to clear my throat to hide it. Jackson furrowed his eyebrows and walked past me, letting himself in.

I followed him into the family room where he paused the music, which had still been playing at an alarming volume. He stared at the laptop for a moment before sitting down on the couch beside it. He turned around to look at me, still standing in the doorway of the family room. I watched his eyes take in the Delvecchios' polo, then they dropped to take in his old pair of boxers, both of which I still had on. I was too drunk to even care.

"I brought you some pizza from the restaurant." He set the bag on the table in front of us, and I slowly walked over to sit next to him.

I wanted to be mad at him; I wanted to keep some distance between us. He was marrying someone else, and I was tired of my old feelings resurfacing. But why did he have to care so much about my well-being? He was making it so hard.

I begrudgingly took the slice that he was holding out for me, forcing myself to eat it. Of course he had to bring pizza!

"What have you been doing all day?" His eyes flicked up and down over my attire again, lingering on the embroidered "Delvecchios' Restaurant" for a second before meeting my eyes.

I ignored him and finished eating my slice. His hands were clasped in his lap as he waited for me to answer. I tucked my knees up to my chin and curled up into the side of the couch, watching him watch me. He was positioned so we were facing each other. An ache was pulsing in my heart. He was looking at me like he cared—like not hearing from me all day hurt him. He didn't hear from me for ten years, and he never once looked for me. So why would he care about twenty-four hours of radio silence?

I reached forward and dragged my finger across the scar on his eyebrow. He caught my hand in his, holding it against his cheek. He closed his eyes, rubbing my wrist with his thumb.

Heat radiated from where he had a hold on me. "I called you, ya know," I whispered. He opened his eyes, looking back and forth between mine.

"No, you didn't. I've been calling you all day."

I shook my head, a tear escaping from my left eye against my will. "Not today."

I exhaled a shaky breath. He was still holding my hand against his face, rubbing those circles with this thumb. "Three years after I left. I called you. I did the whole *67 trick. You actually answered. I think you were at a party, and you sounded fine. You were fine without me, Jackson." He was *fine* without me. He never needed me like I needed him.

Jackson turned his head to kiss the inside of my wrist, and I shut my eyes as if I could hide from him. "I was never fine without you, Addie," he said.

I ripped my hand away from him, anger overcoming all my senses. It was a lie. He never looked for me. He never reached out. And I *had* to leave back then—I had to get away from Peter. It was Jackson that said he would come get me and didn't. And how could he say he wasn't fine without me when he had a fiancée for god's sake.

All Jackson does is hurt you.

I leaned into the couch, burying my face into the fabric so he couldn't see me cry. It wasn't fair how much power he still held over me.

"You never showed," I choked on a sob against the couch, letting my hair fall over my face to cover how pathetic I looked. "You never even tried to find me. You never found me." I kept whispering the last sentence over and over again, trying to convince myself to remember it. To feel it, and to try to forget about my past feelings for him.

I don't know how much time passed as we sat there, but eventually I started to doze off. I assumed Jackson had let himself out until I felt him lift me off the couch. He carried me down the hallway and set me down gently on my old bed. I kept my eyes closed; I didn't want to see the way he was looking at me right now. His eyes were probably filled with so much pity for the girl who couldn't get over her teenage crush.

He pushed my hair out of my eyes and placed it behind my back. Then I felt his thumb graze over my jaw and down my neck, before landing on my collarbone. I couldn't tell him "No touching," because I loved the way his hands were confidently running over my skin, like he knew my body better than anyone else ever had.

It was so soothing, the way he was rubbing my collarbone back and forth. I felt his lips against my temple, down on my cheek, then at the corner of my mouth. I was so tired that the only reaction I had was the tear that ran down my nose.

I let myself fall back into a deep sleep, and I don't know if it was real or not, but I thought I heard Jackson say, "I found you, Addie. I did."

Chapter 30

BEFORE

May, Ten Years Ago

Just like the time we pretended the conversation on New Year's never happened, Jackson and I didn't talk about the argument we had in the car when I dropped him off at Sophie's a few weeks ago. And to be honest, I don't think he even remembered it. Either way, I *couldn't* talk about it, because he was starting to break my heart.

On Monday we went back to school like nothing happened, and for the next two weeks, the only thing we talked about was the restaurant or prom. We hardly worked together anymore, taking opposite shifts throughout the week, and even if we worked a weekend shift, there weren't any moments we were truly alone since Sophie was *still* coming to the restaurant if we worked a shift together. She didn't trust the two of us alone since the fight she witnessed between us in the car. I was driving myself to school now, and taking myself home from the restaurant. Jackson and I were drifting apart, and it was probably for the best.

Jackson, true to his word, still bought my prom ticket and helped me pick out a dress of Julie's for the event. Before the dance, we took pictures at the Delvecchios' house with a group of Sophie's friends.

Jackson was looking handsome in a black tux with a black bow tie to match Sophie's princess-style ball gown. Her red hair was in long curls down her back, and she had on these clear heels that made her look like Cinderella. She was radiant.

I was wearing an old dress of Julie's; a form-fitting light-green gown that tied in a criss-cross up my back. Marie had pulled my white-blonde hair up into a French twist, and I was wearing my black high-top Converse with the embroidered pizza slice.

I stood off to the side during pictures, claiming that Mrs. Delvecchio needed help with the camera, and adjusting where everyone should stand. She forced me to take a picture with Jackson against my wishes, and I could barely manage to smile through the daggers Sophie was throwing at me with her glare. I couldn't shrug his arm off my waist fast enough after hearing the shutter click.

Jackson drove Sophie and I to the dance, Sophie squeezed in between us with the tulle of her dress overflowing onto my lap and Jackson's. It was one of the most uncomfortable situations ever, and not just because of the dress.

When we got to the venue the prom was being held at, things went exactly as I suspected they would go. Everything was awkward, and filled with tension. Sophie and Jackson argued throughout dinner, and their bickering continued into the evening. I tried to ignore it, but it was difficult when I knew they were arguing about me.

***

Toward the end of the night, Jackson and I were sitting at the table, rapping along to the song "The Night Is Still Young" by Nicki Minaj while simultaneously eating our second serving of cupcakes.

My feet were crossed at the ankles on the edge of the table, and I had a hand out like I was spinning a record. Jackson cupped his hands around his mouth, tilting his head up toward the sky while he screamed, "The night is still young, and so are we!" Everyone else was dancing like their lives depended on it.

I was having so much fun with him; it was just like how things used to be when we would sing at the restaurant with Julie. It had been months since we did that together.

Sophie was on the dance floor with her friends, and when the song changed to a slow one, she tapped her way over in her heels. I could *feel* the storm brewing.

"Jackson, come on, just dance with me one time," she begged.

I couldn't look up at her. I felt so bad for her; Jackson had been a dick to her all night, refusing to dance, and huffing and puffing whenever she asked him to take pictures. She had been on the dance floor most of the night, jumping around with her friends, trying to get just a little bit of his attention. It hadn't worked.

After an uncomfortable silence I finally glanced up at her. For once, she didn't look mad—she looked fucking heartbroken. I had looked at Jackson that same way plenty of times, and I couldn't handle seeing it on her face.

"Jackson, go dance with your girlfriend," I said as I ripped his cupcake out of his hand.

Sophie gave me a death glare, even though I was trying to help her out. Even though she was mad at Jackson, that in turn made her mad at me. It wasn't fair.

Jackson stared at me with an angry look and shoved my feet off the table before finally pushing out his chair and joining her on the dance floor, looking like we stole his lunch money. I watched them dance to a slow song, but instead of kissing or pulling each other close like the other couples around them, they were just arguing back and forth about something.

When the song ended, they both headed in different directions, Jackson coming back to the table with a red face while Sophie rushed toward the bathrooms. He loosened his bow tie. "Come on, let's go to the restaurant. I need a drink."

I didn't question him as I grabbed my purse and we left the venue. I was so done with their drama.

I hopped into the passenger seat of his truck, undoing my hair and letting it fall down over my shoulders in loose waves. The song "In Too Deep" by Sum 41 played on his phone on the way there.

By the time we got to Delvecchios', everyone who had closed the restaurant was already gone. We let ourselves in through the back door with my key, turning on the lights as we went. Jackson plugged his phone into the speaker, "Sex" by The 1975 playing around us while we searched for a bottle of wine behind the bar.

We walked across the dining room and sat down on the floor with our backs against the wall—something we hadn't done just the two of us in a long time.

Jackson turned toward me, eyes traveling from my face to my shoes and back up again. "I didn't get a chance to tell you that you look stunning tonight."

My stomach did a huge flip, and with such an explicit song playing in the background, the energy around us felt like it was crackling with tension.

"Thanks," I said as I put my hair behind my ears, trying to act like it was a completely normal compliment from a friend. I took a sip of the wine before giving it to Jackson.

"So, what happened with Sophie at the dance?" I asked, reminding him he had a girlfriend.

Jackson took four large gulps of the wine before passing the bottle back to me.

"It's just always something with her. I don't want to talk about it," Jackson said, grabbing the bottle back impatiently. "Let's just have fun."

I didn't press him, and when the song switched over to "Pursuit Of Happiness" by Kid Cudi, he started bopping his head to the beat with a smile. I couldn't help myself from singing along, too, and he ran to the kitchen to turn the volume all the way up. He came back to join me on the floor, his hip pressed against mine. We took turns drinking the wine until it was almost finished. I felt the alcohol all at once, and we couldn't stop laughing.

The song was blasting from the speakers so loudly that we could barely hear one another giggling and screaming the lyrics. We didn't notice that someone had come in through the back door until it was too late.

The music shut off abruptly, and Jackson cocked an eyebrow as we both stood up with wobbly legs to walk toward the kitchen. I was walking behind him when he stopped in his tracks, causing me to walk straight into his back.

"Watch it, Jackson." I laughed as I went to side-step around him, only to find his mother staring at the two of us from across the room. We were fucked.

My heart started racing as I watched Mrs. Delvecchio's eyes bounce back and forth between me and Jackson, before they settled on the almost finished bottle of wine in Jackson's hands. Shit, shit, shit. We had never been caught stealing the wine before, and he wasn't even trying to hide it. I took in a large breath of air, trying to act as sober as possible.

"Are you kidding me, Jackson?" Marie's nostrils flared, and I could see how red her face was, even with the dimmed lighting in the dining room. I was suddenly terrified of this woman—I had never seen her look like that before. She was hardly five feet tall, but I only felt about two feet tall with the way she was looking at us.

"I'm sorry Mrs. D—" She didn't even let me say her full last name before holding up her hand to stop me from talking.

She walked toward us, and I braced for impact as she grabbed the bottle out of Jackson's hands.

"When will the drinking stop!" Marie screamed so loud I flinched back, my hands involuntarily reaching for my ears to protect them from the sound. "Stealing our wine! Drinking every damn night! And you're supposed to drive Addie home? You could kill her! You could kill yourself, Jackson!"

I was terrified. I had never seen this sweet woman yell like this. The way she yelled instructions in the kitchen during a rush didn't hold a candle to how aggressively she was shouting now. But it didn't feel like anger spewing from her anymore—it felt like *fear*. I wasn't used to this type of screaming. The kind that came from being worried.

"Good!" Jackson yelled.

My mouth dropped open as I swung my head to look at Jackson. How could he say something like that? Good that he could kill himself by drunk driving? How could he act like he had no problem with doing something so reckless—with *dying*? His face was red with anger now, too, his jaw clenched as he stared down at his tiny mother.

I could never have predicted what happened next. Marie screeched so loud that I dropped to a crouch in terror as I watched her throw the wine bottle across the dining room. It shattered against the wall, and the remainder of the wine splattered like blood across the clean tables and floor.

She raised her left hand, and my first reflex was to run. I didn't want to watch her hit him—I *couldn't*. I didn't want to watch him yell at her, either. I couldn't hear him say he wanted to die again. I wasn't just scared—I was absolutely petrified.

I was out the door and down the street, my sneakers smacking across the pavement, when I felt a hand grab my shoulder. This time I was the one to scream at the top of my lungs as I blocked my face, preparing for impact.

"Jesus, Addie. It's just me," I heard Jackson say.

I was crouching on the ground again, my hands covering my ears. Jackson grabbed my wrists to slowly take my hands away from my head, and when I opened my eyes, he was in the same position in front of me. He had a red welt growing on his right cheek; his mom must have slapped him with her left hand—there was a perfect mark from the band of her wedding ring. I couldn't believe she actually hit him. His eyes were heavy with remorse as he looked at me.

"Hey . . . Hey, don't cry."

I didn't even realize I had started crying until Jackson reached forward to wipe his thumbs across my cheeks.

"I can't. I can't be around that," I choked out.

I flashed back to Peter in the kitchen at Christmas, smashing the dishes and destroying everything in a rage. The time he tried to drag me down the street outside of Delvecchios'. Him and my mom having screaming matches over my head as I grew up.

"I'm sorry, Addie. I'm so sorry." And then he was hugging me, rocking us back and forth and trying to calm me down. "Just let us take you home. Come on, Marie's waiting in her car."

I shook my head against him. I couldn't be in the car if he was going to fight with her more. "I don't want to hear you both yell again."

"We won't, I promise. I promise," he whispered against my hair.

I heard the crunch of tires in the road, and Jackson helped me stand up. I hurried to wipe the snot that was leaking from my nose as Marie pulled her car up.

Jackson opened the back door for me, and surprised me when he slid in beside me. He tucked me into his side, and for the first five minutes of the drive, none of us said a word. I could hear Marie sniffling, and every time I heard her try to suppress a sob, it made silent tears fall from my face. Jackson wiped each one away with his thumb, pressing a kiss to the side of my head each time. I thought I should tell him to stop—that his mom could see us—but I couldn't make myself speak.

"I'm sorry you had to hear that, Addison," Marie said as she pulled into the driveway. Everything felt wrong. I felt like I was slipping away from this family; like I was stuck in a bad dream, trying to run toward something but my legs wouldn't move.

"Please," I started to say before I choked on a cry, "don't hit Jackson again."

She choked out a sob and I opened the car door before anything else could be said, rushing toward my front door.

"Addie, wait." I turned around to find Jackson standing on the path with his hands in his pockets. His bow tie was still loosened around his neck, and the top three buttons of his dress shirt were undone, my mascara smeared across the white of it. The porch's automatic light flickered on, and I suppressed another cry when the welt on his cheek was illuminated by the light. Everything was falling apart.

"Jackson, don't ever say you want to die again," I managed to say before turning around and walking through the front door, locking the deadbolt behind me.

Chapter 31

NOW

July

I woke up the next morning with a hangover from hell. It took everything in me just to get out of bed to take a shower. I reeked from wearing that dank old Delvecchios' polo. What the hell possessed me to put that on? The entire bed smelled now.

I slowly showered, cleaning the smell of rotten marinara and the feeling of Jackson's kisses off my skin.

I dry heaved twice, but I couldn't tell if it was from the smell, or the thought of Jackson's mouth on me.

When I got out of the shower, I slipped on a blue ribbed tank top, which I tucked into the waistband of my denim shorts. I braided my blonde hair into two French braids and slapped on a layer of mascara. I put everything from last night into the washing machine, including Jackson's old boxers. Because let's face it, I couldn't throw them out.

In the afternoon, Jackson showed up with a peanut butter banana smoothie and french fries from McDonald's.

"For your hangover," he said bashfully when I opened the door.

"Thanks." I couldn't meet his eyes.

He followed me into the family room, where we sat on opposite sides of the couch. I sat cross-legged, balancing the fries and smoothie between my thighs.

We didn't say anything at first, and he let me eat my food in silence. I purposely ate slowly again, thinking of what I would say first when I decided to speak. Do I say sorry? I felt so awkward. I had acted like a drunk, love-sick puppy last night.

I started to say "I—" At the same time, Jackson started to say, "Are—"

We nervously laughed at each other.

"You go," I said quickly.

"Are you okay?" His brown eyes were filled with sympathy. I wanted to lean across the couch, wrap myself around him, and pretend nothing bad had ever transpired between us. But that wasn't our reality.

I played with one of my braids, pretending to be interested in my split ends. "Listen, I'm really embarrassed about yesterday."

"It was a lot all at once. Nothing to be embarrassed about," Jackson offered.

It *was* a lot. Seeing my room for the first time, and realizing that Peter had left it untouched except for the yearbook. He thought I would come back. The yearbook note where Jackson said he loved me. The old pair of his boxers, the Delvecchios' polo. The fucking photo he taped back together and gave to me. It was all so much. Too many feelings—I didn't even know it was possible to feel so much at once. I could combust from all the pressure I felt in my chest.

"I'm sorry," I said.

Jackson reached over and set his palm on my bare kneecap. He rubbed his thumb back and forth, and I had to close my eyes to convince myself not to slide my hips toward him, to make him touch me higher. I should say, "No touching," but it was no use. I didn't *want* to say it. All of my previous anger for him had dissipated.

"No, I'm sorry," Jackson said gently.

I opened my eyes to look at him, and god, I loved the way those brown eyes were staring back at me. Like I was the only thing in this entire universe that mattered. Maybe in another life it could've been us—we could've been happy, and those could have been the eyes I woke up to every morning. Because that's what it was supposed to be, wasn't it? That was the plan. That's what *he'd* promised.

I set my hand on his, letting myself feel the roughness of his knuckles against my palm before sliding his hand off my knee. "Thanks, Jackson."

He scratched his jaw. "Why don't we get you out of the house today? Get some fresh air."

"Yeah, okay," I agreed.

We got in Jackson's truck, and I didn't even ask where we were going. The windows were down, and the wind was whipping the loose strands of my braids around my face. I embraced it, the sharp hit of it against my skin a good distraction, because having my legs up on Jackson's dash like I was in high school again made me realize that I was falling back in love with him.

"Back To You" by Selena Gomez was playing as I closed my eyes and let myself doze off.

***

When I opened my eyes, we were at a beach. I could just make out a lighthouse off a long pier in the distance.

"Where are we?" I asked as I wiped the sleep from my eyes. Mascara transferred onto my fingers, and I wiped it on my shorts.

"Lake Michigan," Jackson answered.

"We've been on the road for over two hours?" I asked in surprise. I had been asleep for longer than I thought.

"You've never been to Holland before, have you?"

I shook my head no. There was a group of teenagers playing sand volleyball, a mom placing her baby's feet in the water, a dog chasing after a frisbee, and a couple reading books side by side in lawn chairs. It was the perfect day to be out at the beach—not a cloud in the sky.

"Let's go for a walk," Jackson said.

I followed him down to the water's edge, and we both removed our shoes to feel the water. It was colder than I expected, and I jumped back, right into Jackson's frame. He chuckled at me as he put a hand on each of my elbows.

"Walk slowly," he whispered in my ear. I leaned my head back against his neck, feeling the rise and fall of his chest beneath my back.

I didn't want to think about Sophie coming back in a couple days, or that I had work to do on the house, or that I still had to decide what I was doing with it, or what I would do once I got back to North Carolina. I was going to let myself enjoy this time with Jackson, like there was no one else around.

"I'm used to salt water. I've only been in the Atlantic for the past ten years," I said as I let the tide cover my toes before receding back.

"Unsalted is better; no sharks," Jackson said against my cheek. I closed my eyes, letting the heat of the sun wash over us.

I didn't know how long we'd been standing there like that, but I felt one of Jackson's hands leave my elbow. When I slowly opened one of my eyes against the sun, Jackson had his phone out in front of us, taking our picture.

"What are you taking a picture for?" I asked.

"So I can capture a time you were actually nice to me for once," he teased.

I went to push away from him with my hand on his chest, but he caught my wrist. We stared at each other for a moment, dragging our eyes over each other's faces. I looked at his dark hair; there wasn't a single strand of gray yet. My gaze moved down his forehead to the scar on his eyebrow; the long, curled black eyelashes that fluttered as he blinked; the silver hoop in his nose; the faintest scar above his upper lip; the sharpness of his jaw. Jackson was still the most beautiful man I had ever seen. I wanted him. I still loved him—I knew that now, looking at him this closely. Regardless of everything, I *had* fallen back in love with him. But honestly, had I ever really stopped loving him?

He gave my wrist a light tug, pulling my hips into his. Our faces were only inches apart, but instead of kissing me, he dropped my arm and wrapped me in a hug. His arms were around my neck, and my hands were splayed against his back. His face was in my hair, and my face was buried in his chest, right above his heartbeat. We were in the middle of a beach, the waves splashing over our feet with a thousand other people around us, but the only thing that my mind could produce was, *Jackson, Jackson, Jackson. You're my best friend, period. And I love you, period.*

I traced a finger up his spine, feeling the ridges of each vertebra. I was memorizing this moment, and this feeling. Because I didn't know if I would ever get to feel it again.

A dog ran by us, its fur brushing against our legs and forcing us to disconnect. Jackson looked away, running a hand down his mouth before picking up our shoes, which we had abandoned in the sand.

"Let's go play mini-golf," he said before turning around and leaving me no choice but to follow him through the sand.

We left the beach, driving through the town and listening to "Some Protector" by ROLE MODEL. I loved the way he was singing it like it was true—like it was a promise. We arrived at an amusement park that had mini-golf, bumper boats, go-karting, and an arcade. We bought all-day wristbands, even though it was only open for a few more hours.

We rotated between go-karting, bumper boats, playing a round of mini-golf, and then cooling off in the A/C of the arcade before repeating the process.

We were standing in line for the go-karts when the two kids in front of us got turned away for being too short to drive without an adult. We watched as they walked back to their mom—a woman who was in a wheelchair. One of the kids sat down on the ground and started to cry as his mom tried to soothe him. Jackson was slipping under the line barrier and walking toward them before I could ask him where he was going. I looked around quickly before walking back out of line, too.

"Hey, did you guys want to go-kart?" Jackson asked them.

The mom looked up at Jackson, one hand on the head of her son, who was still bawling on the ground.

"We're not big enough, and no one can ride with us," the other kid said, standing next to his mom.

Jackson looked at the mom before throwing a thumb in my direction. "We've been riding all day; we can take the kids for a round. I have two nephews, and Addie here is a nanny." He flashed a smile that said, *I swear we're not trying to be creeps.* Even I had to admit, he was absolutely charming.

"We have great references," I added.

Jackson looked over at me like, *This isn't a fucking job interview.* I shrugged my shoulders as I cringed at myself.

The kid whose face was buried in his hands looked up at his mom. "Please, Mom? Just once?" She was looking down at him with regret, like she really wanted to say no. We were two strangers, and she had no reason to trust us.

"You can watch us from the gate," Jackson said as he attempted to ease her apprehension. She looked up at Jackson again, and he shoved his hand toward her. "I'm Jackson, by the way."

She accepted his hand, and agreed to let the boys go on one race with us. Both boys, who quickly introduced themselves as Elio and Oli, bolted over to the line. We played I spy with them until it was our turn to get in the go-karts.

We raced around the track, the boys waving to their mom from the gate each time we did a lap. When the boys ran back to their mom after, she thanked us before they left to play in the arcade.

I put an arm around Jackson's waist on our way over to the bumper boats, leaning my head against his side like we were a couple. "That was really sweet of you, Jackson."

He rubbed a thumb across the skin above my waistband. "They reminded me so much of my nephews. That was fun."

Jackson had always been a protector; it was one of his best qualities. He had always taken care of the people he loved, including *me*. Why had I forced myself to forget that? I wanted to see him with his nephews now—to be a part of that life with him. It was hard to push away the image once I let myself picture it.

At the bumper boats we drenched each other in water. We were the two oldest people, surrounded by a group of teenagers who were good sports about Jackson spraying every last one of them.

We played a round of mini-golf to dry ourselves in the sun after, Jackson beating me by at least ten points because the asshole ended up getting two holes-in-one back-to-back.

I could feel my shoulders getting sunburnt, and I knew that freckles were likely appearing on my cheeks, but I didn't care. I was having the time of my life with Jackson.

In the arcade, we hogged a game where you had to throw baseballs at clowns and knock them down. We cheated by grabbing more baseballs from the identical game next to it just so we could get all the clowns down and win the jackpot.

We spent the entirety of our tickets on pouches of sour gummy worms, which ended up being way more than we could ever eat. Jackson and I ended up giving them to random people in the park.

On our way back to the beach to watch the sunset, we stopped to get tacos. We ate them in the tailgate of his truck while we watched the last of the beachgoers pack up.

"DAISIES" by Justin Bieber was playing from someone's speaker, and we swayed to the music while we ate our food.

We took one last walk at the water's edge, our shoulders bumping together as we walked through the sand. Jackson was digging for shells, but I couldn't. I didn't know if it was a smart idea to let myself have a memento from this day.

I watched the last of the sun's rays reflect off the water as I spun the wristband from the amusement park around my wrist, knowing I should throw it out sooner rather than later.

We raced back to the truck, kicking up sand and pushing each other to try to beat the other. He grabbed me at the waist and spun me in a circle to prevent me from winning, both of us laughing so hard we barely had the strength to run anymore.

He pulled down the back hatch for us to sit, and he hopped up before grabbing my hand and helping me step up. I sat with my knees pulled up to my chest, leaning against Jackson for warmth as his legs dangled off the edge, his arm wrapped around my shoulder. His fingers were trailing up and down my sunburnt arms, leaving small bursts of warmth beneath my skin. His other hand was holding mine in his lap, his thumb brushing along my knuckles. I let myself have this moment with him.

The orange sky turned to pink before magically turning to a light purple as the sun slipped away. The most beautiful ending to a tragically perfect day.

The lighthouse flickered on, and we watched it for another moment, not ready to leave yet, even though the parking lot was now empty.

I felt a kiss against the side of my head. "Let's go home," Jackson whispered in my ear.

Home.

Maybe this place could actually be my home again. *Jackson* could be my home again. If I knew I could have a day like this with him again, I would stay here in a heartbeat.

I felt euphoric on the drive home. We were singing along to "Bored to Death" by blink-182, nowhere near tired after the day we spent together. I didn't want it to end—I wanted this forever, like it was always supposed to be.

When we pulled onto my street, "Wait" by Knuckle Puck began, and it felt all wrong as we sang the words. It was telling me everything I already knew, but didn't want to believe. I ignored the lyrics, because Jackson *was* attainable, and he was choosing me again. That's what today proved, right? It was a taste of what we could have, and I didn't want to lose him a second time.

We pulled into my driveway, and Jackson put the truck in park. I stared up at the house, pushing away the memory of the last time he dropped me off in this exact same spot ten years ago. I wanted more;

I *needed* so much more. This couldn't be the end again. "Thanks for today, Jackson."

The song "a little more time" by ROLE MODEL began playing, and it felt right for this moment. That was all we needed—just a little more time together, to figure everything out. Jackson let out a long breath of relief.

"I haven't had a day this perfect in a long time," Jackson said as he turned to face me.

I looked at him, and there was that smile again; that genuine smile and those dark-brown eyes that were pleading for me to come to him. The bridge of his nose was sunburnt, his dark hair windswept from the beach, and he looked absolutely perfect sitting across from me in this truck. His eyes dropped down to my lips, and I decided I didn't want to live another second without tasting him again.

Jackson was still the only thing on my mind as I slid closer to him in the truck. Nothing else existed to me when I started to lean in.

Jackson began to fully turn his body toward me, but he bumped the car's horn in the process, startling both of us. We laughed, feeling like inexperienced teenagers about to hook up for the first time. He reached an arm forward and cupped my face in his palm, his thumb rubbing back and forth. I couldn't stop smiling at him as I reached forward to finally touch his collarbone. My hand never made it, because his phone started to ring on the seat between us. *Sophie-my darling fiancée* appeared on the screen. He dropped his hand, and I snapped mine back so quickly that my elbow hit the window. I was punched with a dose of reality.

Jackson still had a fiancée. He was still getting married. And he was *still* the eighteen-year-old boy that had cracked my heart in two. And to top it all off, he was about to become a cheater. This felt like high school all over again—Jackson fucking with my feelings while he had

Sophie. What was I thinking? We were almost thirty; how were we falling into these old patterns?

He looked up at me, an apologetic expression covering his features. He reached for me again and I flinched back, leaning against the door. "Addie, I—"

"No touching," I forced myself to say, even though my voice cracked from holding back hot, angry tears. I opened the truck's door and hopped down, running toward my front door. He was so fucking far out of reach, and I was a fool for thinking any different. I locked the deadbolt the moment I shut it.

Chapter 32

BEFORE

May, Ten Years Ago

Jackson and I worked opposite shifts and were done with classes, so I didn't hear from him for the rest of the week after the disastrous end of prom night. I was nervous to see him on Saturday for our last shift before graduation the next day.

When he came in to work, we didn't bring up what happened with his mom. Marie had pulled me aside earlier in the week and apologized to me about what happened, and I apologized for drinking the wine. We'd hugged and let it go. Thankfully it was a busy shift tonight, so Jackson and I focused on our tasks and not each other.

"Can You Feel My Heart" by Bring Me The Horizon was blasting through the speakers as we closed the restaurant that night. It was another depressing song, and I was worried he was trying to tell me something. Jackson and I still didn't talk, and I missed him, even though he was only two feet away.

At the end of our close, Jackson motioned his head toward the bottles of wine, and I took it as a sign that everything was fine between us.

We had our backs up against the wall again, sitting on the ground and passing the wine bottle back and forth. "Loose Ends" by Real Friends was playing around us. His parents were getting the house ready for his graduation barbecue tomorrow, so there was no risk of either of them catching us drinking tonight.

We still didn't acknowledge what happened after prom last weekend, and I couldn't be the one to bring it up. Marie had already apologized for it, and I was happy to not talk about it again. But I also couldn't forget the way he held me in his arms so soothingly and kept kissing the side of my head, or the way he wiped every single tear off my face as I cried, like I was the one who was hurt when it was him that had been hit.

I felt something brush my leg, and looked down to find Jackson slowly rubbing the back of his index finger against my thigh. I looked up to meet his eyes, but he was watching the movements of his finger.

"So, Sophie and I broke up this week."

I felt a jolt of shock run through my chest at his words, followed by a twinge of nervousness. His eyes finally met mine, and I searched for any sign of sadness behind them.

"Oh, why?"

He pulled his hand back, then grabbed the bottle from me and took a large gulp. "She's jealous that you and I are best friends. She'll never get over it." He shook his head and said under his breath, "What we had was never real, anyways."

I pulled in my lips. "You broke up because of me?" It was pretty obvious; I was the giant wrench in their relationship. But I didn't want to sound conceited by assuming.

He ran a hand through his hair before taking another drink. "Because of how I *feel* about you."

I blinked at him, waiting for him to meet my eyes again so he could further explain. Instead, he changed the topic. "I want to get away from this place. This town, and the family business, and just go anywhere that isn't here."

"Yeah, I want that, too," I admitted. I loved this restaurant, and I loved his family even though he'd grown to resent them. But I hated my brother more, and I'd do anything to get out of here.

"Yeah? Would you come with me?"

My eyes snapped to his, and I couldn't figure out if he was just fucking around, or if he really meant it.

"Are you serious?" I asked in disbelief.

His eyes looked back and forth between mine. "I'm dead serious. End of summer. I'll never be smart enough for college. I just want to get in my car and drive until I find another city with a better restaurant. Work for a few years until I can start my own business." He let out a long breath. "And . . . I want you to come with me."

All I wanted was to be with him, to get back what we'd lost. I didn't even need to think about the question before I answered.

"Okay."

"You really mean it?" He sounded like he was begging, like he couldn't handle it if I said this was all a big joke.

"Of course, Jackson." I had never been more serious in my life. "I'd follow you anywhere."

He stared at me for so long, like he was waiting for me to take it back. Then he said, "You're my best friend, Addie. And I love you."

There was so much heat in his gaze I felt like I could burst into flames and drown in agony. What did that mean exactly?

"You love me, like a best friend?" I asked hesitantly.

His eyes bounced around my face, like he was trying to memorize every second of this moment before he shook his head and whispered, "You're my best friend, period. And I love you, period."

I was on top of him and pressing my lips to his before I could overthink what he was saying. My mind was fuzzy from the wine, but I was almost one hundred percent positive that my best friend was saying he was in love with me.

His fingers tangled in my hair, and I could feel him growing beneath me with each rock of my hips. He pulled my head back to look at me. "I've wanted to kiss you like this since freshman year in that closet." And then his lips were on mine again, frenzied and impatient as I held onto his shoulders.

He flipped us so I was on my back on the dining room carpet, and he was above me. His voice came out strangled as two of his fingers started to slip beneath my waistband. "Can I please touch you, Addie?"

"Yes, yes, please," I said breathlessly. His hand slipped between my thighs, and when he felt me, he groaned against my lips as I tried to catch my breath from everything that was happening. I was finally kissing Jackson again—this was real.

"Don't stop touching me," I begged. I couldn't live a life without his hands on me again.

"I knew you'd feel this good," Jackson murmured against my lips.

I moaned as I rocked against his hand, pleading for more of him.

"Tell me you want me, too, Addie. You want me, too, right?"

"Yes, yes I want you, Jackson." I barely recognized my own voice as I worked to get his shirt off. He never took his hand away from me, and his shirt stayed pooled around his right wrist. Something about him refusing to stop touching me to even fully take off his shirt made a wave of pleasure roll through me. Jackson wanted me. Since our first kiss, Jackson had wanted me just as much as I'd wanted him.

"I love you, Addie. I love you so fucking much," Jackson said as he kissed down my neck and then back up my jaw to find my lips again.

"I love you, too, Jackson." Of course I did. I placed my right hand on his shoulder, rubbing his collarbone with my thumb and tracing the freckle that I'd dreamed about touching for the past four years.

He tried to get my shirt off with his left hand, never removing his right from its place inside me. I ripped my own shirt off, and his hand slipped under my bra immediately to touch me.

My fingers worked on the buttons of his work pants. I had just gotten them unclasped and unzipped when the back door in the kitchen opened.

"Shit," Jackson and I said in unison as we scrambled to get off the floor, kicking over the open wine bottle in the process. His shirt fell off his arm, and as we tried to throw each other our work polos, we mixed them up.

We fumbled to get dressed and I ended up putting on his oversized shirt while he squeezed into mine. We turned around at the same time as Julie walked into the dining room.

"It's always fuckin' Jules," Jackson mumbled as we stood frozen, facing her.

Her eyes bounced back and forth between the two of us until she registered the situation. She let out a groan. "Seriously guys? The one time I try to surprise you? Do you ever listen to me?" Julie mimed a gag. "Button your fucking pants, Jackson."

My eyes flew to his crotch, finding the zipper and button still undone, my shirt halfway tucked into his waistband.

"And fix your hair, Addie," Julie added.

My entire body was on fire—not just from the embarrassment of Julie walking in on us the only two times we had ever hooked up at the restaurant, but because my body was still reeling from each point of contact that Jackson's hands and lips had made a minute ago.

I reached for my hair, finding a tangle of knots at the base of my head where my hair had bunched up on the carpet, and at least half my hair had fallen out of my ponytail. I rushed with flimsy fingers to fix it.

"You guys just couldn't help yourselves, could you?" Julie snapped, all the fun and jokes of her previous tone gone.

"It doesn't fucking matter anymore, Miss Cali," Jackson shot back. My eyes cut to him. Did it not matter because he and Sophie were broken up? Or because soon we would leave this town and never look back?

"What is *that* supposed to mean?" Julie crossed her arms as her eyes flicked between the two of us.

"None of your business." Jackson's eyes looked like a fire had been lit within them—and not the kind that burned for me. The kind that wanted to burn this entire place to the ground.

I watched them argue; Julie saying he was ruining everything, calling Jackson an idiot repeatedly, and him shouting back, calling her a bitch and a princess.

I hadn't even realized I was covering my ears until Jackson pried my hands away from my head and told me it was time to go.

We said our goodbyes to Julie, and she gave me a wary look when I told her I'd see her at graduation tomorrow. We switched our shirts back in the parking lot before we got in our separate cars and drove off in opposite directions.

Chapter 33

BEFORE

May, Ten Years Ago

The day after Jackson and I got caught kissing by Julie, I woke up with a smile on my face. Jackson Delvecchio loved me. I didn't have to pretend I didn't have feelings for him anymore. I could touch him whenever I wanted, and he would touch me back. We didn't have to play games anymore.

I drove to graduation with a smile still stuck on my face. I had splurged on a knee-length white dress with a scoop neck and spaghetti straps, and, per usual, paired it with my high-top black Converse with the embroidered sides. I wore my hair natural and pin-straight, and put on blush and mascara.

I took my seat in the auditorium while we got ready to go outside to the football field for the commencement. I looked around, but couldn't find Jackson among the sea of bodies.

Everyone was talking, the excitement of being done with high school swirling around the room. I felt it in my chest, too; I was done with this school. Jackson and I were together, and in just two short months, it would be just the two of us. Wherever we wanted to be, touching whenever we wanted.

I still didn't spot him when we walked out to the field, but when I searched the crowd for his family, I found them right in the first row, waving at me, so I knew he had to be here somewhere.

The ceremony was humid, and at one point I unzipped my gown and slid off my shoes to cool myself down. The speeches were a blur, because I wasn't paying attention to anything that was being said. All I could think of was Jackson's voice in my head. *Tell me you want me, too, Addie. You want me, too, right?* A shiver ran through me; he was the only thing I wanted.

I slid back into my shoes and carried my gown to the stage while I waited for my name to be called. I zipped up my gown at the last second, walking across the stage as "Addison Bianchi" was announced into the microphone. I could hear Julie's screams and Phil's loud whistle coming from the bleachers. Someone yelled my name, and I knew it was Jackson, somewhere in the rows of chairs on the football field.

I watched Jackson accept his diploma on the stage sometime after me, and I clapped along with his family's screams, even though he couldn't see where I was sitting on the field. I tried to see what row he was in when he walked down the stage, but I lost him again in the mix of students.

When they finished announcing names, we switched our tassels from one side of our cap to the other. I was bouncing with energy; I couldn't wait to get this thing off. I was *done,* and I wanted to go find Jackson.

As soon as we threw our caps in the air, it started to drizzle. Not a full-on rain, but a drop here and there. One on my cheek, one against my arm. I looked around the crowd for Jackson as people passed in a flurry around me, looking for their hats and friends, attempting to take pictures.

When we finally found each other and Jackson's eyes met mine, I felt like we were in a movie. The perfect moment when the lovers finally lock eyes and run toward each other for their happy ending.

I started to head for him, and he broke out into a run, crashing into me and wrapping his arms around me. He spun me in a circle, and it felt so good to have him hold me like this. To not care about anything else except this moment with him.

He walked off the field with me on his back, finding his family and taking a few photos until the rain started to get heavier. His parents said they'd meet us at the house and we took off in a run toward his car, using our diplomas to cover our heads. I never went to look for my cap. I didn't care about it in the slightest.

Jackson's hand was in mine as we ran together, and I wasn't even thinking about the fact that we had driven separately to the ceremony. I couldn't let go of this boy's hand—not when I had waited years to hold it.

We jumped into the truck, and Jackson immediately pulled me in for a kiss, his skin wet from the rain. My hair dripped onto the seats, and his was plastered to his forehead.

"I love that I can touch you now," he said against my lips.

I pushed the fabric of his damp shirt to the side so his collarbone freckle was exposed, then I leaned forward to kiss it. "I've been obsessed with this freckle for years," I admitted.

He grabbed both sides of my face before kissing me hard again.

"You're beautiful," he said against my lips. "I've been obsessed with *you* for years."

We kissed for a few more minutes as the rain pattered against the top of his truck. It was perfect—this truck, and this moment, and this boy.

When Jackson pulled away from me, he put a lock of my hair behind my ear.

"We should probably act normal in front of my parents until the end of summer," Jackson said sadly.

I nodded my head in agreement. I didn't want to cause a problem at the restaurant, not after all the family had done for me over the years.

"No touching," I said with a goofy grin, putting Jackson's hands back on the steering wheel. He laughed before putting the car into drive.

On the way back to the house, "When It Rains" by Paramore was playing, but I decided not to take it as a bad omen.

Chapter 34

NOW

July

Jackson showed up the next morning after our perfect day in Holland with two coffees in hand. I narrowed my eyes at the sight of him on my doorstep before I opened the door.

"Bold," I said as I crossed my arms.

After we nearly kissed last night, I couldn't believe he'd even dare to show his face here again.

"Actually, it's a medium roast," he said as he held a coffee out for me.

How could he be making jokes right now? I wanted to punch the coffee cup right out of his hand, but that stupid small part of my heart still just wanted to kiss him. How could I have such strong feelings that were so polar opposite? The devil wasn't just sitting on my shoulder, he was buried deep in my chest, scratching and clawing, telling me to say and do whatever I wanted.

I ripped the coffee from his hands and tried to shut the door on him, but he stuck a hand out to stop it.

"Can we talk?" Jackson asked.

"No. There's nothing to talk about," I said as I tried to shut the door again. He pushed back harder. For a split second I almost lost my mind and threw the coffee at him.

"Addison—" Jackson started to say, and I gave up the fight at the way he said it, stepping back and causing him to almost faceplant inside. He caught his bearings and I turned around to walk into the family room.

I started getting the paint supplies ready. That was the only task I had to get through today; finish painting this room, and then I didn't have to deal with Jackson or our baggage anymore.

"Will you look at me?" Jackson asked.

"Jackson, please for the love of god, just stop talking to me. Can we just paint? That's all I need you for right now, okay? Can you just do that?" My voice was laced in venom, and I hoped he felt every word like a sting.

He looked at me for a while, clenching and unclenching one of his fists. I almost dared him to say what he wanted, but I gave him a look that I hoped conveyed how much I couldn't stand the sound of his voice. After a moment he looked up at the ceiling, then gave in to my request.

"Fine," he whispered before setting down his coffee and pulling his phone out of his pocket.

I knew he was starting a playlist, and after he chose his songs, he tossed the phone to me. No risk of our hands touching.

I caught it and swiped up on the screen. He didn't even have a passcode. He was one stupid motherfucker. I picked a song, and a notification dropped down that said he had multiple missed calls from Sophie.

"You have like, five missed calls from Sophie," I said as I chose more songs, pressing harder than I had to against the screen. "You should probably call her back."

I threw the phone back to him, smacking him directly in the chest, but he caught it before it fell to the floor.

"I just talked to her last night."

After he almost cheated on her with me. I wanted to hate him so badly.

I took a quick sip of the coffee, and screw Jackson, because it was delicious.

"So, how is she doing?" I forced myself to ask. I picked up a paintbrush, chipping off a piece of dried paint with my fingernail.

"I have a question," Jackson said, ignoring my own question.

I rolled my eyes so he could see my annoyance.

"What's that?" I asked as I dipped the brush into the paint.

"What's your plan after this is done?"

I turned away from him. I was quiet for a little while as I started to paint the wall. I didn't have a plan. My mind was a mess of complicated thoughts. Wren was almost positive she didn't need me to nanny Mia anymore, so I would have to find a new job. I could keep this house, live in it—and then, what? What would I do here? I had no one. Or I could sell it, and use the money to do whatever I wanted. I could start over again if I wanted to, somewhere new just like before. Somewhere Jackson *wasn't*.

I didn't want to admit all that, so I said, "Sell it. Go back to North Carolina."

"That's what I thought," Jackson said softly. How dare he act like he cared at all?

I finally turned to face him. "And you can go back to your fiancée. Happily ever after." I tried to look mad, but we both knew it was a mask.

Jackson blew out a long breath of air then dipped his paintbrush into the can. "I, uh . . . didn't tell you that Sophie and I were on a break while she was away. I bet you thought I was some asshole, trying to cheat on my fiancée."

What . . . ?

They were on a break? Why was he just *now* telling me? I could have kissed him in the car, and I wouldn't have had to feel bad about it. Heck, I could've kissed him on the Fourth of July. When he was on top of me after we fell while painting. In the bathroom without his shirt on. At the beach yesterday. Every moment he touched me since I came back was blinking beneath my skin, alerting me to how much I craved his touch.

"Oh." Was all I said in return.

Did that mean he wanted more with me? My mind was reeling, my brain trying to look at every interaction between us these past two weeks in a new light. I wanted to kiss him *now*, too—until I realized that he said they *were* on a break.

He started to go on. "Yeah, she called me last night to see if I had figured my shit out with you before she came back. I told her nothing is going on with you and I, so . . . we're back together."

I thought he was with her the entire time. That he was repeating the past and trying to cross the line—that he didn't know what he wanted. Did that mean he wanted *me*, but because I rejected him, he was going back to Sophie?

"So, that's it? You're just . . . getting married still?"

"Yes," he answered adamantly.

I huffed like a fucking child. "Why didn't you tell me you were on a break?"

I watched his jaw tick. "Because it didn't matter. You were always going to leave again."

I wanted to yell at him, because no, he *didn't* know that. But he was right, it didn't even matter anymore. I decided I *would* be leaving now. I would sell the house and forget about all of this. All I needed to focus on was painting this wall. Sophie would be home tomorrow, and I wouldn't let Jackson come back to this house. His phone hooked up to the speaker then, at an ear-splitting decibel, which he'd likely done on purpose so that we couldn't talk.

"Let Me Down Slowly" by Alec Benjamin was Jackson's first song choice. I bit my lip to keep from screaming. He was the one who decided he didn't want me, not the other way around. After that was "car" by Royel Otis. Did he really think this was the best thing for us?

When "If It Means A Lot To You" by A Day To Remember started playing, I almost lost it. We both knew we couldn't even go back to being friends—there's no way Sophie would allow it. Why was he doing this to me? It was killing me—absolutely shattering me—that he was fighting the feelings he had for me. I was feeling a hurricane of emotions in my chest, knowing this would likely be the last time Jackson and I ever saw each other.

My first song pick, "I Love You, I'm Sorry" by Gracie Abrams, was starting to play, and I put a hand over my chest to calm my heart rate. Every beat felt so intense it hurt. I pretended to focus hard on the paintbrush strokes, but they came out jagged across the wall. "Alley Rose" by Conan Gray was queued up next, and I sang it with malice to hide the devastation in my chest.

I kept sneaking glances at Jackson, finding him with a stone-faced expression, painting as if he couldn't hear the music. "Fortnight" by

Taylor Swift played next, and this time he sang along, too, with his fist clenched and his other hand white-knuckling the paintbrush. It gave me way too much satisfaction, seeing him struggle with this, too.

"Last Kiss" by Taylor Swift began, and I tried not to look at Jackson while it played. I was mouthing the words, trying my hardest not to cry. I could feel him looking at me as I painted the wall with shaky hands. I didn't want to play this game anymore. I couldn't.

When I finally gained the courage to look over at him, he was closer than he had been a moment ago. I watched as he took three steps toward me, grabbing the sides of my face and lowering his forehead to rest on mine. The end of the song was blaring around us; I could feel it rattling against my heart, like it was bursting from within me.

Our chests were almost touching, and with each heave of our breaths they came in contact. All I had to do was angle up my face, and we would be kissing. I didn't want to fight it anymore—I just wanted to give in. But this time it *would* be cheating, because he was with Sophie again. I hated him. I absolutely despised him for doing this to the both of us.

"You want to kiss me," I whispered up at him. It was a statement, not a question. I wasn't even trying to taunt him. I just needed to hear him say it—to admit to me that he wanted me.

Jackson froze before he took a step back, staring at me with regret before turning around and throwing open the front door. He pounded down the porch steps, the door slamming behind him in the process. I should've let him go; I should have turned around and continued to paint the wall. But, like an idiot, I followed him, because my stupid heart was attached to his.

"Jackson!" I yelled after him when I pulled the door back open. He was pacing back and forth on the curb, grabbing fistfuls of his hair and scoffing at himself.

"I know," he said in a strained voice. It sounded like he was yelling at himself, not me. He actually fucking admitted it. He had a fiancée, and he wanted to kiss *me*.

I could feel the burn starting beneath my skin, the rapid popping of anger.

"And that's exactly why you shouldn't marry her; because the fact that you even *want* to kiss me is wrong," I said, my chest heaving.

"I'm marrying her, Addie," he said defiantly.

It was like a knife to the chest. What was I thinking, wasting my time with him these past three weeks? I should have never let him back in. I couldn't believe I'd let him do this to me, *again*.

"Why? Why are you doing this to me?" I sounded like a wounded child. I couldn't even scream—I was too hurt. I just needed the truth. I was so tired of all the circles we were running in.

"Because . . . Because you know it can't happen." He sounded exasperated, like I was making it all up as I went along. Like everything was inside my head this entire time.

"Why, Jackson? Why not? You're hurting me. You're really fucking hurting me, and you're hurting Sophie."

My throat was on fire; it was taking everything in me to keep it together.

"I want to do the right thing here," he said with his arms splayed out.

"The right thing would be to end it. Call it quits if you don't want to get married!"

"I can't!" He screamed it so loud I flinched back. He looked wounded; I could see the tears in his eyes as his face softened. "I can't," he whispered this time. "I asked her to marry me, okay? I can't hurt her like before. I was horrible to her back then, and I can't be that guy again. And I'm so tired of constantly hurting you. The one time I tried to do the right thing for you, it hurt you."

He didn't even say he wanted to marry her because he loved her. It was just his way of making amends for his past actions. That cut me even deeper. He was choosing her over me.

I couldn't stop myself from crying then. I had no idea what he was talking about when he said he was trying to do the right thing for me; he's always hurt me.

"When, huh? When the fuck did you ever try to do the right thing for me? All you've ever done is hurt me, Jackson. And I'm dumb enough to still want you!"

A tear fell down his jaw. *Ha!* I thought. He needs to hurt, too—to suffer this pain. He would never hurt as deeply as I did.

He let out a painful sob, and my eyes widened. I had never seen Jackson cry before in all the time I'd known him.

"I did, Addie," he cried, sitting down on the curb and placing his hands over his face as his shoulders bounced with his sobs. "I came for you that night. When you called me after graduation, I did come. I tried." He was looking at me now, face raw and red as more tears trickled down his face.

I was frozen to the ground. I didn't think I could take another step if I tried.

"I crashed the truck on my way to you. I was drinking too much at the senior party. That's why I never showed. That's why, okay? And I knew I wasn't a person who deserved you if I was too drunk to be there when you needed me."

I stayed standing, crying as I watched him sit there. I was pained and hurt and just taking it all in.

The scar through his eyebrow. Being sober for the past five years. The new front bumper on the truck. Everything was starting to make sense.

"I love you. I've always loved you, Addie. But I can't cheat on Sophie. It's not right." He wiped his cheeks before standing up, taking two long strides until his arms were wrapped around me.

I sunk into him, letting myself continue to cry as he enveloped me. "I love you. I promise I love you. I've never stopped."

I couldn't even say it back because the sound of a car door slamming broke us apart from each other. I looked up and froze. The worst possible person that could've heard that conversation was stalking toward us, her gaze sizzling with fury. She wasn't supposed to be home until tomorrow.

My blood ran cold when I heard Sophie say, "What the fuck is going on?"

Chapter 35

BEFORE

May, Ten Years ago

By the time we got to Jackson's house for the barbecue, the rain had already stopped. I ignored Julie's eyes on me as we filled our plates, and throughout the meal. She wasn't one to keep her opinions to herself, and I knew she wanted to confront me about catching me and Jackson hooking up.

I was on a high from finally getting with Jackson, and I didn't want a conversation with Julie to ruin it. I also didn't want to be the one to admit that we planned to leave at the end of summer. Who knew, maybe we would end up in California with her. We could go anywhere we wanted.

After we'd sat outside with his family for a while, Jackson claimed that he wanted to play the drums so we could have an excuse to hang out alone in his room. We knew Julie wouldn't follow us, because she couldn't stand the noise.

When we got to his room though, I actually *did* want him to play the drums for me, and he obliged without making me beg.

He let me watch him as he played "Misery Business" by Paramore, and I sang along as I bopped my head to the music. I had been waiting too long to sing this song and mean it.

Jackson knew it, too, because he would smirk up at me every chance he got. He was drenched in sweat after, from the exertion as well as the heat of graduation and the barbecue, so he left to take a shower before joining me back in his bedroom.

We sat on Jackson's bed, our backs against the wall and our legs criss-crossed as we signed each other's yearbooks.

His index finger kept tentatively touching my outer thigh, and with each stroke of his finger, he got closer and closer to the hem of my dress. I couldn't focus on anything when he was touching me like that.

"You're distracting me. I can't think of anything to write," I said, even though I didn't move his hand away. I didn't want him to stop. I had waited too long to have him touch me like this without feeling like it was wrong.

"Just write something generic, like 'Have a great summer, Jackson'," he said with a lazy smile.

I rolled my eyes. "What'd you write in mine?"

His finger kept inching higher and higher. "You'll see later."

He pressed a light kiss to my kneecap, fully eliminating any rational thought from my brain. I tried to write "Addison Bianchi loves Jackson forever" but instead I accidentally wrote "Addison Delvecchio loves Jackson forever," and sloppily drew a slice of pizza next to it.

I set the yearbook on the bed next to me, and watched him. His eyes were locked on mine as he continued this game, stroking his finger back and forth under the hem of my dress. I could feel my breathing getting deeper, and the rise and fall of his chest started to match mine.

His finger finally made its way under my dress, playfully running back and forth on the fabric of my underwear. It moved down between my legs, then back up toward my hips. Back and forth, back and forth, until my body involuntarily started moving toward him.

He finally touched me where I was aching for him, and I arched my back to meet him. A sparkler of pleasure rolled through my body, and I pushed my lips together to refrain from making any sound. He slid his finger in and out, slowly and agonizingly, as his eyes stayed locked on mine. He slipped his thumb under the fabric next, and suddenly I was nothing but jerky limbs against his hand. I whispered his name in a gasp.

Jackson smiled, and I was aching for him to kiss me—to lose all of myself in the sensation of him.

I was close to fully unraveling, and Jackson could sense it. He leaned forward to cover my mouth with his other hand, nodding at me like he was giving me permission to let myself succumb to the feeling. It was the hottest thing I'd ever experienced in my life. He pressed his lips against the hand covering my mouth, whispering for me to *shhh*. I squeezed my eyes shut and let the waves roll through me over and over again as my body jerked beneath him.

I could feel the flush of heat in my cheeks, and when I opened my eyes, Jackson removed his hand to finally kiss me on the lips. A soft sweet peck that left me wanting more, more, *more*.

"Do you have a condom?" I asked breathlessly as I started to crawl on top of him.

He nodded yes and started digging around in the drawer of his bedside dresser, pulling out the packet. I ripped it from his hands, impatient and frenzied as he undid his pants before I slid it on him.

He helped me take off my underwear in a mess of limbs, and shoved them into the drawer he had gotten the condom from.

I lowered myself onto him, and his head fell back to rest against the wall, his mouth slightly parted as he watched me rock back and forth on him. I heard the smallest sound escape from his lips, and I placed my pointer finger there, signaling for him to stay quiet. His hands were gripping my hips so tightly that I was sure I'd have bruises from his touch later.

We didn't even kiss—we stayed in pained silence as we examined every single part of each other. His eyes kept flicking between my face and where our bodies were connected, and I tried to stamp every detail of this moment into my brain: The beads of sweat beginning to form at his hairline that matched the trickle I felt rolling down my spine, the freckle on his collarbone that popped out just below his collar, the fabric of his sheets digging into my knees as they pressed deeper and deeper into his mattress, and my favorite part—the look in Jackson's deep-brown eyes as he watched me.

He mouthed *I love you* beneath my finger, which was still pressed against his lips, and I mouthed it back just as he bit his bottom lip. I could feel his body tightening, and he leaned forward to press his face into my neck to stifle his sounds. His teeth clamped onto my shoulder, and his hands moved to my back to press me closer to him.

I tangled my fingers in his hair, kneading back and forth until his body stilled. He exhaled a long breath before leaning back and putting my hair behind my ears. The kiss he gave me settled something inside me. This was the moment I actually *believed* he was in love with me. Because he was telling me when he was sober. The feeling that passed between us was something I knew I would never experience again in this lifetime.

We both heard footsteps coming up the stairs, and we flew apart. He ripped off the condom and threw it in the drawer that still had my underwear in it, then his fingers flew to his pants to zip and button them. I fixed my dress, then pretended to look at the framed pictures on his dresser while he grabbed his yearbook and placed it on his lap to cover himself.

Two knocks sounded on the door before Jackson managed to say, "Come in."

I could feel liquid dripping down my thigh, and I tightened my legs together in hopes it wouldn't drip to my ankle.

"It's almost time for the senior party," Marie said from the doorway. I kept my back to her, too worried she'd see on my face that I had just lost my virginity to her son. My eyes flicked over to Jackson to see if he looked just as guilty as I was sure I did.

"I'll leave in a second," Jackson said without looking up from the yearbook.

I could feel Marie's eyes on my back, looking back and forth between us. I finally risked a peek over my shoulder at her, and she gave me a genuine smile before shutting the door and leaving. I waited until I heard her steps descending the stairs before turning around.

When my eyes met Jackson's, we both cracked up laughing, him covering his face and shaking his head while I put a fist to my mouth and released a full belly laugh.

"We can never have peace," Jackson joked as I walked toward him on the bed.

"I think I might be bleeding," I said, even though I was still laughing.

I grabbed a tissue from his bedside table and swiped it up my thigh, finding a small trail of blood. Jackson reached forward to hold up my dress for me while I cleaned myself. He didn't say it was gross, or make some stupid teenage boy comment about fucking me too hard. Instead, he grabbed another tissue and helped me clean up the mess.

"Is it obvious that was my first time?" I asked as we bundled up the tissues and shoved them to the bottom of the trash can in his room.

Jackson grabbed my hands, pulling me into a hug. My head was tucked under his chin, and I buried my face into his chest.

"Was it obvious that was mine, too? That barely lasted five minutes," he said into my hair.

"What?" I asked as I leaned away from him to see his face. He smiled at me, not one bit embarrassed. "Are you serious?"

He nodded. "You were my first kiss, Addie. I wanted my first time to be with you, too."

He never slept with Sophie . . . No wonder she hated me so much. Jackson had waited for *me*. He loved me so much that he wanted his first time to be with me.

I felt like I had been thrown into a pool of water; I was being drowned by how much I loved this boy.

He kissed me again, this time walking us backward until we were pressed against his dresser. I giggled before putting my hands on his chest and pushing him away.

"I really do love you, Jackson," I said looking up at him.

"I really do love you, too." He gave me a quick kiss before stepping back. "I wish you were coming to the party."

I never bought a ticket for tonight's senior all-night party because I didn't want to be a third-wheel to Sophie and Jackson. It was too late to buy a ticket by the time I found out they broke up.

I shrugged. "We'll have the entire summer together. Ready to take me home?"

He grabbed my hand and we said our goodbyes to his family.

Julie gave me a tight hug, and promised she'd take me out for breakfast this week while she was in town.

On the way home, we listened to "The Other Side" by Jason Derulo, screaming at the top of our lungs to the lyrics. Jackson turned the volume up as high as it could go. "This one's for the love of my life,

Addison Bianchi!" I laughed and shoved him in the shoulder as we continued to sing. Friends to lovers—the oldest trope in the book.

Peter's car was gone when we pulled into my driveway, and Jackson leaned over to kiss me as "Earned It" by the Weeknd started to play.

I put my hands in his hair, pulling him against me. His hands trailed up my thighs until they were around my waist, rubbing back and forth along my hip bones. He laughed against my lips. "Oh my god, I forgot to give you your underwear back."

"Don't need them," I replied as I dragged my hands down his chest to the button of his pants.

Jackson put a hand on my wrist. "I didn't bring a condom."

He pulled his head back to look at me, and I smiled up at him. I could never get sick of this view. "That's okay, we have all summer to finally do that in the truck."

He smiled back at me before taking off his shirt, then he started kissing down my neck and chest. He lowered his head to kiss the inside of my right thigh, and then the left, alternating a kiss on each one as he got closer and closer to where I wanted him.

Jackson looked up at me before centering himself. "It's you and me, Addison." Then he put his head beneath the hem of my dress. This time we didn't have to try to keep quiet.

The only thought my brain kept repeating was, *Two more months, and then it's just Jackson and me forever.* It was impossible to think anymore once Jackson's mouth touched me. He spent the next thirty minutes learning my body, and how it reacted to him. He paid attention to what made me moan, whimper, tremble, and tighten. And when it mattered most, he put what he'd learned to good use.

After the final waves of pleasure rolled through my body, we switched positions. When I reached to undo his belt, he didn't stop me, and I tasted him in all the ways I'd spent the last four years imagining. I took my time, putting as much effort into learning his body as he had mine. The way he held my hair back so he could watch what I was doing to him drove me wild, and the adoration in his eyes as he bit his lip just confirmed how real this was. He told me he loved me, how good my mouth felt, and moaned my name over and over again. He tensed beneath me before finally relaxing against the seat, and I looked up at him and repeated his words from earlier: "It's you and me, Jackson."

When I finally walked inside the house, I slipped off my shoes and left my yearbook behind them by the front door. I was so exhausted from the emotional high I was on today that I flopped down on the couch without changing.

A part of me wished I was going to the senior all-night party to spend more time with Jackson, but I would see him tomorrow morning. My heart fluttered—not just tomorrow, but the rest of my life would be spent with Jackson Delvecchio.

I let out a yawn and wrapped myself in a blanket, falling into a deep sleep. I could rest easy now that we weren't playing any more games with each other.

We were finally together, and I wholeheartedly believed that one day I would be Addison Delvecchio.

***

I woke up to the sound of the front door opening. I peered up at the clock on the wall, surprised to find that it was one in the morning. I turned from where I was curled up on the couch to see Peter standing in the doorway of the family room, watching me.

"You're just like Mom," he said as he stared down at me.

I rubbed the sleep from my eyes, wondering what he was talking about. I tried to blink him into focus while I spoke. "Peter?"

He was illuminated by the lights in the kitchen, his reddened eyes glazed over as he swayed in the doorway. He was completely obliterated.

"I knew you'd be just like Mom. You're going to leave, too." I couldn't even process what he was trying to say.

He took a step toward me, and I sprung up from the couch. He started undoing his belt, and for a second, I felt a punch of fear that my own brother might try to rape me. My body flung itself into fight or flight mode.

"Woah, what are you talking about?" I took a step back, the backs of my knees hitting against the coffee table.

"I went to your graduation, you know. I saw you with the Delvecchio boy."

My heart was punching against my ribs. I hadn't expected Peter to come to graduation; I hadn't even told him when it was. I put up my hands defensively.

"He's just my friend," I lied "You know this, Peter. We just work together."

Peter folded the belt in half, and a chill swept over me as I realized he took it off so he could hit me with it. I was ready to run, but he was blocking the only exit.

"I saw you with him!" I started to wrack my brain for what he could've seen at the ceremony. Jackson did give me a piggy-back ride from the field to the parking lot, and I had sat with him in his truck. Did we kiss in the truck at the school? I couldn't even remember anymore. I was focusing too much on what Peter was about to do to think about anything else.

Fear crawled over every inch of my body as he took another step toward me. "Just like Mom. You're going to leave me for a man."

I couldn't fully wrap my head around what he was insinuating. Peter hated me, so why was he mad that I was finally leaving him alone? He didn't even know about my plan with Jackson. Why would he even care? This was what he'd always wanted. Right?

I tried to think of something to say to calm him. I moved to take another step back, but I'd forgotten about the coffee table behind me. I fell on top of it, my dress sliding up my body. When Peter saw I wasn't wearing underwear, his nostrils flared.

"I knew it." That was the last thing he said before lunging for me.

The first crack of the belt hit my right arm, and I cried out in pain. This was the first time he had ever intentionally hurt me. That shocked me more than the sensation of the leather.

"Peter, stop!" I tried to fight my way out from beneath him as the belt kept smacking against my skin, hitting a different spot each time. He was too heavy, and he was pressing down on my stomach with his full weight. I could barely get out the words to plead for him to stop.

I clawed at any piece of him I could. Everything was happening in one quick blur. Eventually, he dropped the belt and pinned my arms to my side. I could feel blood trickling down my right arm from where the buckle had struck me.

When I looked in his eyes, I couldn't see any piece of my brother left. I cried beneath him, feeling the tears drip down my temples as his eyes turned sad in a quick moment.

"I hate you, Denise," he said weakly.

I was breathing heavily, trying to catch my breath. He called me by our mom's name.

"I'm not Denise," I said quietly.

Peter stared at me for a while, like he was trying to figure out who I was. He finally let go of me, then fell to the side with a whimper. His body heaved with heavy sobs that had me frozen in place next to him on the floor.

"I hate her. I fucking hate her!" Peter yelled.

He buried his face in his hands, rubbing them up and down. He turned to look at me, and I saw my brother again. Just like that, Peter was back, but he looked like a hurt little boy.

"I'm sorry, Addie."

I didn't respond. I jumped up, grabbing my purse and running outside. I wasn't wearing shoes, but I couldn't even feel the bite of the cement under my feet as I ran down the street.

I didn't stop until I made it down the block, then I got down on my hands and knees, crawling into a heap of bushes on the side of the road. I couldn't even get in my car and drive away, because it was still at the high school.

I finally registered the stinging on my arms from the smack of the leather as I dialed Jackson's number.

When he didn't answer, I felt my breathing grow more rapid, to the point that every inhale was a gasp. I left him a shaky voice mail.

"Jackson, I need you to come get me. Something happened with Peter. I want to leave *now*. I can't wait till August, I wanna go *right now*." My breath caught in my throat and I choked back a sob. "I really need you."

I hung up and tried calling him again. When he didn't answer by the tenth time, I grabbed at the bushes and pulled out a chunk. I picked off pieces of brush until I felt my phone vibrate with a text from Jackson. *I'll be there in twenty minutes. Stay where you are.* I let out a breath of relief. He was coming. He would get me. We were leaving this place for good.

I waited and waited. Twenty minutes turned into thirty, then thirty turned into forty-five. The last time I checked the clock, it was almost three thirty in the morning. I lost count of how many times I had called him. I tried again, only to find that his phone was shut off.

He wasn't coming, and he never would.

I tried dialing Julie's number, but got no response from her either. A sob wracked my body as I dialed Marie's number. "Please," I whispered as the phone rang. "Please . . ." As soon as I heard her voice mail message start playing, I disconnected the call.

I stood up on weak legs, and walked back toward the house slowly. I thought I would pass out from fear when I opened the front door and peered in.

Peter was still on the floor in the family room, but he was sleeping now. The house was a complete disaster. Glasses were broken, framed photos were thrown from every surface, and lamps were overturned. It was even worse than last Christmas.

I tiptoed to my room, grabbing anything of importance and throwing it into a duffel bag. I left the house faster than I ever had before. Pure adrenaline was coursing through me as I ran the two miles to Tostela to get my car.

I started driving away from town with no destination in mind. I would never come back here. I was starting a new life, with or without Jackson.

I had no idea how long I had been on the road when my phone started to ring, interrupting "Breakaway" by Kelly Clarkson, which I'd been blasting through the speakers. I didn't even look to see who it was before I rolled down the window and threw the phone out across the highway. I couldn't let myself be let down again.

This would be the last time I ever let Jackson hurt me.

Chapter 36

NOW

July

I ran back to the house as soon as I heard Sophie yell at Jackson. I really thought she was going to kill me, but she just grabbed Jackson's arm and pulled him toward the car.

I couldn't even finish painting; I was too shaken up. I drove down to Detroit with shaky legs and sat on a bench along the riverfront, watching cars drive back and forth on the Ambassador Bridge. For a while, I wondered if I should drive to Canada—have that be where I start my new life.

I walked up and down the sidewalk, quickly realizing that was a crazy idea. I didn't need a new country. I stopped to pet people's dogs, and to make small talk with the people lounging on the grass. It helped lighten the concavity I felt in my chest.

It was a breezy day with the sun behind the clouds, and I laid down on the grass with my eyes closed, letting my hair blow back and forth across my face. I could feel bugs crawling over my arms and legs, but I didn't squirm. I enjoyed every sensation my body was feeling.

I was going to be okay. I had been hurt before and I had survived. I didn't need anyone but myself. I had always been fine—had always pushed through.

I would finish the house and fly back to North Carolina. I'd stay there until I made a decision about what to do with my life. Even if I wasn't with Jackson, or living with Wren and Mia, I could still build a happy life for myself.

I wanted Wren and Mia now. I wanted my favorite kind of hug, where I'd hold Mia in my arms and Wren would squeeze both of us. Mia was so big now; I couldn't remember the last time I had even picked her up. Just because I wasn't going to be nannying her for much longer, that didn't mean I wouldn't still have them in my life—I knew that. That fact calmed me; that I had stumbled across them one random day, and would get to have them forever, no matter what.

I could live without Peter. My brother had always acted like he hated me, but now I knew deep down that he'd loved me, even though he could never show it. I hoped he was at peace now, somewhere in the sky with his dad again, no longer fighting the demons he suffered from. I wanted him to know I forgave him.

I could continue to live without my mom. That relationship had been nonexistent for most of my life, and I never really needed her anyways. I never missed her like Peter did, because we had been raised so differently; I never even got the chance to get to know her the way he had. I don't think she ever forgave me for being the product of her infidelity.

I thought of Julie and Marie next. The way Marie would call me honey, and Julie would hug me tight like I was her sister. It felt like I was losing them all over again, and I let myself grieve that loss. I wouldn't get back what I had with that family, and even though it hurt, I had lived without them before. I never even knew what love truly felt like until I met the Delvecchios, but now that I'd found that love once, I knew I could find it again.

I could live without Jackson, too. I had been without him all this time; I knew I didn't need him to be happy. But it didn't mean I didn't still *want* him. Either way, I knew I was going to be okay.

I sat up in the grass. It was dusk now, and the trail had grown quiet. I pulled my hair back in a low bun and watched the sky change colors.

I couldn't see the sun setting behind me, but I could feel it. That was all I really needed in this moment. I could pretend this wasn't the end again, because I couldn't see it. But it was, whether I was ready or not.

I drove home with the windows down, my arms prickling with goose bumps from the chill.

I climbed into my old bed with its fresh sheets, ignoring the Delvecchios' polo I'd cleaned and folded neatly on my nightstand. I went to bed feeling at ease.

***

In the morning, I wasn't surprised to find Jackson standing on the front porch, hands in his pockets.

He looked like he hadn't slept at all. There were blue rings under his bloodshot eyes, and his dark hair was mussed like he had repeatedly run his fingers through it. He motioned for me to come outside, and we sat side by side on the front porch. I tucked my knees under my chin, watching as ants crawled between the cracks on the sidewalk.

"I should've told you everything before," he whispered.

I didn't respond; I just waited for him to go on. I was ready to listen, to put everything out on the table.

"You put Julie on your résumé for your job. Wren called her, Addie. I don't know if you ever knew that."

I *didn't* know that. Wren never told me that she'd checked my references. I swallowed deeply.

"She got Wren's name, found her online, and went as far as to see where she lived and everything. Wren had posted a picture of you on Facebook with Mia. That's how Julie confirmed where you were."

I chewed on my lip. I thought I had stayed under the radar since I had no social media, a new phone, and had been living with the Wilsons.

"Okay, so what are you saying? You knew where I was the entire time? And you *still* never came to find me? Is that supposed to make me feel better?" I said, defeated.

He shook his head. "That first week you were gone, before Wren called Julie, my entire family was freaking out. My parents even went to your house. My tiny-ass mom actually screamed at Peter, telling him he better tell us where you went. But he obviously didn't know. I thought you could be dead, or that you'd killed yourself."

I wanted to sarcastically say, "Get over yourself," but I couldn't. I didn't have the energy.

He went on. "When Julie found you, I told her to let it go. I fought with my entire family to leave you alone."

"Why?" It barely came out as a whisper.

"Because I thought you left because of me."

There was that knife, right through the chest again.

"I left because Peter hurt me, and you never showed. Why would I want you to leave me alone?"

I looked up at him, and he had his elbows balanced on his knees, his head in his arms like the weight was too much to hold.

"I got arrested after the accident. Charged with a DUI. My parents ended up sending me to rehab. I had a really bad drinking problem in high school."

I sucked in a breath. I knew Jackson had always turned to the bottle. My own brother was a fucking alcoholic. I should have seen the signs—I should have known how bad it was. Was I really that blinded by my love for him that I never saw it? Or did I just not want to see it, because all I cared about back then was wanting him to want me?

"I didn't kick it the first time. I was sober on and off for five years. I was a mess after you left. The last time I got out of treatment, I ran into Sophie. She was familiar, you know? She had just moved back from college, and we talked for a while. Two years later, we got engaged." He groaned, shaking his head and putting his hands over his face. "She convinced me to buy the restaurant after Phil died. We just bought it last year, *together*. We're fucking business partners now."

I just shook my head. Even though I was furious hearing this, I was more upset than anything. He was tied to her.

"When I finally got my shit together and got with Sophie, Julie told me we should go see you. She thought I hadn't gotten closure on us—that I couldn't start something with Sophie when you were still taking over my every thought. And she was right; you just disappeared, and I was fucked up from it. Truthfully, I didn't want to see you, because I couldn't handle a rejection from you again. I still felt awful over everything. I thought that I destroyed your life. I knew I failed you and let you down. You were my best friend, and I was supposed to protect you, but I wasn't there when you needed me most. I lost the person I cared about more than anything because of my own fuckups.

"But, Julie convinced me, and we drove down. We pulled up to the house, but you were leaving with Mia. We followed you to the beach, and we just sat and watched the two of you for an hour."

He met my eyes now, and through the blur of my tears, I could see that his eyes were glossy, too. "You looked so happy, Addie. I couldn't risk taking that away from you. And I didn't trust my sobriety yet. You didn't need me to save you. So, we left. And I felt at peace knowing you were okay."

I shook my head, wiping at my eyes. He found me. Last week when he told me he'd found me, this was what he was talking about. I'd thought I'd heard him say it, but I couldn't believe that it was true. I was hit with a fresh wave of devastation.

"I never needed you to save me, Jackson. I just wanted you to love me back." That was all I ever wanted from him—and all I wanted even now.

"I always did," he whispered softly.

We sat in silence for a while after that, wiping away our tears, not daring to look at each other.

My chest felt like it had been ripped in half. Everything I had built up in my head and wholeheartedly believed for ten years was wrong. I didn't know what to do with this information. Did it even change anything?

"And I talked to Sophie, I told her everything. Believe it or not, the conversation didn't end terribly."

I figured that meant they were okay. He was marrying her, and his feelings for me were out of his system. "She said she understands. Because she knows how hard it is to let go of your first love."

I nodded, even though my heart shattered into a million pieces. I would never have him. It was never in the cards for us. "I understand, too. Why you can't let her go."

I met his eyes, and he looked back and forth between mine before shaking his head. "Addison . . . I wasn't talking about Sophie."

I didn't understand what he meant by that, and I raised an eyebrow. He leaned forward and smoothed down my eyebrow with his thumb.

"I . . . I was talking about you. She understands why I can't let *you* go. I mean, we've been engaged for over three years. I think we both knew we were never going to get married."

I opened my mouth, but no words came out. It was me? I was his first love? He couldn't let *me* go?

"What do you mean?" I managed to get out.

"I might be Sophie's first love, but you were mine. It's always been you, from the moment I saw you walk through the kitchen doors. God Addie, I've been in love with you since before I kissed you in that closet. It'll never not be you." He paused, and I watched as a tear trickled down his cheek. "But I can't be with you . . . Not until I'm forgiven."

I reached forward and swiped the tear from his cheek with my thumb, leaving my hand cupping his face.

"I forgive you, Jackson."

He closed his eyes and let his head fall into my palm, resting all his weight on it.

"Not you, Addie. Me. *I* have to forgive me first." He swallowed thickly, then opened his eyes. "I broke my sobriety."

I sucked in a gasp at his admission, and he shut his eyes again, pain covering his face.

"The night you were drinking on the couch, I had a drink after you went to sleep. I've been drinking again since that night."

It was a blow to the chest. I was the reason he broke his sobriety, and I was the reason he drank so much in high school.

"This is all my fault," I whispered through a choked sob.

He shook his head quickly. "It's not your fault. It never was. I've been struggling for a while—before you even came back. I just can't seem to get it together," he admitted.

"I can help you; I'll stop drinking, too. You can get sober again."

Everything was slipping through my fingers; he was saying he wanted me though, right? He was finally choosing me again?

He shook his head again. "I'm going back to treatment." Another tear fell from his cheek. "It was never our job to save each other."

I started to cry now, too, and he pulled me into a hug. We stayed there for a while, feeling the rise and fall of each other's breaths, not ready to break apart. Because we knew when we did, that would be it, at least for a while. I focused on his heartbeat, and the way it was in sync with mine—the steady pace of us being together.

There was no telling when we'd find each other again, or if we'd ever get it right. After a while, he was the one to break away. He surprised me by kissing me on the lips—lips I hadn't felt since I was eighteen. I knew a Jackson kiss, but this kiss was slow and tentative, the softest press. It didn't feel like a beginning; it felt like an ending.

"You're my best friend, period. And I love you, period," he whispered against my mouth.

And then he was gone.

Chapter 37

NOW

July

I bought a plane ticket to North Carolina the next day. I couldn't handle driving in my current emotional state.

I felt delirious—like I was watching a bad movie about every worst-case scenario that could've transpired in my life. I tortured myself by listening to "Orange Juice" by Noah Kahan, and "I Know The End" by Phoebe Bridgers in a fucked-up loop.

Wren picked me up from the airport, and the second I saw her, I burst into tears. She wrapped me in a tight hug, right there in the pickup lane. She rubbed my back soothingly, telling me that everything was going to be okay. I knew it would be. But it wasn't right now.

We took Mia to the mall and watched as she picked out a Build-A-Bear, putting in a red heart and excitedly pumping her foot on the lever to fill it with stuffing. She was almost a teenager, and this would probably be one of the last times she would indulge us by doing something like this.

One of the first things I did with Mia when I started nannying her was take her to this same mall to pick out a Build-A-Bear. She still has it at home; a white unicorn with a rainbow horn that's dressed in a ballerina tutu. No shoes, of course, because per Mia you don't need pointe shoes when you have hooves.

We got ice cream and took turns riding the glass elevator up and down, watching each other from the lower level and waving.

Mia wanted to go to her favorite café in the mall for french fries, and she ate two whole sides of unseasoned fries while Wren and I shared a platter of chicken strips.

Later that evening, Mia taught me her new skin care routine that she had perfected while I was in Michigan. I lost count of how many products she used, but I let her do it on my face, too, until my skin was as smooth as a baby's butt.

When we put Mia to bed that night, I let myself cry again. I finally explained everything to Wren, and she listened patiently as I spoke through my tearful gasps.

We were sitting on the couch, and I lost track of how many tissues I had cried through. "It's so stupid; nobody has ever hurt me as much as he has. Why can't I just let him go?"

Wren handed me another tissue, and I blew my nose. She looked at me with soft eyes. "Because you've also never loved someone as much as you love him."

Present tense. Because despite it all, I *still* loved him. I still wanted him.

"It doesn't even matter anymore. I've decided I'm selling the house. I'll be back here by the end of summer."

Wren stared at me for a long time. I finally stopped crying, wiping the last of the tears off my face.

"I think you should stay home," Wren finally said.

"I have to go back to handle the house," I said.

She shook her head. "Not your home here. Your home in Michigan."

I looked at her in disbelief. "That house was never my home."

She gave me a level look. "But it could be. You could make it a home. The Delvecchios are your family. Whether you're with Jackson or not, he's your family."

I couldn't believe what she was saying. All I could do was shake my head no. "Everything is a mess. Sophie owns half the restaurant. Nobody in his family even lives in the state anymore. Trust me, they don't miss me. I'm not their family anymore."

Even I didn't believe the words as they left my mouth.

Wren wiped a tear from the corner of her eye.

"Addie," she whispered. "There's something I need to tell you."

Wren was crying now, grabbing a tissue for herself and laughing through her tears. "You have no idea how much that family loves you."

I switched my position on the couch so that I was fully facing her.

"I never told you the full story of when I called Julie for your reference. She was sobbing, so relieved to hear you were okay. She's the reason I hired you. She told me everything that happened between you and her family. Every year she would contact me to check up on you. I sent her pictures a few times. She asked me to keep it a secret. She just wanted to know you were safe."

I thought my tears were done, but more came running down my cheeks. "Did you know they came to see me? And just left?"

Wren shook her head. "No, I swear I didn't. And I don't think Julie ever told Jackson that her and I stayed in contact. He was just as much in the dark as you were."

I couldn't believe this. They cared. They actually cared about me.

"I just don't know what to do with all this information," I said as I placed my hands on the sides of my head. It was too much... It was all so much. I felt like every time I got to the bottom of the truth, there was another layer popping up.

"Just relax, and give yourself some time to process everything. No major life decision should be made overnight," Wren said as she rubbed my kneecap.

She was right. The last time I made a full one-eighty life choice was on a whim while in a frazzled panic. I needed time to sit with this, to look at every option available to me, and then decide what I would do.

"Okay," I whispered.

***

I stayed in North Carolina for the next month, spending every moment with Wren and Mia.

We had beach days, spent days in the library, and I brought Mia to a carnival. We even drove down to South Carolina for one of George's work conferences and sweat in the sun at Myrtle Beach while watching dolphins.

We celebrated Mia's thirteenth birthday, and Wren and I both sobbed like babies over our favorite teenager. Jackson turned twenty-nine while I was away, and it took everything in me not to call him and see how he was doing.

Before I left to go back to Michigan, Mia let me pick her up in a hug, even though she was more than half my size now. Wren wrapped her arms around both of us, squeezing me so tight it felt like all three of our hearts were beating as one. It felt like everyone else in the airport drop-off lane disappeared—like everything in the world vanished except for the three of us.

"We love you so much," Wren said as she pressed a kiss to my hair.

I held on to them both a little longer, then I pressed a kiss to Mia's head before setting her back down.

"I love you guys," I said, taking them in with watery eyes.

"We'll see you soon, Addie," Mia said with a toothy smile.

She handed me her new Build-A-Bear. "I want you to keep it."

I grabbed the bear from her, holding it against my chest as I gave Mia a smile through my tears. I ran my fingers through her curly hair one last time before turning around and walking through the airport's automatic doors.

Chapter 38

BEFORE

February, Seven Years Ago

It had been almost three years since I got in my car and didn't stop until I hit the Atlantic Ocean. Three years since I left Tostela without looking back.

I woke up reminiscing on that first week I spent here in Wilmington; sleeping in my car every night, and going to different coffee shops and restaurants every day to fill out job applications. I never filled out the address portion—I didn't have one back then. I almost gave up and drove back up to Michigan after so many rejections.

I had bought myself a new phone the day I got here. My very first iPhone—a huge upgrade from the prepaid phone the Delvecchios bought me that first Christmas I spent with them. It had been an entire week without them, and I wondered what they were doing right that second.

I was eating a chocolate croissant in a cafe, contemplating my entire existence now that the Delvecchios weren't a part of it, when the little girl at the table next to me giggled.

I looked over at her and found those big blue eyes staring at me, examining the chocolate I had managed to smear everywhere. I stuck my tongue out at her before grabbing a napkin and cleaning myself up. She covered her mouth with her hand and laughed beneath it. Her mom looked up from her laptop to smile at me.

I made eye contact with the little girl again, and this time she waved.

We played this game back and forth; I'd pretend I was invested in my phone, she'd stare at me, I'd look up like I was surprised to see her, then I'd wave.

When she and her mom got up to leave, the little girl waddled right over to my table.

"You come play with me?" Her little voice was even cuter than the freckles splayed across her cheeks. She couldn't have been older than two.

"Mia . . ." the mom said with a laugh as she grabbed her daughter's hand before turning to me. "She really wants to be your friend, apparently."

I smiled back at the mom before turning to Mia. "I could really use a friend right now, too."

The mom looked me up and down, and I self consciously fixed my hair. I'd only given it a half-assed wash in a library bathroom that morning. I probably looked strung-out and greasy.

"I'm a teacher, and I'm about to go back to work for the first time since Mia was born. My husband and I are looking for a nanny. Would you be interested? Do you have a résumé?"

I couldn't stand up fast enough to introduce myself.

"I'm Addison. Yes, I definitely have a résumé. Um, I can go to the library really quickly and print it for you."

I, in fact, did *not* have a résumé. Delvecchios' Restaurant was the only job I had ever had—was that enough experience to be a nanny?

"No need, I'll give you my email and you can send it over. I'm Wren Wilson by the way." She shook my hand, and I grimaced when I realized how sweaty mine was.

"Okay, great, I'll get that over to you shortly," I said a bit too eagerly.

Mia and Wren said their goodbyes to me, and I ran straight to the library to write up a résumé.

I was following a template I found on Google, but I didn't know who to write for references. Was she actually going to check them? I panicked and wrote Julie's name and number. She was still in California anyways, and she never answered random numbers.

I emailed the résumé to Wren before the day was over. I got a call from her the next day, asking me to come over to chat. She gave me the job, and I've been living with them ever since.

I was sitting with Wren and Mia now, on the morning of my twenty-first birthday. They'd surprised me with sprinkle pancakes, and a mountain of whipped cream. They were both singing to me, and I blew out the single candle, which was leaning over in my lopsided stack of pancakes. I was thankful my birthday fell on a Saturday this year, because Wren would be the one to clean the sticky syrup out of Mia's hair after our breakfast.

Who was I kidding? I'd help anyways. I loved the kid.

After breakfast, I dug through my closet for my old duffel bag so I could start packing for my upcoming spring break trip with the Wilsons. Now that Mia was almost five, Wren and George had decided she was old enough to enjoy Disney World.

When I finally spotted the purple bag, I let out an *aha!* I hadn't used it since I moved in, and it was sandwiched between an old pair of jeans and some bedding I had stuffed in the bottom of my closet.

When I finally wrestled the bag out, it wasn't empty. I unzipped it to clean it out, and found my old pair of high-top Converse.

The tongue was ripped, the laces were frayed, and the sole was detached from the bottom. Some of the threads in the embroidered pizza slice had come undone, but I couldn't bear to get rid of them. I hugged them to my chest, grieving the loss of the people I had left behind.

I hadn't heard from them since the day I left, and I pretended they were out of sight, out of mind. But it was a lie. Every morning when I opened my eyes, I thought about the Delvecchio family.

I rubbed my thumb over the embroidered detail on the side of the shoe. I had drawn a shittier version of this piece of pizza in Jackson's yearbook on the night of graduation. Had he seen it? Did he know it was because of these shoes he had given me five years ago? I hadn't been with anyone since that night after graduation, and I realized then that I didn't want to be. I just wanted *him*.

I had to do something. I had to feel something other than the pain that was radiating from beneath my rib cage.

I drove to a tattoo shop—the first one I could find that accepted walk-ins—and took the first artist that was available.

As the needle pierced my skin and traveled over my rib cage, I remembered the time I went with Jackson for his tattoo. He was right; it wasn't so much pain that you felt, but more of an annoying sting.

Over and over again, the sting followed by the rub of paper towel. I embraced it; I gladly took this feeling over what had been burning inside my heart.

After I paid for my tattoo, I was feeling lighter. I started thinking, what if Jackson *did* try to find me? I threw away my phone, and I didn't have social media. I worked as a live-in nanny—it's not like I had a LinkedIn account or anything. Could he have googled me and seen me listed under Wren's address? What if he actually *had* looked for me, and I didn't know?

I got in my car, using anxious fingers to type *67 before dialing Jackson's number, which I'd had memorized since I was fourteen years old.

With each ring, my heart rate accelerated. What did his voice sound like now? Would he hear me and know right away how much I missed him? Did he miss me too? Did he have some explanation for why he ghosted me that night? Could we get back together? Did he remember that it was my birthday today?

The call connected, and I heard him say, "Hey?" He said it as if it was a question, and I knew right away that he was drunk.

I could hear muffled voices in the background, the sound of music being played, and then static on the phone as if Jackson was trying to cover the receiver while he walked to a quieter room.

Someone called out his name in the background: "Jackson, come here!" It was a girl's voice, and my breath caught in my throat.

Jackson laughed, and my eyes filled with tears. I missed that laugh, and all the times *we* had laughed together. "One sec, I gotta see who this is." He sounded happy; like he was having a good time.

"Hello?" he said again into the phone.

I gripped my cellphone tighter. Jackson didn't need me. He never had. He was partying, having the time of his life, probably about to do a line of coke in the kitchen. He was fine without me. Even from eight hundred and seventeen miles away, he still had the power to hurt me.

I was glad I called, and I was glad when I hung up the phone and tossed it onto the passenger seat.

I could get him out of my system now, because nothing was going to change. I could finally close this chapter. I was officially done with Jackson.

***

I drove to the mall immediately after, jamming to the song "I Hope This Comes Back To Haunt You" by Neck Deep.

I bought myself a new black skirt, a sparkly mesh top, and a brand-new pair of high-top black Converse that weren't embroidered on the sides.

I went out to a club that night, kissed someone whose name I couldn't remember, and let them sleep with me in the bathroom in the back.

It didn't matter that he didn't have hair so dark it was almost black, or that his collarbone didn't have a freckle, or that he wasn't my best friend who once said that he loved me. I couldn't let Jackson Delvecchio be the last person who touched me. I had to let him go.

Even as I thought it, I knew it was a lie. I could never let him go, because I would never love anyone else like I love—present tense *love*—Jackson Delvecchio. Even if he didn't love me back.

Chapter 39

NOW

August

I had been back in Michigan for three days, and was just finishing up the final touches on the family room when I heard a knock at the door. My heart leapt in my chest, hoping it was Jackson back from treatment, telling me that he was feeling better. Because even if we didn't end up together, I *needed* him to be okay.

I took a deep breath and opened the door, finding Julie on the other side instead.

"Oh," I said at the sudden shock of seeing her standing there. Something pinched in my chest, and my eyes filled with tears.

"Oh, honey," Julie said as she wrapped me in a hug. She sounded just like Marie, and suddenly I was fourteen again, sobbing in front of a Delvecchio.

She leaned back and pushed my hair away from my face. "Let's talk."

She followed me into the family room, and we sat on the dilapidated couch.

"So, this is what you and Jackson were up to," she said as she looked around the room, taking in the paintbrushes, rollers, and cans of paint that were still strewn in a mess across the floor.

I nodded, remembering the last time he stood in this room a month ago.

"How is he?" I asked with a scratchy voice.

"He's home—he got out of treatment. I'm here visiting him."

I wondered how long he had been back. Had he decided he didn't want to come see me? He didn't even send me a text.

"Is he, um . . . okay?" I cleared my throat.

Julie gave me a smile, eyes softening. "Yeah, Addie. He's doing great."

I was so happy to hear that, even though it hurt just a little bit. Okay, it hurt a lot bit. I was proud of him for doing something about his problem, though. For attempting to fix it when he knew he was struggling.

I nodded again, not knowing what to say.

"He told me everything that happened," Julie said lightly. I met her eyes, and she was watching for my reaction to her words. Damn lawyer eyes.

"Everything?"

She gave me a grin that crinkled her eyes. "Yes, Addie, everything."

I bit at the inside of my lip. Did she think I was a piece of shit for throwing myself at Jackson when he was technically still with Sophie?

"He didn't cheat. You know that, right?" I could hear the worry in my voice, petrified that I was giving Julie ammo to hate me.

Julie actually let out a laugh. "Relax, Addie. I know."

I leaned back against the couch, letting out a long breath of air.

"I told him not to get back together with Sophie back then, you know. And I told him not to propose, either."

I hated how much I loved hearing this information. It seemed Julie was actually on my side, even though she was the one who told him not to touch me all those years ago. What did she think about us hooking up before graduation? We had never talked about it—I was never alone with her after it happened. I'd always wondered if it was her that tried calling me before I threw my phone out the window ten years ago. At least I finally knew why no one had answered my calls that night, now that Jackson had told me the full story.

"Well, he did it anyways," I said.

Julie smirked at me before shaking her head. "The little shit never listened to my advice, not once."

I chuckled, putting a hand against my forehead.

"Honestly, Sophie isn't bad. She just wanted Jackson to love her like he loved you. But it was never going to happen. I really thought when we drove to see you at Wren's, he'd realize how insane it was that he didn't reach out sooner . . . But he couldn't make himself do it," Julie admitted.

I looked down at the couch, picking at the fabric. "Why didn't you approach me, either?" I was terrified of the answer. I knew why Jackson couldn't make himself come to me, but why hadn't Julie? She kept in contact with Wren this whole time, so why not me?

I could feel Julie staring at me, and when I raised my eyes to hers, she looked so fucking sorry.

"I thought maybe you hated me, too. You didn't just ghost Jackson—you ghosted me, too. You have no idea how much that killed me, Addie. You were like my little sister for so long. If the little pieces I got from Wren were all I had of you, I was fine with it, as long as I knew you were safe. I knew you loved Jackson, but to be honest, I never knew . . . if you loved me, too."

Another blow to the chest. I hurt Julie when she had never, not once, hurt me. What had I done? All of this was on my shoulders, not Jackson's.

"Oh my god, of course I loved you, Julie. I love you like a sister. You're like my fucking family," I said through my tears.

"Good, you brat," Julie said, her tears falling now, too. "And the only reason I didn't want you and Jackson to do anything in high school was because I didn't want things to blow up, and risk you losing our family. But it happened anyways."

Our tears turned to laughter as we realized how dramatic we sounded. I had wasted ten years without her. Julie never wanted to lose me, but I had just up and left her. She wrapped me in a hug, and I squeezed her as tight as I had Wren and Mia. Julie was my family, too—even after all this time.

When she pulled away, she swiped at her cheeks. "Now, can I take you to Jackson? I told him he couldn't have you until I talked to you first."

My heart beat ferociously in my chest. "He wants to see me?"

Julie rolled her eyes and gave me a look that screamed, *Are you kidding me?*

"Come on," she said, grabbing my hand. "He even let me take the truck."

***

We drove to the restaurant, and Julie dropped me off in the back alley so I could walk through the back door to the kitchen. "Text me when you're done. I'll come get you guys."

I turned to tell her to come in with me, that I didn't have her number, and to ask, "Done with what?" But she winked at me and drove away before I could even open my mouth.

I let myself in through the back door, and Jackson was leaning against the dishwasher with his legs crossed at the ankles, just like that first day I ever laid eyes on him fourteen years ago. "About You" by The 1975 was playing through the speakers.

He stood up straighter, putting his phone in his back pocket. He looked amazing—refreshed, and happy. His dark hair was cut a little shorter, and he had on a simple black T-shirt with jeans.

"Um, hi," I said.

"Hey," he said with a smile, slowly walking toward me until I backed into the shelf of empty food containers. He put his hands on either side of me on the shelf, just like he had done back when we were freshman in high school. I set my hands back on the shelf, feeling his thumbs against my hands. I wanted to hike up my leg again, to reenact the memory.

He chuckled at me, clearly reading my mind before pressing a quick kiss to the side of my mouth. He stepped back and leaned against the counter behind him, crossing his arms against his chest.

"How's the house?" he asked, surprising me.

My body was still pulsing from his closeness a second ago, and I had to shake my head to try to unjumble all my thoughts.

"What?" I asked.

Jackson laughed again. "The house, Addie. How is the house coming along?"

I put my hair behind my ears. "It's finished. I just have to clean up the paint supplies."

"So are you putting it on the market?" Jackson asked.

I was no longer playing games. I smiled at him and admitted, "I don't have a plan. I'm still deciding what to do with my life."

Jackson's face lit up with a half-smile. "Yeah?"

I shrugged. "Yeah, I'm kinda waiting to see about this guy. I've had this insane crush on him since I was fourteen. It's pretty pathetic, actually." My face hurt from how hard I was smiling.

Jackson's eyes softened. "Crush, huh?"

I shook my head.

"No, that's a lie."

He quirked an eyebrow at me.

"He's my best friend, actually. And I'm in love with him."

Jackson's smile was so wide and warm that I almost melted to the floor. He motioned his head forward, and I turned to where he was looking, my gaze landing on the Polaroid board.

The empty space I'd left when I ripped down the photo of us at graduation had been filled by the photo Jackson took of us at the beach, back in July during our perfect day in Holland. Jackson was resting his chin on my shoulder, his arm tucked around me, smiling so wide his eyes crinkled. My eyes were closed in the photo, but I was facing toward him with a smile on my lips. We looked happy, and we looked in love. It told me everything I needed to know.

I turned back to Jackson, and he took a step toward me.

"Can I touch you now, Addie?"

"Yes," I whispered.

He was up against me in an instant, pushing me back against the shelf, causing empty containers to fall to the ground around us. A hand was in my hair, his thumb rubbing against my jaw, the other on my hip, keeping us pressed together.

"Don't ever stop touching me again," I pleaded as I lifted his shirt off his head, kissing along his collarbone to the freckle I'd missed so much.

"I'm in love with you, Addison," Jackson said as he kissed down my neck. As if I didn't already know.

I ran my fingers up the back of his head, feeling the strands of his hair. "Say it in my favorite way," I teased.

He stood up straighter, with a smile so beautiful I took a mental picture and buried it deep in my memory bank.

"You're my best friend, period." He leaned forward and kissed me; the kind of Jackson kiss I remembered. The one that felt like a beginning. Then he said against my lips, "And I love you, period."

Epilogue

July, Two Years Later

I gasp when I feel the baby kick under my hand, my eyes shooting up to look at Jackson. He chuckles at me, shaking his head. I had already felt the baby kick three times today, but every time I felt that little foot, I get just as excited as I was the first time.

"Okay, leave the poor thing alone," Jackson says as he guides me away from Julie.

"But I love feeling her little feet!" I whine, my arms outstretched toward Julie's belly, attempting to get one last feel.

Julie clasps her hands over her round bump, rubbing a thumb back and forth. "I promise when she's born you can hog her all you want."

"It's a deal," I say with a megawatt smile.

Jackson and I move to our seats, watching Marie try to get everyone to quiet down so she can announce the rules of the baby shower game we're about to play.

Julie and Britt are having a daughter in a month, and we're all over the moon with excitement.

Jackson grabs my hand under the table, bringing it up and setting our intertwined fingers on the table.

It's been two years, and I still get giddy over the fact that I can hold his hand without worrying about who's around to see.

Once I finished up the house, I put it on the market. I sold it to a family that could create their own happy memories inside it and make it a home.

Jackson no longer owns a portion of Delvecchios' Restaurant. He had a long talk with his family about selling his side of the partnership to Rami. Everyone was ready to let it go—it was no longer the same with Phil gone, anyways. Sophie even graciously let us keep our Polaroids.

Jackson and I decided to move out to California to be closer to Julie and Britt now that they're having a baby, and we've been here for almost a year now.

I enrolled in college earlier this year, and I'm studying education. While I'm in school I'll be helping out with Julie's baby between shifts at the coffee shop Britt owns. She and Jackson are currently in the process of signing a business agreement to make him part-owner.

Before we moved out here, Jackson came with me to North Carolina to stay with Wren and Mia, who is now an angsty teenager. Even though I'm no longer nannying Mia, the Wilsons were true to their promise that we would stay family. They're planning to fly out here for Christmas.

We somehow convinced Marie to move out to California with us, and now almost all the Delvecchios are residents of California. Sam, his wife, and the kids will never leave New York and the east coast; they're New Yorkers through and through. They're here today though, sitting across the table from us.

I'm the happiest I've ever been. I'm surrounded by people who didn't have to love me and choose me, but did anyways. They protect me, they make me feel important, and they're constantly reminding me how happy they are to have me back in their life.

Jackson and I don't run from our problems anymore—we face them head-on, and with the truth. He's still sober, and I gave up drinking, too. When he starts to feel like he's struggling again, he still plays the drums or talks to me about how he's feeling. Usually with my head in his lap as I stare up at him, rubbing my thumb against the freckle on his collarbone as he does the same to my hip bone.

"Ready?" I hear Jackson ask from beside me.

I look down at the game; it's some generic baby shower game where you have to unscramble words.

"Start!" Julie yells out to the room.

I rush to get through it, finishing the last word—"baby bottle"—and holding up my paper.

Britt comes over to grab the paper from me, checking to see if all the answers are right. When she confirms they are, she asks me to stand to get my prize.

"Good job, honey," Marie says, squeezing my arm as I peruse the array of gift baskets.

"Thanks, Mom." That's another thing I'll never get tired of.

"Ah, I figured my smart little sister-in-law would win," Julie says with a sneaky smile.

"*Future* sister-in-law," I remind her.

She swats a hand at me. "Yeah, yeah, whatever you say."

I look over at Jackson, and he smiles at me before giving me a wink.

I roll my eyes at him, placing the gift basket I picked out in front of Nico and Sammy so they can rummage through it.

"Thanks, Aunt Addie!" Nico says with a gap-toothed smile. I press a kiss to his head then ruffle Sammy's hair before sitting back down next to Jackson.

He grabs my left hand again, kissing my finger exactly where an engagement ring will one day go.

I smile back at him, so wide that my eyes crinkle.

I have a feeling I'll become a fiancée tonight. And sometime in the near future, I'll officially become a Delvecchio.

THE END

Afterword

What If It Was Us Playlist

https://open.spotify.com/playlist/6LWQqB3Jf2e7m8ksmq941l?si=ed7fb4ef45a9466d

Acknowledgements

If you've made it this far, thank you for reading, truly. My favorite part about reading a book is the acknowledgements at the end, and finding out what inspired the story, so I'll try to do this part justice.

First off, I need to thank my mom for being the first person to read my stories and reply with "so what now?". Thank you for making me feel like my stories matter.

To my amazing editor Cara Ricketts, for loving these characters just as much as I do, and maybe even knowing them better than me! Ha! You really made me feel like Jackson and Addie were important. (And for putting Sophie deeper in my head, she'll get her happy ending now because of you.) You're stuck with me for life Cara!

Johnny, you're not a reader, but you read this and all my other stories too. Thank you for loving me and listening to the clack of my keyboard day and night.

Reader, I hope you connected with this story in some way, and although I didn't have the same experiences as Addie did, I know too many people that have. But regardless of the cards they've been dealt, they persevered and created such beautiful lives for themselves. Those are the people that inspire me the most, and what push me to keep going when things get rough.

I was blessed to grow up with parents like the Delvecchios, and even though we didn't own an Italian restaurant, I was raised in a household with two loving parents who are STILL in love over thirty years later, and two brothers that inspired the sibling relationship between Julie and Jackson (and both of them live in Michigan with me, thanks for not moving far away even though I did for a time). I didn't realize until I was older how rare our house was, my brothers and I got along and my parents were the type of people who let any child into their home with open arms and offered so much love, regardless of who you were. It was a safe space, and I'll forever be grateful that they taught me how to show kindness and acceptance in that way.

I also come from a humongous Italian family, my grandpa on my mom's side was born into a family of eleven, and my mom herself is the youngest of seven siblings. I grew up surrounded by a chaotic mix of first cousins that are closer in age to my mom than they are to me, and with so many aunts, uncles, and cousins that it was confusing trying to figure out who was actually related to who in what ways, and then piling the great aunts and uncles and distant relatives, it's nearly impossible to remember who everyone is. Just like Jackson felt, it can be overwhelming being surrounded by a sea of family members when half of them don't even know your name.

In the past four years I've learned that blood isn't what makes a family, but *love* does. How special is it to have someone love you because they *choose* to, not because they're told they have to?

Not only did the Delvecchios teach Addie what love was and accept her for who she was, but the family she gained in Wren and Mia too taught her that family is created out of love. I'm lucky enough to have my own Wren and Mia in my life, and while my own Mia is a teenager now too (I'm weepy) and I miss the moments and experiences of babysitting and watching her grow into her own person, I'm so grateful I still have her and my Wren in my life. That's what life is all about right? Evolving with the ones we love around us.

So thank you again for reading this story and being here. I love reading and writing because it's the most vulnerable you can be with the world. Books are the manifestations of what's going on in someone's head, and how weird is it to know you've seen the inside of my brain now? You know who I am now, even if I don't know you. This story isn't just mine anymore, but yours now, so thank you again.

About the author

Anna Lynn was born and raised in Michigan, and when she's not frantically writing stories in the scrivener app, she's drinking coffee like it's a full time job, cleaning teeth as a mobile Dental Hygienist, or reading a book that makes her cry.

https://annalynnauthor.carrd.co/
https://linktr.ee/annalynnauthor

www.ingramcontent.com/pod-product-compliance
Lightning Source LLC
LaVergne TN
LVHW091712070526
838199LV00050B/2367